Robert E. Howard's
CONAN
RED NAILS
contains three of the greatest stories of Conan:
RED NAILS
SHADOWS IN ZAMBOULA
BEYOND THE BLACK RIVER
and Robert E. Howard's masterful essay on the
world of Conan, THE HYBORIAN AGE.

RED NAILS is one of the longest Conan
stories and is the last one that Robert E.
Howard completed and published as a serial in
Weird Tales. It chronicles Conan's adventures
in the demon-haunted city of Xuchotl and his
encounter with Valeria, the fiery adventuress.

"Even as he shifted, he hurled the knife."

Original *Weird Tales* illustration by Harold S. Delay

CONAN
RED NAILS

by Robert E. Howard

edited by Karl Edward Wagner

The Authorized Edition

A BERKLEY MEDALLION BOOK
published by
BERKLEY PUBLISHING CORPORATION

Glenn Lord
P.O. Box 775
Pasadena, Texas 77501

ISBN 0-425-04360-6

*BERKLEY MEDALLION BOOKS are published by
Berkley Publishing Corporation
200 Madison Avenue
New York, N.Y. 10016*

BERKLEY MEDALLION BOOK ® TM 757,375

Printed in the United States of America

Berkley Medallion Edition, OCTOBER, 1977

Second Printing

"A hut wall buckled under the ram-like impact."

Original *Weird Tales* illustration by Hugh Rankin

Contents

"Fierce joy surged through him."

Original *Weird Tales* illustration by Hugh Rankin

Foreword

A FEW MODERN critics have chosen to dismiss *Weird Tales* as a magazine solely devoted to "creepy-crawlies" and yarns of the ghouls-from-the-grave class. Presumably they are merely extending their sneering opinion of H.P. Lovecraft and the Lovecraftian circle of writers to include the entire magazine; clearly they have little cared to prejudice their contempt by reading a fair sampling of issues. During its thirty-two years of existence, *Weird Tales* published stories in every conceivable sub-genre of fantasy—as well as science fiction. Just as *Weird Tales* and the writers that pulp developed were to dominate the field of gothic horror in this century, so was the magazine a major force in the genre of epic fantasy.

As a genre, epic fantasy (or heroic fantasy, as it is also designated) is a fascinating synthesis of horror, adventure, and imagination. While there are as many different concepts and approaches to epic fantasy as with any major genre, the common motif is a universe in which magic works and an individual may kill according to his personal code. When the universe is effectively envisioned and the characters are convincingly realized, epic fantasy can command the reader's attention on multiple levels of enjoyment. When the universe is a cardboard stage set and the characters comic book stereotypes, the result is cliché-ridden melodrama. While it would seem obvious that such holds true for *any* genre, there are some who insist epic fantasy is no more than "swords-and-sorcery" hokum. It is a judgment comparable to dismissing the entire science-fiction genre as "space opera."

While *Weird Tales* was not immune to publishing a few duds, and readers were not averse to pointing these out in the letters column, the magazine presented some of the best epic fantasy ever written. Just as *Weird Tales* had its gallery of stars in the field of horror— H.P. Lovecraft, Robert Bloch, Manly Wade Wellman, Seabury Quinn, Ray Bradbury, Henry S. Whitehead, to name but a few—so did epic fantasy have its stardom: Nictzin Dyalhis, Robert E. Howard, C.L. Moore, Clark Ashton Smith, Henry Kuttner, Clifford Ball, Edmond Hamilton, and others. Particularly from the late 1920's to the close of Farnsworth Wright's editorship a decade later, *Weird Tales* was a fabulous trove of epic fantasy tales, and, in "The Eyrie," the readers were enthusiastic in their approval. Not surprisingly, these dates coincide with the career of Robert E. Howard.

By 1930 Howard had become a regular contributor to *Weird Tales*. He was now twenty-four, and hitting his stride as a writer. *Weird Tales* had started a companion magazine, *Oriental Stories*, a pulp devoted to adventure yarns set in the glamorous Orient (that being any point east of Gibraltar). Howard, who had long sought a market for such fiction, made the jump easily with a series of historical adventure tales, most of them set during the Crusades. They represent his best non-fantasy stories, and Howard loved to write them: "There is no literary work, to me, half as zestful as rewriting history in the guise of fiction. I wish I was able to devote the rest of my life to that kind of work."

With Howard winning acclaim in both magazines, Wright asked his young star for some biographical information. Howard responded in 1931 with a letter describing his "very humdrum and commonplace life":

"Well—my tale is soon told. I come of old pioneer American stock. By nationality I am predominantly Gaelic, in spite of my English name—some three-fourths Irish, while the rest is a mixture of English, Highland Scotch, and Danish. I was born in a little, fading ex-cowtown about forty-five miles west of Ft. Worth. Practically all my life has been spent in the country and small towns, outside of a few brief sojourns in New Orleans and some of the Texas cities. I have only a high school education and not a particularly elaborate one at that. . . .

"My boyhood was spent in the oil country—or rather oil came into the country when I was still a young boy, and remained. I'll say one thing about an oil boom; it will teach a kid that Life's a pretty rotten thing about as quick as anything I can think of.

"I've worked at several jobs, but wasn't a success at any of them; I've picked cotton, helped brand a few yearlings, hauled a little garbage, worked in a grocery store, ditto a dry-goods store, worked in a law office, jerked soda, worked up in a gas office, tried to be a public stenographer, packed a surveyor's rod, worked up oil field news for some Texas and Oklahoma papers, etc., etc., and also etc.

"I've always had a honing to make my living by writing, ever since I can remember, and while I haven't been a howling success in that line, at least I've managed for several years now to get by without grinding at some time clock-punching job. There's freedom in this game; that's the main reason I chose it. As Service says:

> 'In belly-pinch I will pay the price,
> But God, let me be free—
> For once I know in the long ago
> They made a slave of me.'

"Life's not worth living if somebody thinks he's in authority over you.

"You gave me my start in the racket by buying my first story—'Spear and Fang.' I was eighteen years old at the time. Pounding out a living at the writing game is no snap—but the average man's life is no snap, whatever he does. I'm merely one of a huge army, all of whom are bucking the line one way or another for meat for their bellies—which is the main basic principle and reason and eventual goal of Life. Every now and then one of us finds the going too hard and blows his brains out, but it's all in the game, I reckon."

While *Weird Tales* continued to be his major market, Howard was beginning to click with a variety of other pulps, and the writing game was keeping meat in his belly. His earnings from his stories brought him $772.50 in 1929, jumped to $1303.50 in 1930, and just broke $1500 for 1931. The people of Cross Plains still considered him an oddball and wondered when the young man would settle down and get a real job, but $1500 in the throes of the Depression was more money than a lot of Americans saw in a year.

Thus far Howard's epic fantasy tales had almost all been set in the historical past: Solomon Kane in the reign of Elizabeth I, Bran Mak Morn in the early third century, Turlogh Dubh O'Brien in the eleventh century. Only King Kull lived in a mythical age—the

4

Pre-Cataclysmic Age of a hundred thousand years ago (to use the dating in "Kings of the Night"), before Atlantis and Lemuria sank beneath the oceans. Howard had had little luck selling the King Kull series, which he had intended for *Adventure* or *Argosy* in the late 1920's. Wright did buy three of the Kull stories for *Weird Tales* (one of which has Kull leaping forward in time to fight beside Bran Mak Morn), but no others saw print in Howard's lifetime—unfortunate, because Kull was Howard's most complex character, and some (myself one of them) say his best.

But Howard did not abandon his idea of a barbarian adventurer of the mythical past, who battles his way to the throne of a civilized kingdom. Instead he moved his imaginary universe from the Pre-Cataclysmic Age to the Hyborian Age—an epoch still in the unhistoried past, but after the sinking of Atlantis and Lemuria, although the continents had not yet achieved their modern configurations. And the introspective, unstable Kull, a savage from Atlantis, emerged as the less Byronic, man-of-action Conan, a barbarian from Cimmeria.

"I'm working on a new character," Howard wrote in 1932, "providing him with a new epoch—the Hyborian Age—which men have forgotten, but which remains in classical names, and distorted myths. Wright rejected most of the series, but I did sell him one—'The Phoenix on the Sword'—which deals with the adventures of King Conan the Cimmerian in the kingdom of Aquilonia."

A letter from Farnsworth Wright to Howard, dated March 10, 1932, gives further information on Conan's genesis: "I am returning THE FROST-GIANT'S DAUGHTER in a separate envelope, as I do not much care for it. But THE PHOENIX ON THE SWORD has points of real excellence. I hope you will see your way clear to touch it up and resubmit it."

Howard did revise the tale to Wright's satisfaction, and "The Phoenix on the Sword" appeared in the December 1932 issue. Conan was born. And epic fantasy was presented with one of the genre's greatest heroes.

The two stories were both rewrites of earlier tales, dealing with other lead characters.

"The Phoenix on the Sword" was a rewrite of a King Kull story, "By This Axe I Rule!", which Howard had tried without success to sell to the adventure pulps. The Kull version would not be published until 1967, in the Lancer Books paperback, *King Kull*.

"The Frost-Giant's Daughter" was a rewrite of "The Frost King's Daughter," in which the lead character is Amra of Akbitana, who was a proto-Conan of Cimmeria (Amra was the name Conan went by as leader of the black corsairs). "The Frost-Giant's Daughter" finally saw print in an "edited" version in the August 1953 issue of *Fantasy Fiction*. Howard's *own* version (taken verbatim from his manuscript) was not published until 1976, as the other half of *Rogues in the House*, one of the volumes in Donald Grant's deluxe hardcover edition of Conan. However, the earlier version of the tale, featuring Amra of Akbitana, did see print during Howard's lifetime. Howard submitted it to fanzine editor Charles D. Hornig, with a letter dated November 10, 1933: "Here is a short story, 'The Frost King's Daughter,' which I thought you might find suitable for The Fantasy Fan." *The Fantasy Fan*, one of several amateur journals that gladly published discards by famous authors—gratis— ran the story in its March 1934 issue as "Gods of the North." A reading of the Amra version clearly reveals it to be an earlier draft of the Conan version, although the reverse is usually erroneously claimed.

While the above may seem needlessly esoteric, it serves to establish a number of points about the Conan series.

For one thing, Conan sprang forth from the salvage heap, not from the fires of divine inspiration. One wonders how many others of the Conan tales might have been revisions of unsuccessful efforts. In the case of "The Black Stranger," Howard did the reverse— revising a rejected Conan tale in an effort to sell it as a straight pirate yarn, featuring Black Vulmea. This is not to sneer. A professional writer accumulates a stack of unsold manuscripts. The ability to revise and "salvage" an unmarketable story is a measure of his command of fiction and awareness of his own writing flaws.

Another point, plainly Howard was making no effort to present the Conan series in any chronological order based on Conan's career. "The Phoenix on the Sword," which portrays Conan as King of Aquilonia, is one of the last of his adventures—while "The Frost-Giant's Daughter" is arguably the first of his adventures, being the only one that takes place in the frozen wastes of the North.

Moreover, this shows that Wright was not above rejecting a Conan tale—and, in the case of "The Frost-Giant's Daughter," an excellent one. The reason evidently was Wright's own moral hang-ups. In the blurb for "The People of the Black Circle," Wright proclaims: "Rough, and at times uncouth, Conan is a primitive man, who will brave almost certain death against terrific odds to rescue a damsel in distress; yet he will just as quickly give her a resounding slap on the posterior or drop her into a cesspool if she displeases

7

him. But rude though he is, he possesses a sort of primordial chivalry and an innate reverence for womanhood that make him wholly fascinating." Well, as a rule Conan *is* risking his rude neck to save some unclothed damsel from a foul fate, but in "The Frost-Giant's Daughter" (which lacks the overtones of lesbianism and flagellation that several of the stories flaunt) Conan is definitely not in any chivalrous mood—as he chases the near nude Atali across the snows, chopping up her brothers to get to her. The same taboo probably caused Wright to bounce "The Vale of Lost Women" (eventually published in the Spring 1967 issue of *Magazine of Horror*), in which Conan breaks a truce and massacres a village—for which rescue the distressed damsel, Livia, had to barter her virgin body.

All of which should make it evident to new readers that the Conan stories hardly appear in any smooth order, that their history is frequently as convoluted as their plots, and that a definitive collection of the entire series has yet to be published.

Robert E. Howard wrote a total of twenty-one Conan tales. Of these, seventeen were published in *Weird Tales* between December 1932 and October 1936. Four more Conan tales were completed by Howard, but were rejected by Wright, and did not see publication until many years after Howard's suicide on June 11, 1936. These four stories are "The God in the Bowl," "The Black Stranger," "The Frost-Giant's Daughter," and "The Vale of Lost Women."

In addition, a few brief fragments and outlines for never completed Conan tales were much later found among Howard's papers. These furnished a basis for several "posthumous collaborations"—as did several completed, non-fantasy adventure stories, which were

8

"revised" to transform them into Conan tales. Finally, there has been a great outpouring of Conan pastiches, written by various authors to fill in gaps in Conan's career. As one of those who have written Howard pastiches, I feel I have the right to say that pastiche-Conan is *not* the same Conan as Robert E. Howard's indomitable barbarian. Read such, as it pleases you—but don't delude yourself into thinking that this is any more Robert E. Howard's Conan than a Conan story you decided to write yourself.

In writing the Conan stories, Howard drew up a map of the Hyborian Age kingdoms along with a pseudo-history of the period and its peoples. This history, "The Hyborian Age," is reprinted here. Considering that, in addition to his other writing, Howard wrote all twenty-one stories in a period between early 1932 and July of 1935—that the tales range from about 3500 words to 75,000—that some were rewritten salvages and others dashed out in a single draft ("Rogues in the House")—one is astonished that internal inconsistencies are very minor. Howard said that he felt as if Conan were standing at his shoulder, telling him of his adventures—and one wonders.

While Howard never organized the Conan stories into a strict chronology in terms of Conan's lifetime, the stories can be grouped with fair accuracy according to known stages of Conan's career, and to references within them to other adventures. From allusions within the tales and from a few comments in Howard's letters, we know that Conan was born on a battlefield in Cimmeria, that his father was a blacksmith, his people northern barbarians. At fifteen Conan fought in the sack of Vanarium, which the Gundermen had built in an ill-advised attempt to settle Cimmeria's southern frontier. Conan was then six feet tall, weighed 180 pounds, and was already making a name for himself. In his later teens he began wandering across the southern kingdoms of the Hyborian Age. He wandered through most of his world, through civilized lands and waste places—as thief, pirate, mercenary, leader of outlaws and wild tribes, penniless adventurer. When he was about forty, he seized the throne of Aquilonia (evidently not long after events in "Beyond the Black River")—although Howard never tells us of Conan's transition from adventurer to king. In *The Hour of the Dragon* Conan is in his midforties, and we see him no more after that adventure.

Due to contractual difficulties, we are not able to publish all twenty-one of the Conan tales at this time. It is hoped that this matter will be resolved, and that we will at last be free to publish a "definitive" edition of the complete Conan series. There have been two previous attempts to do so—by Gnome Press in hardcover and by Lancer Books in paperback (Sphere Books in Britain). Unfortunately these earlier efforts were burdened with the aforementioned Conan collaborations and pastiches, and Howard's text in the completed stories was tampered with by previous editors. It is this editor's belief that a Conan collection should contain *only* Robert E. Howard's Conan tales, and that *no* editorial emendations should alter the authenticity of Howard's creation.

I have prepared the manuscript for this edition by making photocopies of the Conan stories from the pages of *Weird Tales*. Howard's spelling and punctuation variants are preserved, as are "inconsistencies" and "offensive references" that later editors have deemed it their duty to expunge. Except to correct an obvious typographical error, and to standardize line-drops to indicate transitions (usually done for aesthetic

10

reasons in the pulps, to break up the monotony of the double-columned pages), the text of this edition *exactly* follows the text of the original *Weird Tales* publication.

This edition of Conan contains *no* emendations, *no* collaborations, *no* revisions, *no* pastiches. This is Conan *exactly* as Robert E. Howard presented him, exactly as you would have encountered Conan in *Weird Tales*. For the newer fan who knows Conan only through the watered-down comic book version or the lackluster pastiches, this will be a Conan who will sweep away all your previous conceptions of the Cimmerian.

Due to contractual problems, this edition presents the Conan tales in order of their appearance in *Weird Tales*. While we hope to be able to publish the twenty-one tales in the chronology of Conan's career, the stories are entirely self-standing and complete adventures. Since this present arrangement makes it possible to follow Howard's progress as a writer and the development of Conan as the series progressed, the *Afterword* will offer some critical comments and observations for those who are interested in such.

But now let's step aside for Robert E. Howard. It is late spring of 1935. Despite the wretched Margaret Brundage cover, you have just plunked down a quarter for the May issue of *Weird Tales*. You did that because the issue contains the first half of a new Conan serial, "Beyond the Black River..."

the HYBORIAN WORLD

steppes

Rythunia

Zamora

Brythunia

thia

shadizar

khauran

Zamora

nenian

turan

akif

desert

zamboula

khawarism

aghrapur

Vilayet sea

Isle of
Iron
statues

kapur

Zaporoska R.

Hyper?

Vgia

eshan

neenon

keshia

far

ack kingdoms

punt

Zembabwei

iranistan

to khitai

to vendhya

Beyond the Black River

1.   Conan Loses His Ax

THE STILLNESS OF the forest trail was so primeval that the tread of a soft-booted foot was a startling disturbance. At least it seemed so to the ears of the wayfarer, though he was moving along the path with the caution that must be practised by any man who ventures beyond Thunder River. He was a young man of medium height, with an open countenance and a mop of tousled tawny hair unconfined by cap or helmet. His garb was common enough for that country—a coarse tunic, belted at the waist, short leather breeches beneath, and soft buckskin boots that came short of the knee. A knife-hilt jutted from one boot-top. The broad leather belt supported a short, heavy sword and a buckskin pouch. There was no perturbation in the wide eyes that scanned the green walls which fringed the trail. Though not tall, he was well built, and the arms that the short wide sleeves of the tunic left bare were thick with corded muscle.

He tramped imperturbably along, although the last settler's cabin lay miles behind him, and each step was carrying him nearer the grim peril that hung like a brooding shadow over the ancient forest.

He was not making as much noise as it seemed to him, though he well knew that the faint tread of his booted feet would be like a tocsin of alarm to the fierce ears that might be lurking in the treacherous green fastness. His careless attitude was not genuine; his eyes and ears were keenly alert, especially his ears, for no gaze could penetrate the leafy tangle for more than a few feet in either direction.

But it was instinct more than any warning by the external senses which brought him up suddenly, his hand on his hilt. He stood stock-still in the middle of the trail, unconsciously holding his breath, wondering what he had heard, and wondering if indeed he had heard anything. The silence seemed absolute. Not a squirrel chattered or bird chirped. Then his gaze fixed itself on a mass of bushes beside the trail a few yards ahead of him. There was no breeze, yet he had seen a branch quiver. The short hairs on his scalp prickled, and he stood for an instant undecided, certain that a move in either direction would bring death streaking at him from the bushes.

A heavy chopping crunch sounded behind the leaves. The bushes were shaken violently, and simultaneously with the sound, an arrow arched erratically from among them and vanished among the trees along the trail. The wayfarer glimpsed its flight as he spring frantically to cover.

Crouching behind a thick stem, his sword quivering in his fingers, he saw the bushes part, and a tall figure stepped leisurely into the trail. The traveller stared in surprize. The stranger was clad like himself in regard to boots and breeks, though the latter were of silk instead of leather. But he wore a sleeveless hauberk of dark mesh-mail in place of a tunic, and a helmet perched on his black mane. That helmet held the other's gaze; it was without a crest, but adorned by short bull's horns. No civilized hand ever forged that head-piece. Nor was the face below it that of a civilized man: dark, scarred, with smoldering blue eyes, it was a face as untamed as the primordial forest which formed its background. The man held a broadsword in his right hand, and the edge was smeared with crimson.

"Come on out," he called, in an accent unfamiliar to the wayfarer. "All's safe now. There was only one of the dogs. Come on out."

The other emerged dubiously and stared at the stranger. He felt curiously helpless and futile as he gazed on the proportions of the forest man—the massive iron-clad breast, and the arm that bore the reddened sword, burned dark by the sun and ridged and corded with muscles. He moved with the dangerous ease of a panther; he was too fiercely supple to be a product of civilization, even of that fringe of civilization which composed the outer frontiers.

Turning, he stepped back to the bushes and pulled them apart. Still not certain just what had happened, the wayfarer from the east advanced and stared down into the bushes. A man lay there, a short, dark, thickly-muscled man, naked except for a loin-cloth, a necklace of human teeth and a brass armlet. A short sword was thrust into the girdle of the loin-cloth, and one hand still gripped a heavy black bow. The man had long black hair; that was about all the wayfarer could tell about his head, for his features were a mask of blood and brains. His skull had been split to the teeth.

"A Pict, by the gods!" exclaimed the wayfarer.

The burning blue eyes turned upon him.

"Are you surprized?"

"Why, they told me at Velitrium and again at the settlers' cabins along the road, that these devils sometimes sneaked across the border, but I didn't expect to meet one this far in the interior."

"You're only four miles east of Black River," the stranger informed him. "They've been shot within a mile of Velitrium. No settler between Thunder River and Fort Tuscelan is really safe. I picked up this dog's trail three miles south of the fort this morning, and I've been following him ever since. I came up behind him just as he was drawing an arrow on you. Another instant and there'd have been a stranger in Hell. But I spoiled his aim for him."

The wayfarer was staring wide-eyed at the larger man, dumfounded by the realization that the man had actually tracked down one of the forest-devils and slain him unsuspected. That implied woodsmanship of a quality undreamed, even for Conajohara.

"You are one of the fort's garrison?" he asked.

"I'm no soldier. I draw the pay and rations of an officer of the line, but I do my work in the woods. Valannus knows I'm of more use ranging along the river than cooped up in the fort."

Casually the slayer shoved the body deeper into the thickets with his foot, pulled the bushes together and turned away down the trail. The other followed him.

"My name is Balthus," he offered. "I was at Velitrium last night. I haven't decided whether I'll take up a hide of land, or enter fort-service."

"The best land near Thunder River is already taken," grunted the slayer. "Plenty of good land between Scalp Creek—you crossed it a few miles back—and the fort, but that's getting too devilish close to the river. The Picts steal over to burn and murder—as that one did. They don't always come singly. Some day they'll try to sweep the settlers out of Conajohara. And they may succeed—probably will succeed. This colonization business is mad, anyway. There's plenty of good land east of the Bossonian marches. If the Aquilonians would cut up some of the big estates of their barons, and plant wheat where now only deer are hunted, they wouldn't have to cross the border and take the land of the Picts away from them."

"That's queer talk from a man in the service of the Governor of Conajohara," objected Balthus.

"It's nothing to me," the other retorted. "I'm a mercenary. I sell my sword to the highest bidder. I never planted wheat and never will, so long as there are other harvests to be reaped with the sword. But you Hyborians have expanded as far as you'll be allowed to expand. You've crossed the marches, burned a few villages, exterminated a few clans and pushed back the frontier to Black River; but I doubt if you'll even be able to hold what you've conquered, and you'll never push the frontier any further westward. Your idiotic king doesn't understand conditions here. He won't send you enough reinforcements, and there are not enough settlers to withstand the shock of a concerted attack from across the river."

"But the Picts are divided into small clans," persisted Balthus. "They'll never unite. We can whip any single clan."

"Or any three or four clans," admitted the slayer. "But some day a man will rise and unite thirty or forty clans, just as was done among the Cimmerians, when the Gundermen tried to push the border northward, years ago. They tried to colonize the southern marches of Cimmeria: destroyed a few small clans, built a fort-town, Venarium—you've heard the tale."

"So I have indeed," replied Balthus, wincing. The memory of that red disaster was a black blot in the chronicles of a proud and war-like people. "My uncle was at Venarium when the Cimmerians swarmed over the walls. He was one of the few who escaped that slaughter. I've heard him tell the tale, many a time. The barbarians swept out of the hills in a ravening horde, without warning, and stormed Venarium with such fury none could stand before them. Men, women and children were butchered. Venarium was reduced to a mass of charred ruins, as it is to this day. The Aquilonians were driven back across the marches, and have never since tried to colonize the Cimmerian country. But you speak of Venarium familiarly. Perhaps you were there?"

"I was," grunted the other. "I was one of the horde that swarmed over the walls. I hadn't yet seen fifteen snows, but already my name was repeated about the council fires."

Balthus involuntarily recoiled, staring. It seemed incredible that the man walking tranquilly at his side should have been one of those screeching, blood-mad devils that had poured over the walls of Venarium on that long-gone day to make her streets run crimson.

"Then you, too, are a barbarian!" he exclaimed involuntarily.

The other nodded, without taking offense.

"I am Conan, a Cimmerian."

"I've heard of you." Fresh interest quickened Balthus' gaze. No wonder the Pict had fallen victim to his own sort of subtlety. The Cimmerians were barbarians as ferocious as the Picts, and much more intelligent. Evidently Conan had spent much time among civilized men, though that contact had obviously not softened him, nor weakened any of his primitive instincts. Balthus' apprehension turned to admiration as he marked the easy cat-like stride, the effortless silence with which the Cimmerian moved along the trail. The oiled links of his armor did not clink, and Balthus knew Conan could glide through the deepest thicket or most tangled copse as noiselessly as any naked Pict that ever lived.

"You're not a Gunderman?" It was more assertion than question.

Balthus shook his head. "I'm from the Tauran."

"I've seen good woodsmen from the Tauran. But the Bossonians have sheltered you Aquilonians from the

22

outer wildernesses for too many centuries. You need hardening."

That was true; the Bossonian marches, with their fortified villages filled with determined bowmen, had long served Aquilonia as a buffer against the outlying barbarians. Now among the settlers beyond Thunder River there was growing up a breed of forest-men capable of meeting the barbarians at their own game, but their numbers were still scanty. Most of the frontiersmen were like Balthus—more of the settler than the woodsman type.

The sun had not set, but it was no longer in sight, hidden as it was behind the dense forest wall. The shadows were lengthening, deepening back in the woods as the companions strode on down the trail.

"It will be dark before we reach the fort," commented Conan casually; then: "Listen!"

He stopped short, half crouching, sword ready, transformed into a savage figure of suspicion and menace, poised to spring and rend. Balthus had heard it too—a wild scream that broke at its highest note. It was the cry of a man in dire fear or agony.

Conan was off in an instant, racing down the trail, each stride widening the distance between him and his straining companion. Balthus puffed a curse. Among the settlements of the Tauran he was accounted a good runner, but Conan was leaving him behind with maddening ease. Then Balthus forgot his exasperation as his ears were outraged by the most frightful cry he had ever heard. It was not human, this one; it was a demoniacal caterwauling of hideous triumph that seemed to exult over fallen humanity and find echo in black gulfs beyond human ken.

Balthus faltered in his stride, and clammy sweat

beaded his flesh. But Conan did not hesitate; he darted around a bend in the trail and disappeared, and Balthus, panicky at finding himself alone with that awful scream still shuddering through the forest in grisly echoes, put on an extra burst of speed and plunged after him.

The Aquilonian slid to a stumbling halt, almost colliding with the Cimmerian who stood in the trail over a crumpled body. But Conan was not looking at the corpse which lay there in the crimson-soaked dust. He was glaring into the deep woods on either side of the trail.

Balthus muttered a horrified oath. It was the body of a man which lay there in the trail, a short, fat man, clad in the gilt-worked boots and (despite the heat) the ermine-trimmed tunic of a wealthy merchant. His fat, pale face was set in a stare of frozen horror; his thick throat had been slashed from ear to ear as if by a razor-sharp blade. The short sword still in its scabbard seemed to indicate that he had been struck down without a chance to fight for his life.

"A Pict?" Balthus whispered, as he turned to peer into the deepening shadows of the forest.

Conan shook his head and straightened to scowl down at the dead man.

"A forest devil. This is the fifth, by Crom!"

"What do you mean?"

"Did you ever hear of a Pictish wizard called Zogar Sag?"

Balthus shook his head uneasily.

"He dwells in Gwawela, the nearest village across the river. Three months ago he hid beside this road and stole a string of pack-mules from a pack-train bound for the fort—drugged their drivers, somehow. The mules belonged to this man"—Conan casually indicat-

24

ed the corpse with his foot—"Tiberias, a merchant of Velitrium. They were loaded with ale-kegs, and old Zogar stopped to guzzle before he got across the river. A woodsman named Soractus trailed him, and led Valannus and three soldiers to where he lay dead drunk in a thicket. At the importunities of Tiberias, Valannus threw Zogar Sag into a cell, which is the worst insult you can give a Pict. He managed to kill his guard and escape, and sent back word that he meant to kill Tiberias and the five men who captured him in a way that would make Aquilonians shudder for centuries to come.

"Well, Soractus and the soliders are dead. Soractus was killed on the river, the soldiers in the very shadow of the fort. And now Tiberias is dead. No Pict killed any of them. Each victim—except Tiberias, as you see—lacked his head—which no doubt is now ornamenting the altar of Zogar Sag's particular god."

"How do you know they weren't killed by the Picts?" demanded Balthus.

Conan pointed to the corpse of the merchant.

"You think that was done with a knife or a sword? Look closer and you'll see that only a talon could have made a gash like that. The flesh is ripped, not cut."

"Perhaps a panther—" began Balthus, without conviction.

Conan shook his head impatiently.

"A man from the Tauran couldn't mistake the mark of a panther's claws. No. It's a forest devil summoned by Zogar Sag to carry out his revenge. Tiberias was a fool to start for Velitrium alone, and so close to dusk. But each one of the victims seemed to be smitten with madness just before doom overtook him. Look here; the signs are plain enough. Tiberias came riding along the trail on his mule, maybe with a bundle of choice otter pelts behind his saddle to sell in Velitrium, and the *thing* sprang on him from behind that bush. See where the branches are crushed down.

"Tiberias gave one scream, and then his throat was torn open and he was selling his otter skins in Hell. The mule ran away into the woods. Listen! Even now you can hear him thrashing about under the trees. The demon didn't have time to take Tiberias' head; it took fright as we came up."

"As *you* came up," amended Balthus. "It must not be a very terrible creature if it flees from one armed man. But how do you know it was not a Pict with some kind of a hook that rips instead of slicing? Did you see it?"

"Tiberias was an armed man," grunted Conan. "If Zogar Sag can bring demons to aid him, he can tell them which men to kill and which to let alone. No, I didn't see it. I only saw the bushes shake as it left the trail. But if you want further proof, look here!"

The slayer had stepped into the pool of blood in which the dead man sprawled. Under the bushes at the edge of the path there was a footprint, made in blood on the hard loam.

"Did a man make that?" demanded Conan.

Balthus felt his scalp prickle. Neither man nor any beast that he had ever seen could have left that strange, monstrous three-toed print, that was curiously combined of the bird and the reptile, yet a true type of neither. He spread his fingers above the print, careful not to touch it, and grunted explosively. He could not span the mark.

"What is it?" he whispered. "I never saw a beast that left a spoor like that."

"Nor any other sane man," answered Conan grimly. "It's a swamp demon—they're thick as bats in the swamps beyond Black River. You can hear them

26

howling like damned souls when the wind blows strong from the south on hot nights."

"What shall we do?" asked the Aquilonian, peering uneasily into the deep blue shadows. The frozen fear on the dead countenance haunted him. He wondered what hideous head the wretch had seen thrust grinning from among the leaves to chill his blood with terror.

"No use to try to follow a demon," grunted Conan, drawing a short woodman's ax from his girdle. "I tried tracking him after he killed Soractus. I lost his trail within a dozen steps. He might have grown himself wings and flown away, or sunk down through the earth to Hell. I don't know. I'm not going after the mule, either. It'll either wander back to the fort, or to some settler's cabin."

As he spoke Conan was busy at the edge of the trail with his ax. With a few strokes he cut a pair of saplings nine or ten feet long, and denuded them of their branches. Then he cut a length from a serpent-like vine that crawled among the bushes near by, and making one end fast to one of the poles, a couple of feet from the end, whipped the vine over the other sapling and interlaced it back and forth. In a few moments he had a crude but strong litter.

"The demon isn't going to get Tiberias' head if I can help it," he growled. "We'll carry the body into the fort. It isn't more than three miles. I never liked the fat fool, but we can't have Pictish devils making so cursed free with white men's heads."

The Picts were a white race, though swarthy, but the border men never spoke of them as such.

Balthus took the rear end of the litter, onto which Conan unceremoniously dumped the unfortunate merchant, and they moved on down the trail as swiftly as possible. Conan made no more noise laden with their grim burden than he had made when unencumbered. He had made a loop with the merchant's belt at the end of the poles, and was carrying his share of the load with one hand, while the other gripped his naked broadsword, and his restless gaze roved the sinister walls about them. The shadows were thickening. A darkening blue mist blurred the outlines of the foliage. The forest deepened in the twilight, became a blue haunt of mystery sheltering unguessed things.

They had covered more than a mile, and the muscles in Balthus' sturdy arms were beginning to ache a little, when a cry rang shuddering from the woods whose blue shadows were deepening into purple.

Conan started convulsively, and Balthus almost let go the poles.

"A woman!" cried the younger man. "Great Mitra, a woman cried out then!"

"A settler's wife straying in the woods," snarled Conan, setting down his end of the litter. "Looking for a cow, probably, and—stay here!"

He dived like a hunting wolf into the leafy wall. Balthus' hair bristled.

"Stay here alone with this corpse and a devil hiding in the woods?" he yelped. "I'm coming with you!"

And suiting action to words, he plunged after the Cimmerian. Conan glanced back at him, but made no objection, though he did not moderate his pace to accommodate the shorter legs of his companion. Balthus wasted his wind in swearing as the Cimmerian drew away from him again, like a phantom between the trees, and then Conan burst into a dim glade and halted crouching, lips snarling, sword lifted.

"What are we stopping for?" panted Balthus, dashing the sweat out of his eyes and gripping his short sword.

"That scream came from this glade, or near by," answered Conan. "I don't mistake the location of sounds, even in the woods. But where—"

Abruptly the sound rang out again—*behind them*; in the direction of the trail they had just quitted. It rose piercingly and pitifully, the cry of a woman in frantic terror—and then, shockingly, it changed to a yell of mocking laughter that might have burst from the lips of a fiend of lower Hell.

"What in Mitra's name—" Balthus' face was a pale blur in the gloom.

With a scorching oath Conan wheeled and dashed back the way he had come, and the Aquilonian stumbled bewilderedly after him. He blundered into the Cimmerian as the latter stopped dead, and rebounded from his brawny shoulders as though from an iron statue. Gasping from the impact, he heard Conan's breath hiss through his teeth. The Cimmerian seemed frozen in his tracks.

Looking over his shoulder, Balthus felt his hair stand up stiffly. Something was moving through the deep bushes that fringed the trail—something that neither walked nor flew, but seemed to glide like a serpent. But it was not a serpent. Its outlines were indistinct, but it was taller than a man, and not very bulky. It gave off a glimmer of weird light, like a faint blue flame. Indeed, the eery fire was the only tangible thing about it. It might have been an embodied flame moving with reason and purpose through the blackening woods.

Conan snarled a savage curse and hurled his ax with ferocious will. But the thing glided on without altering its course. Indeed it was only a few instants' fleeting glimpse they had of it—a tall, shadowy thing of misty flame floating through the thickets. Then it was gone, and the forest crouched in breathless stillness.

With a snarl Conan plunged through the intervening foliage and into the trail. His profanity, as Balthus floundered after him, was lurid and impassioned. The Cimmerian was standing over the litter on which lay the body of Tiberias. And that body no longer possessed a head.

"Tricked us with its damnable caterwauling!" raved Conan, swinging his great sword about his head in his wrath. "I might have known! I might have guessed a trick! Now there'll be five heads to decorate Zogar's altar."

"But what thing is it that can cry like a woman and laugh like a devil, and shines like witch-fire as it glides through the trees?" gasped Balthus, mopping the sweat from his pale face.

"A swamp devil," responded Conan morosely. "Grab those poles. We'll take in the body, anyway. At least our load's a bit lighter."

With which grim philosophy he gripped the leathery loop and stalked down the trail.

2. *The Wizard of Gwawela*

FORT TUSCELAN STOOD on the eastern bank of Black River, the tides of which washed the foot of the stockade. The latter was of logs, as were all the buildings within, including the donjon (to dignify it by that appellation), in which were the governor's quarters, overlooking the stockade and the sullen river. Beyond that river lay a huge forest, which approached jungle-like density along the spongy shores. Men paced the runways along the log parapet day and night, watching that dense green wall. Seldom a menacing figure appeared, but the sentries knew that they too were watched, fiercely, hungrily, with the mercilessness of ancient hate. The forest beyond the river might seem desolate and vacant of life to the ignorant eye, but life teemed there, not alone of bird and beast and reptile, but also of men, the fiercest of all the hunting beasts.

There, at the fort, civilization ended. Fort Tuscelan was the last outpost of a civilized world; it represented the westernmost thrust of the dominant Hyborian races. Beyond the river the primitive still reigned in shadowy forests, brush-thatched huts where hung the grinning skulls of men, and mud-walled enclosures where fires flickered and drums rumbled, and spears were whetted in the hands of dark, silent men with tangled black hair and the eyes of serpents. Those eyes often glared through the bushes at the fort across the river. Once dark-skinned men had built their huts where that fort stood; yes, and their huts had risen where now stood the fields and log cabins of fair-haired settlers, back beyond Velitrium, that raw, turbulent frontier town on the banks of Thunder River, to the shores of that other river that bounds the Bossonian marches. Traders had come, and priests of Mitra who walked with bare feet and empty hands, and died horribly, most of them; but soldiers had followed, and men with axes in their hands and women and children in ox-drawn wains. Back to Thunder River, and still back, beyond Black River the aborigines had been pushed, with slaughter and massacre. But the dark-skinned people did not forget that once Conajohara had been theirs.

The guard inside the eastern gate bawled a challenge. Through a barred aperture torchlight flickered, glinting on a steel head-piece and suspicious eyes beneath it.

"Open the gate," snorted Conan. "You see it's I. don't you?"

Military discipline put his teeth on edge.

The gate swung inward and Conan and his companion passed through. Balthus noted that the gate was flanked by a tower on each side, the summits of which rose above the stockade. He saw loopholes for arrows.

The guardsmen grunted as they saw the burden borne between the men. Their pikes jangled against each other as they thrust shut the gate, chin on shoulder, and Conan asked testily: "Have you never seen a headless body before?"

The faces of the soldiers were pallid in the torchlight.

"That's Tiberias," blurted one. "I recognize that fur-trimmed tunic. Valerius here owes me five lunas. I told him Tiberias had heard the loon call when he rode through the gate on his mule, with his glassy stare. I wagered he'd come back without his head."

Conan grunted enigmatically, motioned Balthus to ease the litter to the ground, and then strode off toward the governor's quarters, with the Aquilonian at his heels. The tousle-headed youth stared about him eagerly and curiously, noting the rows of barracks along the walls, the stables, the tiny merchants' stalls, the towering blockhouse, and the other buildings, with the open square in the middle where the soldiers drilled, and where, now, fires danced and men off duty lounged. These were now hurrying to join the morbid crowd gathered about the litter at the gate. The rangy figures of Aquilonian pikemen and forest runners mingled with the shorter, stockier forms of Bossonian archers.

He was not greatly surprized that the governor received them himself. Autocratic society with its rigid caste laws lay east of the marches. Valannus was still a young man, well knit, with a finely chiseled countenance already carved into sober cast by toil and responsibility.

"You left the fort before daybreak, I was told," he said to Conan. "I had begun to fear that the Picts had caught you at last."

"When they smoke my head the whole river will know it," grunted Conan. "They'll hear Pictish women wailing their dead as far as Velitrium—I was on a lone scout. I couldn't sleep. I kept hearing drums talking across the river."

"They talk each night," reminded the governor, his fine eyes shadowed, as he stared closely at Conan. He had learned the unwisdom of discounting wild men's instincts.

"There was a difference last night," growled Conan. "There has been ever since Zogar Sag got back across the river."

"We should either have given him presents and sent him home, or else hanged him," sighed the governor. "You advised that, but—"

"But it's hard for you Hyborians to learn the ways of

33

the outlands," said Conan. "Well, it can't be helped now, but there'll be no peace on the border so long as Zogar lives and remembers the cell he sweated in. I was following a warrior who slipped over to put a few white notches on his bow. After I split his head I fell in with this lad whose name is Balthus and who's come from the Tauran to help hold the frontier."

Valannus approvingly eyed the young man's frank countenance and strongly-knit frame.

"I am glad to welcome you, young sir. I wish more of your people would come. We need men used to forest life. Many of our soldiers and some of our settlers are from the eastern provinces and know nothing of woodcraft, or even of agricultural life."

"Not many of that breed this side of Velitrium," grunted Conan. "That town's full of them, though. But listen, Valannus, we found Tiberias dead on the trail." And in a few words he related the grisly affair.

Valannus paled. "I did not know he had left the fort. He must have been mad!"

"He was," answered Conan. "Like the other four; each one, when his time came, went mad and rushed into the woods to meet his death like a hare running down the throat of a python. *Something* called to them from the deeps of the forest, something the men call a loon, for lack of a better name, but only the doomed ones could hear it. Zogar Sag has made a magic that Aquilonian civilization can't overcome."

To this thrust Valannus made no reply; he wiped his brow with a shaky hand.

"Do the soldiers know of this?"

"We left the body by the eastern gate."

"You should have concealed the fact, hidden the corpse somewhere in the woods. The soldiers are nervous enough already."

34

"They'd have found it out some way. If I'd hidden the body, it would have been returned to the fort as the corpse of Soractus was—tied up outside the gate for the men to find in the morning."

Valannus shuddered. Turning, he walked to a casement and stared silently out over the river, black and shiny under the glint of the stars. Beyond the river the jungle rose like an ebony wall. The distant screech of a panther broke the stillness. The night pressed in, blurring the sounds of the soldiers outside the blockhouse, dimming the fires. A wind whispered through the black branches, rippling the dusky water. On its wings came a low, rhythmic pulsing, sinister as the pad of a leopard's foot.

"After all," said Valannus, as if speaking his thoughts aloud, "what do we know—what does anyone know—of the things that jungle may hide? We have dim rumors of great swamps and rivers, and a forest that stretches on and on over everlasting plains and hills to end at last on the shores of the western ocean. But what things lie between this river and that ocean we dare not even guess. No white man has ever plunged deep into that fastness and returned alive to tell us what he found. We are wise in our civilized knowledge, but our knowledge extends just so far—to the western bank of that ancient river! Who knows what shapes earthly and unearthly may lurk beyond the dim circle of light our knowledge has cast?

"Who knows what gods are worshipped under the shadows of that heathen forest, or what devils crawl out of the black ooze of the swamps? Who can be sure that all the inhabitants of that black country are natural? Zogar Sag—a sage of the eastern cities would sneer at his primitive magic-making as the mummery of a fakir; yet he has driven mad and killed five men in a manner no man can explain. I wonder if he himself is wholly human."

"If I can get within ax-throwing distance of him I'll settle that question," growled Conan, helping himself to the governor's wine and pushing a glass toward Balthus, who took it hesitatingly, and with an uncertain glance toward Valannus.

The governor turned toward Conan and stared at him thoughtfully.

"The soldiers, who do not believe in ghosts or devils," he said, "are almost in a panic of fear. You, who believe in ghosts, ghouls, goblins, and all manner of uncanny things, do not seem to fear any of the things in which you believe."

"There's nothing in the universe cold steel won't cut," answered Conan. "I threw my ax at the demon, and he took no hurt, but I might have missed, in the dusk, or a branch deflected its flight. I'm not going out of my way looking for devils; but I wouldn't step out of my path to let one go by."

Valannus lifted his head and met Conan's gaze squarely.

"Conan, more depends on you than you realize. You know the weakness of this province—a slender wedge thrust into the untamed wilderness. You know that the lives of all the people west of the marches depend on this fort. Were it to fall, red axes would be splintering the gates of Velitrium before a horseman could cross the marches. His majesty, or his majesty's advisers, have ignored my plea that more troops be sent to hold the frontier. They know nothing of border conditions, and are averse to expending any more money in this direction. The fate of the frontier depends upon the men who now hold it.

"You know that most of the army which conquered

Conajohara has been withdrawn. You know the force left me is inadequate, especially since that devil Zogar Sag managed to poison our water supply, and forty men died in one day. Many of the others are sick, or have been bitten by serpents or mauled by wild beasts which seem to swarm in increasing numbers in the vicinity of the fort. The soldiers believe Zogar's boast that he could summon the forest beasts to slay his enemies.

"I have three hundred pikemen, four hundred Bossonian archers, and perhaps fifty men who, like yourself, are skilled in woodcraft. They are worth ten times their number of soldiers, but there are so few of them. Frankly, Conan, my situation is becoming precarious. The soldiers whisper of desertion; they are low-spirited, believing Zogar Sag has loosed devils on us. They fear the black plague with which he threatened us—the terrible black death of the swamplands. When I see a sick soldier I sweat with fear of seeing him turn black and shrivel and die before my eyes.

"Conan, if the plague is loosed upon us, the soldiers will desert in a body! The border will be left unguarded and nothing will check the sweep of the dark-skinned hordes to the very gates of Velitrium—maybe beyond! If we can not hold the fort, how can they hold the town?

"Conan, Zogar Sag must die, if we are to hold Conajohara. You have penetrated the unknown deeper than any other man in the fort; you know where Gwawela stands, and something of the forest trails across the river. Will you take a band of men tonight and endeavor to kill or capture him? Oh, I know it's mad. There isn't more than one chance in a thousand that any of you will come back alive. But if we don't get him, it's death for us all. You can take as many men as you wish."

37

"A dozen men are better for a job like that than a regiment," answered Conan. "Five hundred men couldn't fight their way to Gwawela and back, but a dozen might slip in and out again. Let me pick my men. I don't want any soldiers."

"Let me go!" eagerly exclaimed Balthus. "I've hunted deer all my life on the Tauran."

"All right. Valannus, we'll eat at the stall where the foresters gather, and I'll pick my men. We'll start within an hour, drop down the river in a boat to a point below the village and then steal upon it through the woods. If we live, we should be back by daybreak."

3.   The Crawlers in the Dark

THE RIVER WAS a vague trace between walls of ebony. The paddles that propelled the long boat creeping along in the dense shadow of the eastern bank dipped softly into the water, making no more noise than the beak of a heron. The broad shoulders of the man in front of Balthus were a blur in the dense gloom. He knew that not even the keen eyes of the man who knelt in the prow would discern anything more than a few feet ahead of them. Conan was feeling his way by instinct and an intensive familiarity with the river.

No one spoke. Balthus had had a good look at his companions in the fort before they slipped out of the stockade and down the bank into the waiting canoe. They were of a new breed growing up in the world on the raw edge of the frontier—men whom grim necessity had taught woodcraft. Aquilonians of the western provinces to a man, they had many points in common. They dressed alike—in buckskin boots, leathern breeks and deerskin shirts, with broad girdles that held axes and short swords; and they were all gaunt and scarred and hard-eyed; sinewy and taciturn.

They were wild men, of a sort, yet there was still a wide gulf between them and the Cimmerian. They were sons of civilization, reverted to a semi-barbarism. He was a barbarian of a thousand generations of barbarians. They had acquired stealth and craft, but he had been born to these things. He excelled them even in lithe economy of motion. They were wolves, but he was a tiger.

Balthus admired them and their leader and felt a pulse of pride that he was admitted into their company. He was proud that his paddle made no more noise than did theirs. In that respect at least he was their equal, though woodcraft learned in hunts on the Tauran could never equal that ground into the souls of men on the savage border.

Below the fort the river made a wide bend. The lights of the outpost were quickly lost, but the canoe held on its way for nearly a mile, avoiding snags and floating logs with almost uncanny precision.

Then a low grunt from their leader, and they swung its head about and glided toward the opposite shore. Emerging from the black shadows of the brush that fringed the bank and coming into the open of the midstream created a peculiar illusion of rash exposure. But the stars gave little light, and Balthus knew that unless one were watching for it, it would be all but impossible for the keenest eye to make out the shadowy shape of the canoe crossing the river.

They swung in under the overhanging bushes of the western shore and Balthus groped for and found a projecting root which he grasped. No word was spoken. All instructions had been given before the scouting-party left the fort. As silently as a great panther Conan slid over the side and vanished in the bushes. Equally noiseless, nine men followed him. To Balthus, grasping the root with his paddle across his knee, it seemed incredible that ten men should thus fade into the tangled forest without a sound.

He settled himself to wait. No word passed between him and the other man who had been left with him. Somewhere, a mile or so to the northwest, Zogar Sag's village stood girdled with thick woods. Balthus understood his orders; he and his companion were to wait for the return of the raiding-party. If Conan and his men had not returned by the first tinge of dawn, they were to race back up the river to the fort and report that the forest had again taken its immemorial toll of the invading race. The silence was oppressive. No sound came from the black woods, invisible beyond the ebony masses that were the overhanging bushes. Balthus no longer heard the drums. They had been silent for hours. He kept blinking, unconsciously trying to see through the deep gloom. The dank night-smells of the river and the damp forest oppressed him. Somewhere, near by, there was a sound as if a big fish had flopped and splashed the water. Balthus thought it must have leaped so close to the canoe that it had struck the side, for a slight quiver vibrated the craft. The boat's stern began to swing, slightly away from the shore. The man behind him must have let go of the projection he was gripping. Balthus twisted his head to hiss a warning, and could just make out the figure of his companion, a slightly blacker bulk in the blackness.

The man did not reply. Wondering if he had fallen asleep, Balthus reached out and grasped his shoulder. To his amazement, the man crumpled under his touch and slumped down in the canoe. Twisting his body half about, Balthus groped for him, his heart shooting into his throat. His fumbling fingers slid over the man's throat—only the youth's convulsive clenching of his jaws choked back the cry that rose to his lips. His fingers encountered a gaping, oozing wound—his companion's throat had been cut from ear to ear.

In that instant of horror and panic Balthus started up—and then a muscular arm out of the darkness locked fiercely about his throat, strangling his yell. The canoe rocked wildly. Balthus' knife was in his hand, though he did not remember jerking it out of his boot, and he stabbed fiercely and blindly. He felt the blade sink deep, and a fiendish yell rang in his ear, a yell that was horribly answered. The darkness seemed to come to life about him. A bestial clamor rose on all sides, and other arms grappled him. Borne under a mass of hurtling bodies the canoe rolled sidewise, but before he went under with it, something cracked against Balthus' head and the night was briefly illuminated by a blinding burst of fire before it gave way to a blackness where not even stars shone.

4. The Beasts of Zogar Sag

FIRES DAZZLED BALTHUS again as he slowly recovered his senses. He blinked, shook his head. Their glare hurt his eyes. A confused medley of sound rose about him, growing more distinct as his senses cleared. He lifted his head and stared stupidly about him. Black figures hemmed him in, etched against crimson tongues of flame.

Memory and understanding came in a rush. He was bound upright to a post in an open space, ringed by fierce and terrible figures. Beyond that ring fires burned, tended by naked, dark-skinned women. Beyond the fires he saw huts of mud and wattle, thatched with brush. Beyond the huts there was a stockade with a broad gate. But he saw these things only incidentally. Even the cryptic dark women with their curious coiffures were noted by him only absently. His full attention was fixed in awful fascination on the men who stood glaring at him.

Short men, broad-shouldered, deep-chested, lean-hipped, they were naked except for scanty loin-clouts. The firelight brought out the play of their swelling muscles in bold relief. Their dark faces were immobile, but their narrow eyes glittered with the fire that burns in the eyes of a stalking tiger. Their tangled manes were bound back with bands of copper. Swords and axes were in their hands. Crude bandages banded the limbs of some, and smears of blood were dried on their dark skins. There had been fighting, recent and deadly.

His eyes wavered away from the steady glare of his captors, and he repressed a cry of horror. A few feet away there rose a low, hideous pyramid: it was built of gory human heads. Dead eyes glared glassily up at the black sky. Numbly he recognized the countenances which were turned toward him. They were the heads of the men who had followed Conan into the forest. He could not tell if the Cimmerian's head were among them. Only a few faces were visible to him. It looked to him as if there must be ten or eleven heads at least. A deadly sickness assailed him. He fought a desire to retch. Beyond the heads lay the bodies of half a dozen Picts, and he was aware of a fierce exultation at the sight. The forest runners had taken toll, at least.

Twisting his head away from the ghastly spectacle, he became aware that another post stood near him—a stake painted black as was the one to which he was bound. A man sagged in his bonds there, naked except for his leathern breeks, whom Balthus recognized as one of Conan's woodsmen. Blood trickled from his mouth, oozed sluggishly from a gash in his side. Lifting his head as he licked his livid lips, he muttered, making himself heard with difficulty above the fiendish clamor of the Picts: "So they got you, too!"

"Sneaked up in the water and cut the other fellow's throat," groaned Balthus. "We never heard them till they were on us. Mitra, how can anything move so silently?"

"They're devils," mumbled the frontiersman. "They must have been watching us from the time we left midstream. We walked into a trap. Arrows from all sides were ripping into us before we knew it. Most of us dropped at the first fire. Three or four broke through the bushes and came to hand-grips. But there were too many. Conan might have gotten away. I haven't seen his head. Been better for you and me if they'd killed us outright. I can't blame Conan. Ordinarily we'd have gotten to the village without being discovered. They don't keep spies on the river bank as far down as we landed. We must have stumbled into a big party coming up the river from the south. Some devilment is up. Too many Picts here. These aren't all Gwaweli; men from the western tribes here and from up and down the river."

Balthus stared at the ferocious shapes. Little as he knew of Pictish ways, he was aware that the number of men clustered about them was out of proportion to the size of the village. There were not enough huts to have accommodated them all. Then he noticed that there was a difference in the barbaric tribal designs painted on their faces and breasts.

"Some kind of devilment," muttered the forest runner. "They might have gathered here to watch Zogar's magic-making. He'll make some rare magic with our carcasses. Well, a border-man doesn't expect to die in bed. But I wish we'd gone out along with the rest."

The wolfish howling of the Picts rose in volume and exultation, and from a movement in their ranks, an eager surging and crowding, Balthus deduced that someone of importance was coming. Twisting his head about, he saw that the stakes were set before a long building, larger than the other huts, decorated by human skulls dangling from the eaves. Through the door of that structure now danced a fantastic figure.

"Zogar!" muttered the woodsman, his bloody countenance set in wolfish lines as he unconsciously strained at his cords. Balthus saw a lean figure of middle height, almost hidden in ostrich plumes set on a harness of leather and copper. From amidst the plumes peered a hideous and malevolent face. The plumes puzzled Balthus. He knew their source lay half the width of a world to the south. They fluttered and rustled evilly as the shaman leaped and cavorted.

With fantastic bounds and prancings he entered the ring and whirled before his bound and silent captives. With another man it would have seemed ridiculous—a foolish savage prancing meaninglessly in a whirl of feathers. But that ferocious face glaring out from the billowing mass gave the scene a grim significance. No man with a face like that could seem ridiculous or like anything except the devil he was.

Suddenly he froze to statuesque stillness; the plumes rippled once and sank about him. The howling warriors fell silent. Zogar Sag stood erect and motionless, and he seemed to increase in height—to grow and expand. Balthus experienced the illusion that the Pict was towering above him, staring contemptuously down from a great height, though he knew the shaman was not as tall as himself. He shook off the illusion with difficulty.

The shaman was talking now, a harsh, guttural intonation that yet carried the hiss of a cobra. He thrust his head on his long neck toward the wounded man on the stake; his eyes shone red as blood in the firelight. The frontiersman spat full in his face.

With a fiendish howl Zogar bounded convulsively into the air, and the warriors gave tongue to a yell that shuddered up to the stars. They rushed toward the man on the stake, but the shaman beat them back. A snarled command sent men running to the gate. They hurled it open, turned and raced back to the circle. The ring of men split, divided with desperate haste to right and left. Balthus saw the women and naked children scurrying to the huts. They peeked out of doors and windows. A broad lane was left to the open gate, beyond which loomed the black forest, crowding sullenly in upon the clearing, unlighted by the fires.

A tense silence reigned as Zogar Sag turned toward

the forest, raised on his tiptoes and sent a weird inhuman call shuddering out into the night. Somewhere, far out in the black forest, a deeper cry answered him. Balthus shuddered. From the timbre of that cry he knew it never came from a human throat. He remembered what Valannus had said—that Zogar boasted that he could summon wild beasts to do his bidding. The woodsman was livid beneath his mask of blood. He licked his lips spasmodically.

The village held its breath. Zogar Sag stood still as a statue, his plumes trembling faintly about him. But suddenly the gate was no longer empty.

A shuddering gasp swept over the village and men crowded hastily back, jamming one another between the huts. Balthus felt the short hair stir on his scalp. The creature that stood in the gate was like the embodiment of nightmare legend. Its color was of a curious pale quality which made it seem ghostly and unreal in the dim light. But there was nothing unreal about the low-hung savage head, and the great curved fangs that glistened in the firelight. On noiseless padded feet it approached like a phantom out of the past. It was a survival of an older, grimmer age, the ogre of many an ancient legend—a saber-tooth tiger. No Hyborian hunter had looked upon one of those primordial brutes for centuries. Immemorial myths lent the creatures a supernatural quality, induced by their ghostly color and their fiendish ferocity.

The beast that glided toward the men on the stakes was longer and heavier than a common, striped tiger, almost as bulky as a bear. Its shoulders and forelegs were so massive and mightily muscled as to give it a curiously top-heavy look, though its hind-quarters were more powerful than that of a lion. Its jaws were massive, but its head was brutishly shaped. Its brain capacity was small. It had room for no instincts except those of destruction. It was a freak of carnivorous development, evolution run amuck in a horror of fangs and talons.

This was the monstrosity Zogar Sag had summoned out of the forest. Balthus no longer doubted the actuality of the shaman's magic. Only the black arts could establish a domination over that tiny-brained, mighty-thewed monster. Like a whisper at the back of his consciousness rose the vague memory of the name of an ancient god of darkness and primordial fear, to whom once both men and beasts bowed and whose children—men whispered—still lurked in dark corners of the world. New horror tinged the glare he fixed on Zogar Sag.

The monster moved past the heap of bodies and the pile of gory heads without appearing to notice them. He was no scavenger. He hunted only the living, in a life dedicated solely to slaughter. An awful hunger burned greenly in the wide, unwinking eyes; the hunger not alone of belly-emptiness, but the lust of death-dealing. His gaping jaws slavered. The shaman stepped back; his hand waved toward the woodsman.

The great cat sank into a crouch, and Balthus numbly remembered tales of its appalling ferocity: of how it would spring upon an elephant and drive its sword-like fangs so deeply into the titan's skull that they could never be withdrawn, but would keep it nailed to its victim, to die by starvation. The shaman cried out shrilly, and with an ear-shattering roar the monster sprang.

Balthus had never dreamed of such a spring, such a hurtling of incarnated destruction embodied in that giant bulk of iron thews and ripping talons. Full on the woodsman's breast it struck, and the stake splintered and snapped at the base, crashing to the earth under the impact. Then the saber-tooth was gliding toward the gate, half dragging, half carrying a hideous crimson hulk that only faintly resembled a man. Balthus glared almost paralyzed, his brain refusing to credit what his eyes had seen.

In that leap the great beast had not only broken off the stake, it had ripped the mangled body of its victim from the post to which it was bound. The huge talons in that instant of contact had disemboweled and partially dismembered the man, and the giant fangs had torn away the whole top of his head, shearing through the skull as easily as through flesh. Stout rawhide thongs had given way like paper; where the thongs had held, flesh and bones had not. Balthus retched suddenly. He had hunted bears and panthers, but he had never dreamed the beast lived which could make such a red ruin of a human frame in the flicker of an instant.

The saber-tooth vanished through the gate, and a few moments later a deep roar sounded through the forest, receding in the distance. But the Picts still shrank back against the huts, and the shaman still stood facing the gate that was like a black opening to let in the night.

Cold sweat burst suddenly out on Balthus' skin. What new horror would come through that gate to make carrion-meat of *his* body? Sick panic assailed him and he strained futilely at his thongs. The night pressed in very black and horrible outside the firelight. The fires themselves glowed lurid as the fires of hell. He felt the eyes of the Picts upon him—hundreds of hungry, cruel eyes that reflected the lust of souls utterly without humanity as he knew it. They no longer seemed men; they were devils of this black jungle, as inhuman as the creatures to which the fiend in the

49

nodding plumes screamed through the darkness.

Zogar sent another call shuddering through the night, and it was utterly unlike the first cry. There was a hideous sibilance in it—Balthus turned cold at the implication. If a serpent could hiss that loud, it would make just such a sound.

This time there was no answer—only a period of breathless silence in which the pound of Balthus' heart strangled him; and then there sounded a swishing outside the gate, a dry rustling that sent chills down Balthus' spine. Again the firelit gate held a hideous occupant.

Again Balthus recognized the monster from ancient legends. He saw and knew the ancient and evil serpent which swayed there, its wedge-shaped head, huge as that of a horse, as high as a tall man's head, and its palely gleaming barrel rippling out behind it. A forked tongue darted in and out, and the firelight glittered on bared fangs.

Balthus became incapable of emotion. The horror of his fate paralyzed him. That was the reptile that the ancients called Ghost Snake, the pale, abominable terror that of old glided into huts by night to devour whole families. Like the python it crushed its victim, but unlike other constrictors its fangs bore venom that carried madness and death. It too had long been considered extinct. But Valannus had spoken truly. No white man knew what shapes haunted the great forests beyond Black River.

It came on silently, rippling over the ground, its hideous head on the same level, its neck curving back slightly for the stroke. Balthus gazed with glazed, hypnotized stare into that loathsome gullet down which he would soon be engulfed, and he was aware of no sensation except a vague nausea.

And then something that glinted in the firelight streaked from the shadows of the huts, and the great reptile whipped about and went into instant convulsions. As in a dream Balthus saw a short throwing-spear transfixing the mighty neck, just below the gaping jaws; the shaft protruded from one side, the steel head from the other.

Knotting and looping hideously, the maddened reptile rolled into the circle of men who strove back from him. The spear had not severed its spine, but merely transfixed its great neck muscles. Its furiously lashing tail mowed down a dozen men and its jaws snapped convulsively, splashing others with venom that burned like liquid fire. Howling, cursing, screaming, frantic, they scattered before it, knocking each other down in their flight, trampling the fallen, bursting through the huts. The giant snake rolled into a fire, scattering sparks and brands, and the pain lashed it to more frenzied efforts. A hut wall buckled under the ram-like impact of its flailing tail, disgorging howling people.

Men stampeded through the fires, knocking the logs right and left. The flames sprang up, then sank. A reddish dim glow was all that lighted that nightmare scene where the giant reptile whipped and rolled, and men clawed and shrieked in frantic flight.

Balthus felt something jerk at his wrists, and then, miraculously, he was free, and a strong hand dragged him behind the post. Dazedly he saw Conan, felt the forest man's iron grip on his arm.

There was blood on the Cimmerian's mail, dried blood on the sword in his right hand; he loomed dim and gigantic in the shadowy light.

"Come on! Before they get over their panic!"

Balthus felt the haft of an ax shoved into his hand.

Zogar Sag had disappeared. Conan dragged Balthus after him until the youth's numb brain awoke, and his legs began to move of their own accord. Then Conan released him and ran into the building where the skulls hung. Balthus followed him. He got a glimpse of a grim stone altar, faintly lighted by the glow outside; five human heads grinned on that altar, and there was a grisly familiarity about the features of the freshest; it was the head of the merchant Tiberias. Behind the altar was an idol, dim, indistinct, bestial, yet vaguely man-like in outline. Then fresh horror choked Balthus as the shape heaved up suddenly with a rattle of chains, lifting long misshapen arms in the gloom.

Conan's sword flailed down, crunching through flesh and bone, and then the Cimmerian was dragging Balthus around the altar, past a huddled shaggy bulk on the floor, to a door at the back of the long hut. Through this they burst, out into the enclosure again. But a few yards beyond them loomed the stockade.

It was dark behind the altar-hut. The mad stampede of the Picts had not carried them in that direction. At the wall Conan halted, gripped Balthus and heaved him at arm's length into the air as he might have lifted a child. Balthus grasped the points of the upright logs set in the sun-dried mud and scrambled up on them, ignoring the havoc done his skin. He lowered a hand to the Cimmerian, when around a corner of the altar-hut sprang a fleeing Pict. He halted short, glimpsing the man on the wall in the faint glow of the fires. Conan hurled his ax with deadly aim, but the warrior's mouth was already open for a yell of warning, and it rang loud above the din, cut short as he dropped with a shattered skull.

Blinding terror had not submerged all ingrained instincts. As that wild yell rose above the clamor, there was an instant's lull, and then a hundred throats bayed ferocious answer and warriors came leaping to repel the attack presaged by the warning.

Conan leaped high, caught, not Balthus' hand but his arm near the shoulder, and swung himself up. Balthus set his teeth against the strain, and then the Cimmerian was on the wall beside him, and the fugitives dropped down on the other side.

5. *The Children of Jhebbal Sag*

"WHICH WAY IS the river?" Balthus was confused.

"We don't dare try for the river now," grunted Conan. "The woods between the village and the river are swarming with warriors. Come on! We'll head in the last direction they'll expect us to go—west!"

Looking back as they entered the thick growth, Balthus beheld the wall dotted with black heads as the savages peered over. The Picts were bewildered. They had not gained the wall in time to see the fugitives take cover. They had rushed to the wall expecting to repel an attack in force. They had seen the body of the dead warrior. But no enemy was in sight.

Balthus realized that they did not yet know their prisoner had escaped. From other sounds he believed that the warriors, directed by the shrill voice of Zogar Sag, were destroying the wounded serpent with arrows. The monster was out of the shaman's control. A moment later the quality of the yells was altered. Screeches of rage rose in the night.

Conan laughed grimly. He was leading Balthus along a narrow trail that ran west under the black branches, stepping as swiftly and surely as if he trod a well-lighted thoroughfare. Balthus stumbled after him, guiding himself by feeling the dense wall on either hand.

"They'll be after us now. Zogar's discovered you're gone, and he knows my head wasn't in the pile before the altar-hut. The dog! If I'd had another spear I'd have thrown it through him before I struck the snake. Keep to the trail. They can't track us by torchlight, and there are a score of paths leading from the village. They'll follow those leading to the river first—throw a cordon of warriors for miles along the bank, expecting us to try to break through. We won't take to the woods until we have to. We can make better time on this trail. Now buckle down to it and run as you never ran before."

"They got over their panic cursed quick!" panted Balthus, complying with a fresh burst of speed.

"They're not afraid of anything, very long," grunted Conan.

For a space nothing was said between them. The fugitives devoted all their attention to covering distance. They were plunging deeper and deeper into the wilderness and getting farther away from civilization at every step, but Balthus did not question Conan's wisdom. The Cimmerian presently took time to grunt: "When we're far enough away from the village we'll swing back to the river in a big circle. No other village within miles of Gwawela. All the Picts are gathered in that vicinity. We'll circle wide around them. They can't track us until daylight. They'll pick up our path then, but before dawn we'll leave the trail and take to the woods."

They plunged on. The yells died out behind them. Balthus' breath was whistling through his teeth. He felt a pain in his side, and running became torture. He blundered against the bushes on each side of the trail. Conan pulled up suddenly, turned and stared back down the dim path.

Somewhere the moon was rising, a dim white glow amidst a tangle of branches.

"Shall we take to the woods?" panted Balthus.

"Give me your ax," murmured Conan softly. "Something is close behind us."

"Then we'd better leave the trail!" exclaimed Balthus.

Conan shook his head and drew his companion into

a dense thicket. The moon rose higher, making a dim light in the path.

"We can't fight the whole tribe!" whispered Balthus.

"No human being could have found our trail so quickly, or followed us so swiftly," muttered Conan. "Keep silent."

There followed a tense silence in which Balthus felt that his heart could be heard pounding for miles away. Then abruptly, without a sound to announce its coming, a savage head appeared in the dim path. Balthus' heart jumped into his throat; at first glance he feared to look upon the awful head of the saber-tooth. But this head was smaller, more narrow; it was a leopard which stood there, snarling silently and glaring down the trail. What wind there was was blowing toward the hiding men, concealing their scent. The beast lowered his head and snuffed the trail, then moved forward uncertainly. A chill played down Balthus' spine. The brute was undoubtedly trailing them.

And it was suspicious. It lifted its head, its eyes glowing like balls of fire, and growled low in its throat. And at that instant Conan hurled the ax.

All the weight of arm and shoulder was behind the throw, and the ax was a streak of silver in the dim moon. Almost before he realized what had happened, Balthus saw the leopard rolling on the ground in its death-throes, the handle of the ax standing up from its head. The head of the weapon had split its narrow skull.

Conan bounded from the bushes, wrenched his ax free and dragged the limp body in among the trees, concealing it from the casual glance.

"Now let's go, and go fast!" he grunted, leading the way southward, away from the trail. "There'll be warriors coming after that cat. As soon as he got his wits back Zogar sent him after us. The Picts would follow him, but he'd leave them far behind. He'd circle the village until he hit our trail and then come after us like a streak. They couldn't keep up with him, but they'll have an idea as to our general direction. They'd follow, listening for his cry. Well, they won't hear that, but they'll find the blood on the trail, and look around and find the body in the brush. They'll pick up our spoor there, if they can. Walk with care."

He avoided clinging briars and low-hanging branches effortlessly, gliding between trees without touching the stems and always planting his feet in the places calculated to show least evidence of his passing; but with Balthus it was slower, more laborious work.

No sound came from behind them. They had covered more than a mile when Balthus said: "Does Zogar Sag catch leopard-cubs and train them for bloodhounds?"

Conan shook his head. "That was a leopard he called out of the woods."

"But," Balthus persisted, "if he can order the beasts to do his bidding, why doesn't he rouse them all and have them after us? The forest is full of leopards; why send only one after us?"

Conan did not reply for a space, and when he did it was with a curious reticence.

"He can't command all the animals. Only such as remember Jhebbal Sag."

"Jhebbal Sag?" Balthus repeated the ancient name hesitantly. He had never heard it spoken more than three or four times in his whole life.

"Once all living things worshipped him. That was long ago, when beasts and men spoke one language. Men have forgotten him; even the beasts forget. Only a few remember. The men who remember Jhebbal Sag and the beasts who remember are brothers and speak the same tongue."

Balthus did not reply; he had strained at a Pictish stake and seen the nighted jungle give up its fanged horrors at a shaman's call.

"Civilized men laugh," said Conan. "But not one can tell me how Zogar Sag can call pythons and tigers and leopards out of the wilderness and make them do his bidding. They would say it is a lie, if they dared. That's the way with civilized men. When they can't explain something by their half-baked science, they refuse to believe it."

The people on the Tauran were closer to the primitive than most Aquilonians; superstitions persisted, whose sources were lost in antiquity. And Balthus had seen that which still prickled his flesh. He could not refute the monstrous thing which Conan's words implied.

"I've heard that there's an ancient grove sacred to Jhebbal Sag somewhere in this forest," said Conan. "I don't know. I've never seen it. But more beasts *remember* in this country than any I've ever seen."

"Then others will be on our trail?"

"They are now," was Conan's disquieting answer. "Zogar would never leave our tracking to one beast alone."

"What are we to do, then?" asked Balthus uneasily, grasping his ax as he stared at the gloomy arches above him. His flesh crawled with the momentary expectation of ripping talons and fangs leaping from the shadows.

"Wait!"

Conan turned, squatted and with his knife began scratching a curious symbol in the mold. Stooping to look at it over his shoulder, Balthus felt a crawling of the flesh along his spine, he knew not why. He felt no wind against his face, but there was a rustling of leaves above them and a weird moaning swept ghostily through the branches. Conan glanced up inscrutably, then rose and stood staring somberly down at the symbol he had drawn.

"What is it?" whispered Balthus. It looked archaic and meaningless to him. He supposed that it was his ignorance of artistry which prevented his identifying it as one of the conventional designs of some prevailing culture. But had he been the most erudite artist in the world, he would have been no nearer the solution.

"I saw it carved in the rock of a cave no human had visited for a million years," muttered Conan, "in the uninhabited mountains beyond the Sea of Vilayet, half a world away from this spot. Later I saw a black witch-finder of Kush scratch it in the sand of a nameless river. He told me part of its meaning—it's sacred to Jhebbal Sag and the creatures which worship him. Watch!"

They drew back among the dense foliage some yards away and waited in tense silence. To the east drums muttered and somewhere to north and west other drums answered. Balthus shivered, though he knew long miles of black forest separated him from the grim beaters of those drums whose dull pulsing was a sinister overture that set the dark stage for bloody drama.

Balthus found himself holding his breath. Then with a slight shaking of the leaves, the bushes parted and a magnificent panther came into view. The moonlight dappling through the leaves shone on its glossy coat rippling with the play of the great muscles beneath it.

With its head held low it glided toward them. It was smelling out their trail. Then it halted as if frozen, its muzzle almost touching the symbol cut in the mold.

For a long space it crouched motionless; it flattened its long body and laid its head on the ground before the mark. And Balthus felt the short hairs stir on his scalp. For the attitude of the great carnivore was one of awe and adoration.

Then the panther rose and backed away carefully, belly almost to the ground. With his hind-quarters among the bushes he wheeled as if in sudden panic and was gone like a flash of dappled light.

Balthus mopped his brow with a trembling hand and glanced at Conan.

The barbarian's eyes were smoldering with fires that never lit the eyes of men bred to the ideas of civilization. In that instant he was all wild, and had forgotten the man at his side. In his burning gaze Balthus glimpsed and vaguely recognized pristine images and half-embodied memories, shadows from Life's dawn, forgotten and repudiated by sophisticated races—ancient, primeval fantasms unnamed and nameless.

Then the deeper fires were masked and Conan was silently leading the way deeper into the forest.

"We've no more to fear from the beasts," he said after a while, "but we've left a sign for men to read. They won't follow our trail very easily, and until they find that symbol they won't know for sure we've turned south. Even then it won't be easy to smell us out without the beasts to aid them. But the woods south of the trail will be full of warriors looking for us. If we keep moving after daylight, we'll be sure to run into some of them. As soon as we find a good place we'll hide and wait until another night to swing back and make the river. We've got to warn Valannus, but it won't help him any if we get ourselves killed."

"Warn Valannus?"

"Hell, the woods along the river are swarming with Picts! That's why they got us. Zogar's brewing warmagic; no mere raid this time. He's done something no Pict has done in my memory—united as many as fifteen or sixteen clans. His magic did it; they'll follow a wizard farther than they will a war-chief. You saw the mob in the village; and there were hundreds hiding along the river bank that you didn't see. More coming, from the farther villages. He'll have at least three thousand fighting-men. I lay in the bushes and heard their talk as they went past. They mean to attack the fort; when, I don't know, but Zogar doesn't dare delay long. He's gathered them and whipped them into a frenzy. If he doesn't lead them into battle quickly, they'll fall to quarreling with one another. They're like blood-mad tigers.

"I don't know whether they can take the fort or not. Anyway, we've got to get back across the river and give the warning. The settlers on the Velitrium road must either get into the fort or back to Velitrium. While the Picts are besieging the fort, war-parties will range the road far to the east—might even cross Thunder River and raid the thickly settled country behind Velitrium."

As he talked he was leading the way deeper and deeper into the ancient wilderness. Presently he grunted with satisfaction. They had reached a spot where the underbrush was more scattered, and an outcropping of stone was visible, wandering off southward. Balthus felt more secure as they followed it. Not even a Pict could trail them over naked rock.

"How did you get away?" he asked presently.

Conan tapped his mail-shirt and helmet.

"If more borderers would wear harness there'd be fewer skulls hanging on the altar-huts. But most men make noise if they wear armor. They were waiting on each side of the path, without moving. And when a Pict stands motionless, the very beasts of the forest pass him without seeing him. They'd seen us crossing the river and got in their places. If they'd gone into ambush after we left the bank, I'd have had some hint of it. But they were waiting, and not even a leaf trembled. The devil himself couldn't have suspected anything. The first suspicion I had was when I heard a shaft rasp against a bow as it was pulled back. I dropped and yelled for the men behind me to drop, but they were too slow, taken by surprize like that.

"Most of them fell at the first volley that raked us from both sides. Some of the arrows crossed the trail and struck Picts on the other side. I heard them howl." He grinned with vicious satisfaction. "Such of us as were left plunged into the woods and closed with them. When I saw the others were all down or taken, I broke through and outfooted the painted devils through the darkness. They were all around me. I ran and crawled and sneaked, and sometimes I lay on my belly under the bushes while they passed me on all sides.

"I tried for the shore and found it lined with them, waiting for just such a move. But I'd have cut my way through and taken a chance on swimming, only I heard the drums pounding in the village and knew they'd taken somebody alive.

"They were all so engrossed in Zogar's magic that I was able to climb the wall behind the altar-hut. There was a warrior supposed to be watching at that point, but he was squatting behind the hut and peering around the corner at the ceremony. I came up behind him and broke his neck with my hands before he knew what was happening. It was his spear I threw into the snake, and that's his ax you're carrying."

"But what was that—that thing you killed in the

altar-hut?" asked Balthus, with a shiver at the memory of the dim-seen horror.

"One of Zogar's gods. One of Jhebbal's children that didn't remember and had to be kept chained to the altar. A bull ape. The Picts think they're sacred to the Hairy One who lives on the moon—the gorilla-god of Gullah.

"It's getting light. Here's a good place to hide until we see how close they're on our trail. Probably have to wait until night to break back to the river."

A low hill pitched upward, girdled and covered with thick trees and bushes. Near the crest Conan slid into a tangle of jutting rocks, crowned by dense bushes. Lying among them they could see the jungle below without being seen. It was a good place to hide or defend. Balthus did not believe that even a Pict could have trailed them over the rocky ground for the past four or five miles, but he was afraid of the beasts that obeyed Zogar Sag. His faith in the curious symbol wavered a little now. But Conan had dismissed the possibility of beasts tracking them.

A ghostly whiteness spread through the dense branches; the patches of sky visible altered in hue, grew from pink to blue. Balthus felt the gnawing of hunger, though he had slaked his thirst at a stream they had skirted. There was complete silence, except for an occasional chirp of a bird. The drums were no longer to be heard. Balthus' thoughts reverted to the grim scene before the altar-hut.

"Those were ostrich plumes Zogar Sag wore," he said. "I've seen them on the helmets of knights who rode from the East to visit the barons of the marches. There are no ostriches in this forest, are there?"

"They came from Kush," answered Conan. "West of here, many marches, lies the seashore. Ships from

Zingara occasionally come and trade weapons and ornaments and wine to the coastal tribes for skins and copper ore and gold dust. Sometimes they trade ostrich plumes they got from the Stygians, who in turn got them from the black tribes of Kush, which lies south of Stygia. The Pictish shamans place great store by them. But there's much risk in such trade. The Picts are too likely to try to seize the ship. And the coast is dangerous to ships. I've sailed along it when I was with the pirates of the Barachan Isles, which lie southwest of Zingara."

Balthus looked at his companion with admiration.

"I knew you hadn't spent your life on this frontier. You've mentioned several far places. You've traveled widely?"

"I've roamed far; farther than any other man of my race ever wandered. I've seen all the great cities of the Hyborians, the Shemites, the Stygians and the Hyrkanians. I've roamed in the unknown countries south of the black kingdoms of Kush, and east of the Sea of Vilayet. I've been a mercenary captain, a corsair, a *kozak*, a penniless vagabond, a general—hell, I've been everything except a king, and I may be that, before I die." The fancy pleased him, and he grinned hardly. Then he shrugged his shoulders and stretched his mighty figure on the rocks. "This is as good life as any. I don't know how long I'll stay on the frontier; a week, a month, a year. I have a roving foot. But it's as well on the border as anywhere."

Balthus set himself to watch the forest below them. Momentarily he expected to see fierce painted faces thrust through the leaves. But as the hours passed no stealthy footfall disturbed the brooding quiet. Balthus believed the Picts had missed their trail and given up the chase. Conan grew restless.

"We should have sighted parties scouring the woods for us. If they've quit the chase, it's because they're after bigger game. They may be gathering to cross the river and storm the fort."

"Would they come this far south if they lost the trail?"

"They've lost the trail, all right; otherwise they'd have been on our necks before now. Under ordinary circumstances they'd scour the woods for miles in every direction. Some of them should have passed within sight of this hill. They must be preparing to cross the river. We've got to take a chance and make for the river."

Creeping down the rocks Balthus felt his flesh crawl between his shoulders as he momentarily expected a withering blast of arrows from the green masses about them. He feared that the Picts had discovered them and were lying about in ambush. But Conan was convinced no enemies were near, and the Cimmerian was right.

"We're miles to the south of the village," grunted Conan. "We'll hit straight through for the river. I don't know how far down the river they've spread. We'll hope to hit it below them."

With haste that seemed reckless to Balthus they hurried eastward. The woods seemed empty of life. Conan believed that all the Picts were gathered in the vicinity of Gwawela, if, indeed, they had not already crossed the river. He did not believe they would cross in the daytime, however.

"Some woodsman would be sure to see them and give the alarm. They'll cross above and below the fort, out of sight of the sentries. Then others will get in canoes and make straight across for the river wall. As soon as they attack, those hidden in the woods on the east shore will assail the fort from the other sides.

They've tried that before, and got the guts shot and hacked out of them. But this time they've got enough men to make a real onslaught of it."

They pushed on without pausing, though Balthus gazed longingly at the squirrels flitting among the branches, which he could have brought down with a cast of his ax. With a sigh he drew up his broad belt. The everlasting silence and gloom of the primitive forest was beginning to depress him. He found himself thinking of the open groves and sun-dappled meadows of the Tauran, of the bluff cheer of his father's steep-thatched, diamond-paned house, of the fat cows browsing through the deep, lush grass, and the hearty fellowship of the brawny, bare-armed plowmen and herdsmen.

He felt lonely, in spite of his companion. Conan was as much a part of this wilderness as Balthus was alien to it. The Cimmerian might have spent years among the great cities of the world; he might have walked with the rulers of civilization; he might even achieve his wild whim some day and rule as king of a civilized nation; stranger things had happened. But he was no less a barbarian. He was concerned only with the naked fundamentals of life. The warm intimacies of small, kindly things, the sentiments and delicious trivialities that make up so much of civilized men's lives were meaningless to him. A wolf was no less a wolf because a whim of chance caused him to run with the watch-dogs. Bloodshed and violence and savagery were the natural elements of the life Conan knew; he could not, and would never, understand the little things that are so dear to civilized men and women.

The shadows were lengthening when they reached the river and peered through the masking bushes. They could see up and down the river for about a mile each way. The sullen stream lay bare and empty. Conan scowled across at the other shore.

"We've got to take another chance here. We've got to swim the river. We don't know whether they've crossed or not. The woods over there may be alive with them. We've got to risk it. We're about six miles south of Gwawela."

He wheeled and ducked as a bowstring twanged. Something like a white flash of light streaked through the bushes. Balthus knew it was an arrow. Then with a tigerish bound Conan was through the bushes. Balthus caught the gleam of steel as he whirled his sword, and heard a death scream. The next instant he had broken through the bushes after the Cimmerian.

A Pict with a shattered skull lay face-down on the ground, his fingers spasmodically clawing at the grass. Half a dozen others were swarming about Conan, swords and axes lifted. They had cast away their bows, useless at such deadly close quarters. Their lower jaws were painted white, contrasting vividly with their dark faces, and the designs on their muscular breasts differed from any Balthus had ever seen.

One of them hurled his ax at Balthus and rushed after it with lifted knife. Balthus ducked and then caught the wrist that drove the knife licking at his throat. They went to the ground together, rolling over and over. The Pict was like a wild beast, his muscles hard as steel strings.

Balthus was striving to maintain his hold on the wild man's wrist and bring his own ax into play, but so fast and furious was the struggle that each attempt to strike was blocked. The Pict was wrenching furiously to free his knife hand, was clutching at Balthus' ax, and driving his knees at the youth's groin. Suddenly he attempted to shift his knife to his free hand, and in that instant Balthus, struggling up on one knee, split the painted head with a desperate blow of his ax.

He sprang up and glared wildly about for his companion, expecting to see him overwhelmed by numbers. Then he realized the full strength and ferocity of the Cimmerian. Conan bestrode two of his attackers, shorn half asunder by that terrible broadsword. As Balthus looked he saw the Cimmerian beat down a thrusting shortsword, avoid the stroke of an ax with a cat-like sidewise spring which brought him within arm's length of a squat savage stooping for a bow. Before the Pict could straighten, the red sword flailed down and clove him from shoulder to mid-breastbone, where the blade stuck. The remaining warriors rushed in, one from either side. Balthus hurled his ax with an accuracy that reduced the attackers to one, and Conan, abandoning his efforts to free his sword, wheeled and met the remaining Pict with his bare hands. The stocky warrior, a head shorter than his tall enemy, leaped in, striking with his ax, at the same time stabbing murderously with his knife. The knife broke on the Cimmerian's mail, and the ax checked in midair as Conan's fingers locked like iron on the descending arm. A bone snapped loudly, and Balthus saw the Pict wince and falter. The next instant he was swept off his feet, lifted high above the Cimmerian's head—he writhed in midair for an instant, kicking and thrashing, and then was dashed headlong to the earth with such force that he rebounded, and then lay still, his limp posture telling of splintered limbs and a broken spine.

"Come on!" Conan wrenched his sword free and snatched up an ax. "Grab a bow and a handful of arrows, and hurry! We've got to trust to our heels again. That yell was heard. They'll be here in no time. If we tried to swim now, they'd feather us with arrows before we reached midstream!"

6.   Red Axes of the Border

CONAN DID NOT plunge deeply into the forest. A few hundred yards from the river, he altered his slanting course and ran parallel with it. Balthus recognized a grim determination not to be hunted away from the river which they must cross if they were to warn the men in the fort. Behind them rose more loudly the yells of the forest men. Balthus believed the Picts had reached the glade where the bodies of the slain men lay. Then further yells seemed to indicate that the savages were streaming into the woods in pursuit. They had left a trail any Pict could follow.

Conan increased his speed, and Balthus grimly set his teeth and kept on his heels, though he felt he might collapse any time. It seemed centuries since he had eaten last. He kept going more by an effort of will than anything else. His blood was pounding so furiously in his ear-drums that he was not aware when the yells died out behind them.

Conan halted suddenly. Balthus leaned against a tree and panted.

"They've quit!" grunted the Cimmerian, scowling.

"Sneaking—up—on—us!" gasped Balthus.

Conan shook his head.

"A short chase like this they'd yell every step of the way. No. They've gone back. I thought I heard somebody yelling behind them a few seconds before the noise began to get dimmer. They've been recalled. And that's good for us, but damned bad for the men in the fort. It means the warriors are being summoned out of the woods for the attack. These men we ran into were warriors from a tribe down the river. They were undoubtedly headed for Gwawela to join in the assault on the fort. Damn it, we're farther away than ever, now. We've got to get across the river."

Turning east he hurried through the thickets with no attempt at concealment. Balthus followed him, for the first time feeling the sting of lacerations on his breast and shoulder where the Pict's savage teeth had scored him. He was pushing through the thick bushes that fringed the bank when Conan pulled him back. Then he heard a rhythmic splashing, and peering through the leaves, saw a dugout canoe coming up the river, its single occupant paddling hard against the current. He was a strongly built Pict with a white heron feather thrust in a copper band that confined his square-cut mane.

"That's a Gwawela man," muttered Conan. "Emissary from Zogar. White plume shows that. He's carried a peace talk to the tribes down the river and now he's trying to get back and take a hand in the slaughter."

The lone ambassador was now almost even with their hiding-place, and suddenly Balthus almost jumped out of his skin. At his very ear had sounded the harsh gutturals of a Pict. Then he realized that Conan had called to the paddler in his own tongue. The man started, scanned the bushes and called back something, then cast a startled glance across the river, bent low and sent the canoe shooting in toward the western bank. Not understanding, Balthus saw Conan take from his hand the bow he had picked up in the glade, and notch an arrow.

The Pict had run his canoe in close to the shore, and staring up into the bushes, called out something. His answer came in the twang of the bow-string, the streaking flight of the arrow that sank to the feathers in his broad breast. With a choking gasp he slumped sidewise and rolled into the shallow water. In an instant

Conan was down the bank and wading into the water to grasp the drifting canoe. Balthus stumbled after him and somewhat dazedly crawled into the canoe. Conan scrambled in, seized the paddle and sent the craft shooting toward the eastern shore. Balthus noted with envious admiration the play of the great muscles beneath the sun-burnt skin. The Cimmerian seemed an iron man, who never knew fatigue.

"What did you say to the Pict?" asked Balthus.

"Told him to pull into shore; said there was a white forest runner on the bank who was trying to get a shot at him."

"That doesn't seem fair," Balthus objected. "He thought a friend was speaking to him. You mimicked a Pict perfectly—"

"We needed his boat," grunted Conan, not pausing in his exertions. "Only way to lure him to the bank. Which is worse—to betray a Pict who'd enjoy skinning us both alive, or betray the men across the river whose lives depend on our getting over?"

Balthus mulled over this delicate ethical question for a moment, then shrugged his shoulder and asked: "How far are we from the fort?"

Conan pointed to a creek which flowed into Black River from the east, a few hundred yards below them.

"That's South Creek; it's ten miles from its mouth to the fort. It's the southern boundary of Conajohara. Marshes miles wide south of it. No danger of a raid from across them. Nine miles above the fort North Creek forms the other boundary. Marshes beyond that, too. That's why an attack must come from the west, across Black River. Conajohara's just like a spear, with a point nineteen miles wide, thrust into the Pictish wilderness."

"Why don't we keep to the canoe and make the trip

by water?"

"Because, considering the current we've got to brace, and the bends in the river, we can go faster afoot. Besides, remember Gwawela is south of the fort; if the Picts are crossing the river we'd run right into them."

Dusk was gathering as they stepped upon the eastern bank. Without pause Conan pushed on northward, at a pace that made Balthus' sturdy legs ache.

"Valannus wanted a fort built at the mouths of North and South Creeks," grunted the Cimmerian. "Then the river could be patrolled constantly. But the Government wouldn't do it.

"Soft-bellied fools sitting on velvet cushions with naked girls offering them iced wine on their knees—I know the breed. They can't see any farther than their palace wall. Diplomacy—hell! They'd fight Picts with theories of territorial expansion. Valannus and men like him have to obey the orders of a set of damned fools. They'll never grab any more Pictish land, any more than they'll ever rebuild Venarium. The time may come when they'll see the barbarians swarming over the walls of the Eastern cities!"

A week before, Balthus would have laughed at any such preposterous suggestion. Now he made no reply. He had seen the unconquerable ferocity of the men who dwelt beyond the frontiers.

He shivered, casting glances at the sullen river, just visible through the bushes, at the arches of the trees which crowded close to its banks. He kept remembering that the Picts might have crossed the river and be lying in ambush between them and the fort. It was fast growing dark.

A slight sound ahead of them jumped his heart into his throat, and Conan's sword gleamed in the air. He lowered it when a dog, a great, gaunt, scarred beast, slunk out of the bushes and stood staring at them.

"That dog belonged to a settler who tried to build his cabin on the bank of the river a few miles south of the fort," grunted Conan. "The Picts slipped over and killed him, of course, and burned his cabin. We found him dead among the embers, and the dog lying senseless among three Picts he'd killed. He was almost cut to pieces. We took him to the fort and dressed his wounds, but after he recovered he took to the woods and turned wild.—What now, Slasher, are you hunting the men who killed your master?"

The massive head swung from side to side and the eyes glowed greenly. He did not growl or bark. Silently as a phantom he slid in behind them.

"Let him come," muttered Conan. "He can smell the devils before we can see them."

Balthus smiled and laid his hand caressingly on the dog's head. The lips involuntarily writhed back to display the gleaming fangs; then the great beast bent his head sheepishly, and his tail moved with jerky uncertainty, as if the owner had almost forgotten the emotions of friendliness. Balthus mentally compared the great gaunt hard body with the fat sleek hounds tumbling vociferously over one another in his father's kennel yard. He sighed. The frontier was no less hard for beasts than for men. This dog had almost forgotten the meaning of kindness and friendliness.

Slasher glided ahead, and Conan let him take the lead. The last tinge of dusk faded into stark darkness. The miles fell away under their steady feet. Slasher seemed voiceless. Suddenly he halted, tense, ears lifted. An instant later the men heard it—a demoniac yelling up the river ahead of them, faint as a whisper.

Conan swore like a madman.

"They've attacked the fort! We're too late! Come on!"

He increased his pace, trusting to the dog to smell out ambushes ahead. In a flood of tense excitement Balthus forgot his hunger and weariness. The yells grew louder as they advanced, and above the devilish screaming they could hear the deep shouts of the soldiers. Just as Balthus began to fear they would run into the savages who seemed to be howling just ahead of them, Conan swung away from the river in a wide semicircle that carried them to a low rise from which they could look over the forest. They saw the fort, lighted with torches thrust over the parapets on long poles. These cast a flickering, uncertain light over the clearing, and in that light they saw throngs of naked, painted figures along the fringe of the clearing. The river swarmed with canoes. The Picts had the fort completely surrounded.

An incessant hail of arrows rained against the stockade from the woods and the river. The deep twanging of the bow-strings rose above the howling. Yelling like wolves, several hundred naked warriors with axes in their hands ran from under the trees and raced toward the eastern gate. They were within a hundred and fifty yards of their objective when a withering blast of arrows from the wall littered the ground with corpses and sent the survivors fleeing back to the trees. The men in the canoes rushed their boats toward the river-wall, and were met by another shower of clothyard shafts and a volley from the small ballistas mounted on towers on that side of the stockade. Stones and logs whirled through the air and splintered and sank half a dozen canoes, killing their occupants, and the other boats drew back out of range. A deep roar of triumph rose from the walls of the fort, answered by bestial howling from all quarters.

"Shall we try to break through?" asked Balthus, trembling with eagerness.

Conan shook his head. He stood with his arms folded, his head slightly bent, a somber and brooding figure.

"The fort's doomed. The Picts are blood-mad, and won't stop until they're all killed. And there are too many of them for the men in the fort to kill. We couldn't break through, and if we did, we could do nothing but die with Valannus."

"There's nothing we can do but save our own hides, then?"

"Yes. We've got to warn the settlers. Do you know why the Picts are not trying to burn the fort with fire-arrows? Because they don't want a flame that might warn the people to the east. They plan to stamp out the fort, and then sweep east before anyone knows of its fall. They may cross Thunder River and take Velitrium before the people know what's happened. At least they'll destroy every living thing between the fort and Thunder River.

"We've failed to warn the fort, and I see now it would have done no good if we had succeeded. The fort's too poorly manned. A few more charges and the Picts will be over the walls and breaking down the gates. But we can start the settlers toward Velitrium. Come on! We're outside the circle the Picts have thrown around the fort. We'll keep clear of it."

They swung out in a wide arc, hearing the rising and falling of the volume of the yells, marking each charge and repulse. The men in the fort were holding their own; but the shrieks of the Picts did not diminish in savagery. They vibrated with a timbre that held assurance of ultimate victory.

Before Balthus realized they were close to it, they broke into the road leading east.

"Now run!" grunted Conan. Balthus set his teeth. It was nineteen miles to Velitrium, a good five to Scalp Creek beyond which began the settlements. It seemed to the Aquilonian that they had been fighting and running for centuries. But the nervous excitement that rioted through his blood stimulated him to herculean efforts.

Slasher ran ahead of them, his head to the ground, snarling low, the first sound they had heard from him.

"Picts ahead of us!" snarled Conan, dropping to one knee and scanning the ground in the starlight. He shook his head, baffled. "I can't tell how many. Probably only a small party. Some that couldn't wait to take the fort. They've gone ahead to butcher the settlers in their beds! Come on!"

Ahead of them presently they saw a small blaze through the trees, and heard a wild and ferocious chanting. The trail bent there, and leaving it, they cut across the bend, through the thickets. A few moments later they were looking on a hideous sight. An ox-wain stood in the road piled with meager household furnishings; it was burning; the oxen lay near with their throats cut. A man and a woman lay in the road, stripped and mutilated. Five Picts were dancing about them with fantastic leaps and bounds, waving bloody axes; one of them brandished the woman's red-smeared gown.

At the sight a red haze swam before Balthus. Lifting his bow he lined the prancing figure, black against the fire, and loosed. The slayer leaped convulsively and fell dead with the arrow through his heart. Then the two white men and the dog were upon the startled survivors. Conan was animated merely by his fighting spirit and an old, old racial hate, but Balthus was afire with wrath.

He met the first Pict to oppose him with a ferocious swipe that split the painted skull, and sprang over his falling body to grapple with the others. But Conan had already killed one of the two he had chosen, and the leap of the Aquilonian was a second late. The warrior was down with the long sword through him even as Balthus' ax was lifted. Turning toward the remaining Pict, Balthus saw Slasher rise from his victim, his great jaws dripping blood.

Balthus said nothing as he looked down at the pitiful forms in the road beside the burning wain. Both were young, the woman little more than a girl. By some whim of chance the Picts had left her face unmarred, and even in the agonies of an awful death it was beautiful. But her soft young body had been hideously slashed with many knives—a mist clouded Balthus' eyes and he swallowed chokingly. The tragedy momentarily overcame him. He felt like falling upon the ground and weeping and biting the earth.

"Some young couple just hitting out on their own," Conan was saying as he wiped his sword unemotionally. "On their way to the fort when the Picts met them. Maybe the boy was going to enter the service; maybe take up land on the river. Well, that's what will happen to every man, woman and child this side of Thunder River if we don't get them into Velitrium in a hurry."

Balthus' knees trembled as he followed Conan. But there was no hint of weakness in the long easy stride of the Cimmerian. There was a kinship between him and the great gaunt brute that glided beside him. Slasher no longer growled with his head to the trail. The way was clear before them. The yelling on the river came faintly to them, but Balthus believed the fort was still holding.

Conan halted suddenly, with an oath.

He showed Balthus a trail that led north from the road. It was an old trail, partly grown with new young growth, and this growth had recently been broken down. Balthus realized this fact more by feel than sight, though Conan seemed to see like a cat in the dark. The Cimmerian showed him where broad wagon tracks turned off the main trail, deeply indented in the forest mold.

"Settlers going to the licks after salt," he grunted. "They're at the edges of the marsh, about nine miles from here. Blast it! They'll be cut off and butchered to a man! Listen! One man can warn the people on the road. Go ahead and wake them up and herd them into Velitrium. I'll go and get the men gathering the salt. They'll be camped by the licks. We won't come back to the road. We'll head straight through the woods."

With no further comment Conan turned off the trail and hurried down the dim path, and Balthus, after staring after him for a few moments, set out along the road. The dog had remained with him, and glided softly at his heels. When Balthus had gone a few rods he heard the animal growl. Whirling, he glared back the way he had come, and was startled to see a vague ghostly glow vanishing into the forest in the direction Conan had taken. Slasher rumbled deep in his throat, his hackles stiff and his eyes balls of green fire. Balthus remembered the grim apparition that had taken the head of the merchant Tiberias not far from that spot, and he hesitated. The thing must be following Conan. But the giant Cimmerian had repeatedly demonstrated his ability to take care of himself, and Balthus felt his duty lay toward the helpless settlers who slumbered in the path of the red hurricane. The horror of the fiery phantom was overshadowed by the horror of those limp, violated bodies beside the burning ox-wain.

He hurried down the road, crossed Scalp Creek and came in sight of the first settler's cabin—a long, low structure of ax-hewn logs. In an instant he was pounding on the door. A sleepy voice inquired his pleasure.

"Get up! The Picts are over the river!"

That brought instant response. A low cry echoed his words and then the door was thrown open by a woman in a scanty shift. Her hair hung over her bare shoulders in disorder; she held a candle in one hand and an ax in the other. Her face was colorless, her eyes wide with terror.

"Come in!" she begged. "We'll hold the cabin."

"No. We must make for Velitrium. The fort can't hold them back. It may have fallen already. Don't stop to dress. Get your children and come on."

"But my man's gone with the others after salt!" she wailed, wringing her hands. Behind her peered three tousled youngsters, blinking and bewildered.

"Conan's gone after them. He'll fetch them through safe. We must hurry up the road to warn the other cabins."

Relief flooded her countenance.

"Mitra be thanked!" she cried. "If the Cimmerian's gone after them, they're safe if mortal man can save them!"

In a whirlwind of activity she snatched up the smallest child and herded the others through the door ahead of her. Balthus took the candle and ground it out under his heel. He listened an instant. No sound came up the dark road.

"Have you got a horse?"

"In the stable," she groaned. "Oh, hurry!"

He pushed her aside as she fumbled with shaking

hands at the bars. He led the horse out and lifted the children on its back, telling them to hold to its mane and to one another. They stared at him seriously, making no outcry. The woman took the horse's halter and set out up the road. She still gripped her ax and Balthus knew that if cornered she would fight with the desperate courage of a she-panther.

He held behind, listening. He was oppressed by the belief that the fort had been stormed and taken; that the dark-skinned hordes were already streaming up the road toward Velitrium, drunken on slaughter and mad for blood. They would come with the speed of starving wolves.

Presently they saw another cabin looming ahead. The woman started to shriek a warning, but Balthus stopped her. He hurried to the door and knocked. A woman's voice answered him. He repeated his warning, and soon the cabin disgorged its occupants—an old woman, two young women and four children. Like the other woman's husband, their men had gone to the salt licks the day before, unsuspecting of any danger. One of the young women seemed dazed, the other prone to hysteria. But the old woman, a stern old veteran of the frontier, quieted them harshly; she helped Balthus get out the two horses that were stabled in a pen behind the cabin and put the children on them. Balthus urged that she herself mount with them, but she shook her head and made one of the younger women ride.

"She's with child," grunted the old woman. "I can walk—and fight, too, if it comes to that."

As they set out, one of the young women said: "A young couple passed along the road about dusk; we advised them to spend the night at our cabin, but they were anxious to make the fort tonight. Did—did—"

"They met the Picts," answered Balthus briefly, and

the woman sobbed in horror.

They were scarcely out of sight of the cabin when some distance behind them quavered a long high-pitched yell.

"A wolf!" exclaimed one of the women.

"A painted wolf with an ax in his hand," muttered Balthus. "Go! Rouse the other settlers along the road and take them with you. I'll scout along behind."

Without a word the old woman herded her charges ahead of her. As they faded into the darkness, Balthus could see the pale ovals that were the faces of the children twisted back over their shoulders to stare toward him. He remembered his own people on the Tauran and a moment's giddy sickness swam over him. With momentary weakness he groaned and sank down in the road; his muscular arm fell over Slasher's massive neck and he felt the dog's warm moist tongue touch his face.

He lifted his head and grinned with a painful effort.

"Come on, boy," he mumbled, rising. "We've got work to do."

A red glow suddenly became evident through the trees. The Picts had fired the last hut. He grinned. How Zogar Sag would froth if he knew his warriors had let their destructive natures get the better of them. The fire would warn the people farther up the road. They would be awake and alert when the fugitives reached them. But his face grew grim. The women were traveling slowly, on foot and on the overloaded horses. The swift-footed Picts would run them down within a mile, unless—he took his position behind a tangle of fallen logs beside the trail. The road west of him was lighted by the burning cabin, and when the Picts came he saw them first—black furtive figures etched against the distant glare.

Drawing a shaft to the head, he loosed and one of the figures crumpled. The rest melted into the woods on either side of the road. Slasher whimpered with the killing lust beside him. Suddenly a figure appeared on the fringe of the trail, under the trees, and began gliding toward the fallen timbers. Balthus' bow-string twanged and the Pict yelped, staggered and fell into the shadows with the arrow through his thigh. Slasher cleared the timbers with a bound and leaped into the bushes. They were violently shaken and then the dog slunk back to Balthus' side, his jaws crimson.

No more appeared in the trail; Balthus began to fear they were stealing past his position through the woods, and when he heard a faint sound to his left he loosed blindly. He cursed as he heard the shaft splinter against a tree, but Slasher glided away as silently as a phantom, and presently Balthus heard a thrashing and a gurgling; then Slasher came like a ghost through the bushes, snuggling his great, crimson-stained head against Balthus' arm. Blood oozed from a gash in his shoulder, but the sounds in the wood had ceased for ever.

The men lurking on the edges of the road evidently sensed the fate of their companion, and decided that an open charge was preferable to being dragged down in the dark by a devil-beast they could neither see nor hear. Perhaps they realized that only one man lay behind the logs. They came with a sudden rush, breaking cover from both sides of the trail. Three dropped with arrows through them—and the remaining pair hesitated. One turned and ran back down the road, but the other lunged over the breastwork, his eyes and teeth gleaming in the dim light, his ax lifted. Balthus' foot slipped as he sprang up, but the slip saved his life. The descending ax shaved a lock of hair from his head, and the Pict rolled down the logs from the force of his wasted blow. Before he could regain his feet Slasher tore his throat out.

Then followed a tense period of waiting, in which time Balthus wondered if the man who had fled had been the only survivor of the party. Obviously it had been a small band that had either left the fighting at the fort, or was scouting ahead of the main body. Each moment that passed increased the chances for safety of the women and children hurrying toward Velitrium.

Then without warning a shower of arrows whistled over his retreat. A wild howling rose from the woods along the trail. Either the survivor had gone after aid, or another party had joined the first. The burning cabin still smoldered, lending a little light. Then they were after him, gliding through the trees beside the trail. He shot three arrows and threw the bow away. As if sensing his plight, they came on, not yelling now, but in deadly silence except for a swift pad of many feet.

He fiercely hugged the head of the great dog growling at his side, muttered: "All right, boy, give 'em hell!" and sprang to his feet, drawing his ax. Then the dark figures flooded over the breastworks and closed in a storm of flailing axes, stabbing knives and ripping fangs.

7. *The Devil in the Fire*

WHEN CONAN TURNED from the Velitrium road he expected a run of some nine miles and set himself to the task. But he had not gone four when he heard the sounds of a party of men ahead of him. From the noise they were making in their progress he knew they were not Picts. He hailed them.

"Who's there?" challenged a harsh voice. "Stand where you are until we know you, or you'll get an arrow through you."

"You couldn't hit an elephant in this darkness," answered Conan impatiently. "Come on, fool; it's I— Conan. The Picts are over the river."

"We suspected as much," answered the leader of the men, as they strode forward—tall, rangy men, stern-faced, with bows in their hands. "One of our party wounded an antelope and tracked it nearly to Black River. He heard them yelling down the river and ran back to our camp. We left the salt and the wagons, turned the oxen loose and came as swiftly as we could. If the Picts are besieging the fort, war-parties will be ranging up the road toward our cabins."

"Your families are safe," grunted Conan. "My companion went ahead to take them to Velitrium. If we go back to the main road we may run into the whole horde. We'll strike southeast, through the timber. Go ahead. I'll scout behind."

A few moments later the whole band was hurrying southeastward. Conan followed more slowly, keeping just within ear-shot. He cursed the noise they were making; that many Picts or Cimmerians would have moved through the woods with no more noise than the wind makes as it blows through the black branches.

He had just crossed a small glade when he wheeled, answering the conviction of his primitive instincts that he was being followed. Standing motionless among the bushes he heard the sounds of the retreating settlers fade away. Then a voice called faintly back along the way he had come: "Conan! Conan! Wait for me, Conan!"

"Balthus!" he swore bewilderedly. Cautiously he called: "Here I am!"

"Wait for me, Conan!" the voice came more distinctly.

Conan moved out of the shadows, scowling. "What the devil are you doing here?—*Crom*!"

He half crouched, the flesh prickling along his spine. It was not Balthus who was emerging from the other side of the glade. A weird glow burned through the trees. It moved toward him, shimmering weirdly—a green witch-fire that moved with purpose and intent.

It halted some feet away and Conan glared at it, trying to distinguish its fire-misted outlines. The quivering flame had a solid core; the flame was but a green garment that masked some animate and evil entity; but the Cimmerian was unable to make out its shape or likeness. Then, shockingly, a voice spoke to him from amidst the fiery column.

"Why do you stand like a sheep waiting for the butcher, Conan?"

The voice was human but carried strange vibrations that were not human.

"Sheep?" Conan's wrath got the best of his momentary awe. "Do you think I'm afraid of a damned Pictish swamp devil? A friend called me."

"I called in his voice," answered the other. "The men you follow belong to my brother; I would not rob his knife of their blood. But you are mine. Oh, fool, you have come from the far gray hills of Cimmeria to meet your doom in the forests of Conajohara."

"You've had your chance at me before now," snorted Conan. "Why didn't you kill me then, if you could?"

"My brother had not painted a skull black for you and hurled it into the fire that burns for ever on Gullah's black altar. He had not whispered your name to the black ghosts that haunt the uplands of the Dark Land. But a bat has flown over the Mountains of the Dead and drawn your image in blood on the white tiger's hide that hangs before the long hut where sleep the Four Brothers of the Night. The great serpents coil about their feet and the stars burn like fire-flies in their hair."

"Why have the gods of darkness doomed me to death?" growled Conan.

Something—a hand, foot or talon, he could not tell which, thrust out from the fire and marked swiftly on the mold. A symbol blazed there, marked with fire, and faded, but not before he recognized it.

"You dared make the sign which only a priest of Jhebbal Sag dare make. Thunder rumbled through the black Mountain of the Dead and the altar-hut of Gullah was thrown down by a wind from the Gulf of Ghosts. The loon which is messenger to the Four Brothers of the Night flew swiftly and whispered your name in my ear. Your race is run. You are a dead man already. Your head will hang in the altar-hut of my brother. Your body will be eaten by the black-winged, sharp-beaked Children of Jhil."

"Who the devil is your brother?" demanded Conan. His sword was naked in his hand, and he was subtly loosening the ax in his belt.

"Zogar Sag; a child of Jhebbal Sag who still visits his sacred groves at times. A woman of Gwawela slept in a grove holy to Jhebbal Sag. Her babe was Zogar Sag. I too am a son of Jhebbal Sag, out of a fire-being from a far realm. Zogar Sag summoned me out of the Misty Lands. With incantations and sorcery and his own blood he materialized me in the flesh of his own planet. We are one, tied together by invisible threads. His thoughts are my thoughts; if he is struck, I am bruised. If I am cut, he bleeds. But I have talked enough. Soon your ghost will talk with the ghosts of the Dark Land, and they will tell you of the old gods which are not dead, but sleep in the outer abysses, and from time to time awake."

"I'd like to see what you look like," muttered Conan, working his ax free, "you who leave a track like a bird, who burn like a flame and yet speak with a human voice."

"You shall see," answered the voice from the flame, "see, and carry the knowledge with you into the Dark Land."

The flames leaped and sank, dwindling and dimming. A face began to take shadowy form. At first Conan thought it was Zogar Sag himself who stood wrapped in green fire. But the face was higher than his own, and there was a demoniac aspect about it— Conan had noted various abnormalities about Zogar Sag's features—an obliqueness of the eyes, a sharpness of the ears, a wolfish thinness of the lips: these peculiarities were exaggerated in the apparition which swayed before him. The eyes were red as coals of living fire.

More details came into view: a slender torso, covered with snaky scales, which was yet man-like in shape, with man-like arms, from the waist upward; below, long crane-like legs ended in splay, three-toed feet like those of some huge bird. Along the monstrous limbs the blue fire fluttered and ran. He saw it as through a glistening mist.

Then suddenly it was towering over him, though he had not seen it move toward him. A long arm, which for the first time he noticed was armed with curving, sickle-like talons, swung high and swept down at his neck. With a fierce cry he broke the spell and bounded aside, hurling his ax. The demon avoided the cast with an unbelievably quick movement of its narrow head and was on him again with a hissing rush of leaping flames.

But fear had fought for it when it slew its other victims, and Conan was not afraid. He knew that any being clothed in material flesh can be slain by material weapons, however grisly its form may be.

One flailing talon-armed limb knocked his helmet from his head. A little lower and it would have decapitated him. But fierce joy surged through him as his savagely driven sword sank deep in the monster's groin. He bounded backward from a flailing stroke, tearing his sword free as he leaped. The talons raked his breast, ripping through mail-links as if they had been cloth. But his return spring was like that of a starving wolf. He was inside the lashing arms and driving his sword deep in the monster's belly—felt the arms lock about him and the talons ripping the mail from his back as they sought his vitals—he was lapped and dazzled by blue flame that was chill as ice—then he had torn fiercely away from the weakening arms and his sword cut the air in a tremendous swipe.

The demon staggered and fell sprawling sidewise, its head hanging only by a shred of flesh. The fires that veiled it leaped fiercely upward, now red as gushing blood, hiding the figure from view. A scent of burning flesh filled Conan's nostrils. Shaking the blood and sweat from his eyes, he wheeled and ran staggering through the woods. Blood trickled down his limbs. Somewhere, miles to the south, he saw the faint glow of flames that might mark a burning cabin. Behind him, toward the road, rose a distant howling that spurred him to greater efforts.

8. *Conajohara No More*

THERE HAD BEEN fighting on Thunder River; fierce fighting before the walls of Velitrium; ax and torch had been plied up and down the bank, and many a settler's cabin lay in ashes before the painted horde was rolled back.

A strange quiet followed the storm, in which people gathered and talked in hushed voices, and men with red-stained bandages drank their ale silently in the taverns along the river bank.

There, to Conan the Cimmerian, moodily quaffing from a great wine-glass, came a gaunt forester with a bandage about his head and his arm in a sling. He was the one survivor of Fort Tuscelan.

"You went with the soldiers to the ruins of the fort?" Conan nodded.

"I wasn't able," murmured the other. "There was no fighting?"

"The Picts had fallen back across Black River. Something must have broken their nerve, though only the devil who made them knows what."

The woodsman glanced at his bandaged arm and sighed.

"They say there were no bodies worth disposing of."

Conan shook his head. "Ashes. The Picts had piled them in the fort and set fire to the fort before they crossed the river. Their own dead and the men of Valannus."

"Valannus was killed among the last—in the hand-to-hand fighting when they broke the barriers. They tried to take him alive, but he made them kill him. They took ten of the rest of us prisoners when we were so weak from fighting we could fight no more. They butchered nine of us then and there. It was when Zogar Sag died that I got my chance to break free and run for it."

"Zogar Sag's dead?" ejaculated Conan.

"Aye. I saw him die. That's why the Picts didn't press the fight against Velitrium as fiercely as they did against the fort. It was strange. He took no wounds in battle. He was dancing among the slain, waving an ax with which he'd just brained the last of my comrades. He came at me, howling like a wolf—and then he staggered and dropped the ax, and began to reel in a circle screaming as I never heard a man or beast scream before. He fell between me and the fire they'd built to roast me, gagging and frothing at the mouth, and all at once he went rigid and the Picts shouted that he was dead. It was during the confusion that I slipped my cords and ran for the woods.

"I saw him lying in the firelight. No weapon had touched him. Yet there were red marks like the wounds of a sword in the groin, belly and neck—the last as if his head had been almost severed from his body. What do you make of that?"

Conan made no reply, and the forester, aware of the reticence of barbarians on certain matters, continued: "He lived by magic, and somehow, he died by magic. It was the mystery of his death that took the heart out of the Picts. Not a man who saw it was in the fighting before Velitrium. They hurried back across Black River. Those that struck Thunder River were warriors who had come on before Zogar Sag died. They were not enough to take the city by themselves.

"I came along the road, behind their main force, and I know none followed me from the fort. I sneaked through their lines and got into the town. You brought the settlers through all right, but their women and children got into Velitrium just ahead of those painted devils. If the youth Balthus and old Slasher hadn't held them up awhile, they'd have butchered every woman and child in Conajohara. I passed the place where Balthus and the dog made their last stand. They were lying amid a heap of dead Picts—I counted seven, brained by his ax, or disemboweled by the dog's fangs, and there were others in the road with arrows sticking in them. Gods, what a fight that must have been!"

"He was a man," said Conan. "I drink to his shade, and to the shade of the dog, who knew no fear." He quaffed part of the wine, then emptied the rest upon the floor, with a curious heathen gesture, and smashed the goblet. "The heads of ten Picts shall pay for his, and seven heads for the dog, who was a better warrior than many a man."

And the forester, staring into the moody, smoldering blue eyes, knew the barbaric oath would be kept.

"They'll not rebuild the fort?"

"No; Conajohara is lost to Aquilonia. The frontier has been pushed back. Thunder River will be the new border."

The woodsman sighed and stared at his calloused hand, worn from contact with ax-haft and sword-hilt. Conan reached his long arm for the wine-jug. The forester stared at him, comparing him with the men about them, the men who had died along the lost river, comparing him with those other wild men over that river. Conan did not seem aware of his gaze.

"Barbarism is the natural state of mankind," the borderer said, still staring somberly at the Cimmerian. "Civilization is unnatural. It is a whim of circumstance. And barbarism must always ultimately triumph."

Shadows in Zamboula

1. A Drum Begins

"PERIL HIDES IN the house of Aram Baksh!"

The speaker's voice quivered with earnestness and his lean, black-nailed fingers clawed at Conan's mightily-muscled arm as he croaked his warning. He was a wiry, sun-burnt man with a straggling black beard, and his ragged garments proclaimed him a nomad. He looked smaller and meaner than ever in contrast to the giant Cimmerian with his black brows, broad chest, and powerful limbs. They stood in a corner of the Sword-Makers' Bazar, and on either side of them flowed past the many-tongued, many-colored stream of the Zamboula streets, which is exotic, hybrid, flamboyant and clamorous.

Conan pulled his eyes back from following a bold-eyed, red-lipped Ghanara whose short slit skirt bared her brown thigh at each insolent step, and frowned down at his importunate companion.

"What do you mean by peril?" he demanded.

The desert man glanced furtively over his shoulder before replying, and lowered his voice.

"Who can say? But desert men and travelers *have* slept in the house of Aram Baksh, and never been seen or heard of again. What became of them? *He* swore they rose and went their way—and it is true that no citizen of the city has ever disappeared from his house. But no one saw the travelers again, and men say that goods and equipment recognized as theirs have been seen in the bazars. If Aram did not sell them, after doing away with their owners, how came they there?"

"I have no goods," growled the Cimmerian, touching the shagreen-bound hilt of the broadsword that hung at his hip. "I have even sold my horse."

"But it is not always rich strangers who vanish by night from the house of Aram Baksh!" chattered the Zuagir. "Nay, poor desert men have slept there—because his score is less than that of the other taverns—and have been seen no more. Once a chief of the Zuagirs whose son had thus vanished complained to the satrap, Jungir Khan, who ordered the house searched by soldiers."

"And they found a cellar full of corpses?" asked Conan in good-humored derision.

"Nay! They found naught! And drove the chief from the city with threats and curses! But"—he drew closer to Conan and shivered—"something else was found! At the edge of the desert, beyond the houses, there is a clump of palm-trees, and within that grove there is a pit. And within that pit have been found human bones, charred and blackened! Not once, but many times!"

"Which proves what?" grunted the Cimmerian.

"Aram Baksh is a demon! Nay, in this accursed city which Stygians built and which Hyrkanians rule—where white, brown and black folk mingle together to produce hybrids of all unholy hues and breeds—who can tell who is a man, and who a demon in disguise? Aram Baksh is a demon in the form of a man! At night he assumes his true guise and carries his guests off into the desert where his fellow demons from the waste meet in conclave."

"Why does he always carry off strangers?" asked Conan skeptically.

"The people of the city would not suffer him to slay their people, but they care naught for the strangers who fall into his hands. Conan, you are of the West, and know not the secrets of this ancient land. But, since the beginning of happenings, the demons of the desert have worshipped Yog, the Lord of the Empty Abodes, with fire—fire that devours human victims.

"Be warned! You have dwelt for many moons in the tents of the Zuagirs, and you are our brother! Go not to the house of Aram Baksh!"

"Get out of sight!" Conan said suddenly. "Yonder comes a squad of the city-watch. If they see you they may remember a horse that was stolen from the satrap's stable—"

The Zuagir gasped; and moved convulsively. He ducked between a booth and a stone horse-trough, pausing only long enough to chatter: "Be warned, my brother! There are demons in the house of Aram Baksh!" Then he darted down a narrow alley and was gone.

Conan shifted his broad sword-belt to his liking, and calmly returned the searching stares directed at him by the squad of watchmen as they swung past. They eyed him curiously and suspiciously, for he was a man who stood out even in such a motley throng as crowded the winding streets of Zamboula. His blue eyes and alien features distinguished him from the Eastern swarms, and the straight sword at his hip added point to the racial difference.

The watchmen did not accost him, but swung on down the street, while the crowd opened a lane for them. They were Pelishtim, squat, hook-nosed, with blue-black beards sweeping their mailed breasts—mercenaries hired for work the ruling Turanians considered beneath themselves, and no less hated by the mongrel population for that reason.

Conan glanced at the sun, just beginning to dip behind the flat-topped houses on the western side of the bazar, and hitching once more at his belt, moved off in the direction of Aram Baksh's tavern.

With a hillman's stride he moved through the ever-shifting colors of the streets, where the ragged tunics of whining beggars brushed against the ermine-trimmed khalats of lordly merchants, and the pearl-sewn satin of rich courtezans. Giant black slaves slouched along, jostling blue-bearded wanderers from the Shemitish cities, ragged nomads from the surrounding deserts, traders and adventurers from all the lands of the East.

The native population was no less heterogenous. Here, centuries ago, the armies of Stygia had come, carving an empire out of the eastern desert. Zamboula was but a small trading-town then, lying amidst a ring of oases, and inhabited by descendants of nomads. The Stygians built it into a city and settled it with their own people, and with Shemite and Kushite slaves. The ceaseless caravans, threading the desert from east to west and back again, brought riches and more mingling of races. Then came the conquering Turanians, riding out of the East to thrust báck the boundaries of Stygia, and now for a generation Zamboula had been Turan's westernmost outpost, ruled by a Turanian satrap.

The babel of a myriad tongues smote on the Cimmerian's ears as the restless pattern of the Zamboula streets weaved about him—cleft now and then by a squad of clattering horsemen, the tall, supple warriors of Turan, with dark hawk-faces, clinking metal and curved swords. The throng scampered from under their horses' hoofs, for they were the lords of Zamboula. But tall, somber Stygians, standing back in the shadows, glowered darkly, remembering their ancient glories. The hybrid population cared little whether the king who controlled their destinies dwelt in dark Khemi or gleaming Aghrapur. Jungir Khan ruled Zamboula, and men whispered that Nafertari, the satrap's mistress, ruled Jungir Khan; but the people went their way, flaunting their myriad colors in the streets, bargaining, disputing, gambling, swilling, loving, as the people of Zamboula have done for all the centuries its towers and minarets have lifted over the sands of the Kharamun.

Bronze lanterns, carved with leering dragons, had been lighted in the streets before Conan reached the house of Aram Baksh. The tavern was the last occupied house on the street, which ran west. A wide garden, enclosed by a wall, where date-palms grew thick, separated it from the houses farther east. To the west of the inn stood another grove of palms, through which the street, now become a road, wound out into the desert. Across the road from the tavern stood a row of deserted huts, shaded by straggling palm-trees, and occupied only by bats and jackals. As Conan came down the road he wondered why the beggars, so plentiful in Zamboula, had not appropriated these empty houses for sleeping-quarters. The lights ceased some distance behind him. Here were no lanterns, except the one hanging before the tavern gate: only the stars, the soft dust of the road underfoot, and the rustle of the palm-leaves in the desert breeze.

Aram's gate did not open upon the road, but upon the alley which ran between the tavern and the garden of the date-palms. Conan jerked lustily at the rope which depended from the bell beside the lantern, augmenting its clamor by hammering on the iron-bound teakwood gate with the hilt of his sword. A wicket opened in the gate and a black face peered through.

"Open, blast you," requested Conan. "I'm a guest. I've paid Aram for a room, and a room I'll have, by Crom!"

The black craned his neck to stare into the starlit road behind Conan; but he opened the gate without comment, and closed it again behind the Cimmerian, locking it and bolting it. The wall was unusually high; but there were many thieves in Zamboula, and a house on the edge of the desert might have to be defended against a nocturnal nomad raid. Conan strode through a garden where great pale blossoms nodded in the starlight, and entered the tap-room, where a Stygian with the shaven head of a student sat at a table brooding over nameless mysteries, and some nondescripts wrangled over a game of dice in a corner.

Aram Baksh came forward, walking softly, a portly man, with a black beard that swept his breast, a jutting hook-nose, and small black eyes which were never still.

"You wish food?" he asked. "Drink?"

"I ate a joint of beef and a loaf of bread in the *suk*," grunted Conan. "Bring me a tankard of Ghazan wine— I've got just enough left to pay for it." He tossed a copper coin on the wine-splashed board.

"You did not win at the gaming-tables?"

"How could I, with only a handful of silver to begin with? I paid you for the room this morning, because I knew I'd probably lose. I wanted to be sure I had a roof over my head tonight. I notice nobody sleeps in the streets in Zamboula. The very beggars hunt a niche they can barricade before dark. The city must be full of a particularly bloodthirsty brand of thieves."

He gulped the cheap wine with relish, and then followed Aram out of the tap-room. Behind him the players halted their game to stare after him with a cryptic speculation in their eyes. They said nothing, but the Stygian laughed, a ghastly laugh of inhuman cynicism and mockery. The others lowered their eyes uneasily, avoiding one another's glance. The arts studied by a Stygian scholar are not calculated to make him share the feelings of a normal human being.

Conan followed Aram down a corridor lighted by

copper lamps, and it did not please him to note his host's noiseless tread. Aram's feet were clad in soft slippers and the hallway was carpeted with thick Turanian rugs; but there was an unpleasant suggestion of stealthiness about the Zamboulan.

At the end of the winding corridor Aram halted at a door, across which a heavy iron bar rested in powerful metal brackets. This Aram lifted and showed the Cimmerian into a well-appointed chamber, the windows of which, Conan instantly noted, were small and strongly set with twisted bars of iron, tastefully gilded. There were rugs on the floor, a couch, after the Eastern fashion, and ornately carven stools. It was a much more elaborate chamber than Conan could have procured for the price nearer the center of the city—a fact that had first attracted him, when, that morning, he discovered how slim a purse his roisterings for the past few days had left him. He had ridden into Zamboula from the desert a week before.

Aram had lighted a bronze lamp, and he now called Conan's attention to the two doors. Both were provided with heavy bolts.

"You may sleep safely tonight, Cimmerian," said Aram, blinking over his bushy beard from the inner doorway.

Conan grunted and tossed his naked broadsword on the couch.

"Your bolts and bars are strong; but I always sleep with steel by my side."

Aram made no reply; he stood fingering his thick beard for a moment as he stared at the grim weapon. Then silently he withdrew, closing the door behind him. Conan shot the bolt into place, crossed the room, opened the opposite door and looked out. The room was on the side of the house that faced the road running west from the city. The door opened into a small court that was enclosed by a wall of its own. The end-walls, which shut it off from the rest of the tavern compound, were high and without entrances; but the wall that flanked the road was low, and there was no lock on the gate.

Conan stood for a moment in the door, the glow of the bronze lamp behind him, looking down the road to where it vanished among the dense palms. Their leaves rustled together in the faint breeze; beyond them lay the naked desert. Far up the street, in the other direction, lights gleamed and the noises of the city came faintly to him. Here was only starlight, the whispering of the palm-leaves, and beyond that low wall, the dust of the road and the deserted huts thrusting their flat roofs against the low stars. Somewhere beyond the palm groves a drum began.

The garbled warnings of the Zuagir returned to him, seeming somehow less fantastic than they had seemed in the crowded, sunlit streets. He wondered again at the riddle of those empty huts. Why did the beggars shun them? He turned back into the chamber, shut the door and bolted it.

The light began to flicker, and he investigated, swearing when he found the palm-oil in the lamp was almost exhausted. He started to shout for Aram, then shrugged his shoulders and blew out the light. In the soft darkness he stretched himself fully clad on the couch, his sinewy hand by instinct searching for and closing on the hilt of his broadsword. Glancing idly at the stars framed in the barred windows, with the murmur of the breeze through the palms in his ears, he sank into slumber with a vague consciousness of the muttering drum, out on the desert—the low rumble and mutter of a leather-covered drum, beaten with soft, rhythmic strokes of an open black hand....

2.   *The Night Skulkers*

IT WAS THE stealthy opening of a door which awakened the Cimmerian. He did not awake as civilized men do, drowsy and drugged and stupid. He awoke instantly, with a clear mind, recognizing the sound that had interrupted his sleep. Lying there tensely in the dark he saw the outer door slowly open. In a widening crack of starlit sky he saw framed a great black bulk, broad, stooping shoulders and a misshapen head blocked out against the stars.

Conan felt the skin crawl between his shoulders. He had bolted that door securely. How could it be opening now, save by supernatural agency? And how could a human being possess a head like that outlined against the stars? All the tales he had heard in the Zuagir tents of devils and goblins came back to bead his flesh with clammy sweat. Now the monster slid noiselessly into the room, with a crouching posture and a shambling gait; and a familiar scent assailed the Cimmerian's nostrils, but did not reassure him, since Zuagir legendry represented demons as smelling like that.

Noiselessly Conan coiled his long legs under him; his naked sword was in his right hand, and when he struck it was as suddenly and murderously as a tiger lunging out of the dark. Not even a demon could have avoided that catapulting charge. His sword met and clove through flesh and bone, and something went heavily to the floor with a strangling cry. Conan crouched in the dark above it, sword dripping in his hand. Devil or beast or man, the thing was dead there on the floor. He sensed death as any wild thing senses it. He glared through the half-open door into the starlit court beyond. The gate stood open, but the court was empty.

Conan shut the door but did not bolt it. Groping in the darkness he found the lamp and lighted it. There was enough oil in it to burn for a minute or so. An instant later he was bending over the figure that sprawled on the floor in a pool of blood.

It was a gigantic black man, naked but for a loin-cloth. One hand still grasped a knotty-headed bludgeon. The fellow's kinky wool was built up into horn-like spindles with twigs and dried mud. This barbaric coiffure had given the head its misshapen appearance in the starlight. Provided with a clue to the riddle, Conan pushed back the thick red lips, and grunted as he stared down at teeth filed to points.

He understood now the mystery of the strangers who had disappeared from the house of Aram Baksh; the riddle of the black drum thrumming out there beyond the palm groves, and of that pit of charred bones—that pit where strange meat might be roasted under the stars, while black beasts squatted about to glut a hideous hunger. The man on the floor was a cannibal slave from Darfar.

There were many of his kind in the city. Cannibalism was not tolerated openly in Zamboula. But Conan knew now why people locked themselves in so securely at night, and why even beggars shunned the open alleys and doorless ruins. He grunted in disgust as he visualized brutish black shadows skulking up and down the nighted streets, seeking human prey—and such men as Aram Baksh to open the doors to them. The innkeeper was not a demon; he was worse. The slaves from Darfar were notorious thieves; there was no doubt that some of their pilfered loot found its way into the hands of Aram Baksh. And in return he sold them human flesh.

Conan blew out the light, stepped to the door and

opened it, and ran his hand over the ornaments on the outer side. One of them was movable and worked the bolt inside. The room was a trap to catch human prey like rabbits. But this time instead of a rabbit it had caught a saber-toothed tiger.

Conan returned to the other door, lifted the bolt and pressed against it. It was immovable and he remembered the bolt on the other side. Aram was taking no chances either with his victims or the men with whom he dealt. Buckling on his sword-belt, the Cimmerian strode out into the court, closing the door behind him. He had no intention of delaying the settlement of his reckoning with Aram Baksh. He wondered how many poor devils had been bludgeoned in their sleep and dragged out of that room and down the road that ran through the shadowed palm groves to the roasting-pit.

He halted in the court. The drum was still muttering, and he caught the reflection of a leaping red glare through the groves. Cannibalism was more than a perverted appetite with the black men of Darfar; it was an integral element of their ghastly cult. The black vultures were already in conclave. But whatever flesh filled their bellies that night, it would not be his.

To reach Aram Baksh he must climb one of the walls which separated the small enclosure from the main compound. They were high, meant to keep out the man-eaters; but Conan was no swamp-bred black man; his thews had been steeled in boyhood on the sheer cliffs of his native hills. He was standing at the foot of the nearer wall when a cry echoed under the trees.

In an instant Conan was crouching at the gate, glaring down the road. The sound had come from the shadows of the huts across the road. He heard a frantic choking and gurgling such as might result from a desperate attempt to shriek, with a black hand fastened over the victim's mouth. A close-knit clump of figures emerged from the shadows beyond the huts, and started down the road—three huge black men carrying a slender, struggling figure between them. Conan caught the glimmer of pale limbs writhing in the starlight, even as, with a convulsive wrench, the captive slipped from the grasp of the brutal fingers and came flying up the road, a supple young woman, naked as the day she was born. Conan saw her plainly before she ran out of the road and into the shadows between the huts. The blacks were at her heels, and back in the shadows the figures merged and an intolerable scream of anguish and horror rang out.

Stirred to red rage by the ghoulishness of the episode, Conan raced across the road.

Neither victim nor abductors were aware of his presence until the soft swish of the dust about his feet brought them about, and then he was almost upon them, coming with gusty fury of a hill wind. Two of the blacks turned to meet him, lifting their bludgeons. But they failed to estimate properly the speed at which he was coming. One of them was down, disemboweled, before he could strike, and wheeling cat-like, Conan evaded the stroke of the other's cudgel and lashed in a whistling counter-cut. The black's head flew into the air; the headless body took three staggering steps, spurting blood and clawing horribly at the air with groping hands, and then slumped to the dust.

The remaining cannibal gave back with a strangled yell, hurling his captive from him. She tripped and rolled in the dust, and the black fled in blind panic toward the city. Conan was at his heels. Fear winged the black feet, but before they reached the easternmost hut, he sensed death at his back, and bellowed like an ox in the slaughter-yards.

"Black dog of hell!" Conan drove his sword between the dusky shoulders with such vengeful fury that the broad blade stood out half its length from the black breast. With a choking cry the black stumbled headlong, and Conan braced his feet and dragged out his sword as his victim fell.

Only the breeze disturbed the leaves. Conan shook his head as a lion shakes its mane and growled his unsatiated blood-lust. But no more shapes slunk from the shadows, and before the huts the starlit road stretched empty. He whirled at the quick patter of feet behind him, but it was only the girl, rushing to throw herself on him and clasp his neck in a desperate grasp, frantic from terror of the abominable fate she had just escaped.

"Easy, girl," he grunted. "You're all right. How did they catch you?"

She sobbed something unintelligible. He forgot all about Aram Baksh as he scrutinized her by the light of the stars. She was white, though a very definite brunette, obviously one of Zamboula's many mixed breeds. She was tall, with a slender, supple form, as he was in a good position to observe. Admiration burned in his fierce eyes as he looked down on her splendid bosom and her lithe limbs, which still quivered from fright and exertion. He passed an arm around her flexible waist and said, reassuringly: "Stop shaking, wench; you're safe enough."

His touch seemed to restore her shaken sanity. She tossed back her thick, glossy locks and cast a fearful glance over her shoulder, while she pressed closer to the Cimmerian as if seeking security in the contact.

"They caught me in the streets," she muttered, shuddering. "Lying in wait, beneath a dark arch— black men, like great, hulking apes! Set have mercy on me! I shall dream of it!"

"What were you doing out on the streets this time of night?" he inquired, fascinated by the satiny feel of her sleek skin under his questing fingers.

She raked back her hair and stared blankly up into his face. She did not seem aware of his caresses.

"My lover," she said. "My lover drove me into the streets. He went mad and tried to kill me. As I fled from him I was seized by those beasts."

"Beauty like yours might drive a man mad," quoth Conan, running his fingers experimentally through her glossy tresses.

She shook her head, like one emerging from a daze. She no longer trembled, and her voice was steady.

"It was the spite of a priest—of Totrasmek, the high priest of Hanuman, who desires me for himself—the dog!"

"No need to curse him for that," grinned Conan. "The old hyena has better taste than I thought."

She ignored the bluff compliment. She was regaining her poise swiftly.

"My lover is a—a young Turanian soldier. To spite me, Totrasmek gave him a drug that drove him mad. Tonight he snatched up a sword and came at me to slay me in his madness, but I fled from him into the streets. The negroes seized me and brought me to this—*what was that?*"

Conan had already moved. Soundlessly as a shadow he drew her behind the nearest hut, beneath the straggling palms. They stood in tense stillness, while the low mutterings both had heard grew louder until voices were distinguishable. A group of negroes, some nine or ten, were coming along the road from the direction of the city. The girl clutched Conan's arm and he felt the terrified quivering of her supple body against his.

108

Now they could understand the gutturals of the black men.

"Our brothers are already assembled at the pit," said one. "We have had no luck. I hope they have enough for us."

"Aram promised us a man," muttered another, and Conan mentally promised Aram something.

"Aram keeps his word," grunted yet another. "Many a man we have taken from his tavern. But we pay him well. I myself have given him ten bales of silk I stole from my master. It was good silk, by Set!"

The blacks shuffled past, bare splay feet scuffing up the dust, and their voices dwindled down the road.

"Well for us those corpses are lying behind these huts," muttered Conan. "If they look in Aram's death-room they'll find another. Let's begone."

"Yes, let us hasten!" begged the girl, almost hysterical again. "My lover is wandering somewhere in the streets alone. The negroes may take him."

"A devil of a custom this is!" growled Conan, as he led the way toward the city, paralleling the road but keeping behind the huts and straggling trees. "Why don't the citizens clean out these black dogs?"

"They are valuable slaves," murmured the girl. "There are so many of them they might revolt if they were denied the flesh for which they lust. The people of Zamboula know they skulk the streets at night, and all are careful to remain within locked doors, except when something unforeseen happens, as it did to me. The blacks prey on anything they catch, but they seldom catch anybody but strangers. The people of Zamboula are not concerned with the strangers that pass through the city.

"Such men as Aram Baksh sell these strangers to the blacks. He would not dare attempt such a thing with a citizen."

Conan spat in disgust, and a moment later led his companion out into the road which was becoming a street, with still, unlighted houses on each side. Slinking in the shadows was not congenial to his nature.

"Where do you want to go?" he asked. The girl did not seem to object to his arm about her waist.

"To my house, to rouse my servants," she answered. "To bid them search for my lover. I do not wish the city—the priests—anyone—to know of his madness. He—he is a young officer with a promising future. Perhaps we can drive this madness from him if we can find him."

"If *we* find him?" rumbled Conan. "What makes you think I want to spend the night scouring the streets for a lunatic?"

She cast a quick glance into his face, and properly interpreted the gleam in his blue eyes. Any woman could have known that he would follow her wherever she led—for a while, at least. But being a woman, she concealed her knowledge of that fact.

"Please," she began with a hint of tears in her voice, "I have no one else to ask for help—you have been kind—"

"All right!" he grunted. "All right! What's the young reprobate's name?"

"Why—Alafdhal. I am Zabibi, a dancing-girl. I have danced often before the satrap, Jungir Khan, and his mistress Nafertari, and before all the lords and royal ladies of Zamboula. Totrasmek desired me, and because I repulsed him, he made me the innocent tool of his vengeance against Alafdhal. I asked a love potion of Totrasmek, not suspecting the depth of his guile and hate. He gave me a drug to mix with my lover's wine, and he swore that when Alafdhal drank it, he would

110

love me even more madly than ever, and grant my every wish. I mixed the drug secretly with my lover's wine. But having drunk, my lover went raving mad and things came about as I have told you. Curse Totrasmek, the hybrid snake—ahhh!"

She caught his arm convulsively and both stopped short. They had come into a district of shops and stalls, all deserted and unlighted, for the hour was late. They were passing an alley, and in its mouth a man was standing, motionless and silent. His head was lowered, but Conan caught the weird gleam of eery eyes regarding them unblinkingly. His skin crawled, not with fear of the sword in the man's hand, but because of the uncanny suggestion of his posture and silence. They suggested madness. Conan pushed the girl aside and drew his sword.

"Don't kill him!" she begged. "In the name of Set, do not slay him! You are strong—overpower him!"

"We'll see," he muttered, grasping his sword in his right hand and clenching his left into a mallet-like fist.

He took a wary step toward the alley—and with a horrible moaning laugh the Turanian charged. As he came he swung his sword, rising on his toes as he put all the power of his body behind the blows. Sparks flashed blue as Conan parried the blade, and the next instant the madman was stretched senseless in the dust from a thundering buffet of Conan's left fist.

The girl ran forward.

"Oh, he is not—he is not—"

Conan bent swiftly, turned the man on his side and ran quick fingers over him.

"He's not hurt much," he grunted. "Bleeding at the nose, but anybody's likely to do that, after a clout on the jaw. He'll come to after a bit, and maybe his mind will be right. In the meantime I'll tie his wrists with his sword-belt—so. Now where do you want me to take him?"

"Wait!" She knelt beside the senseless figure, seized the bound hands and scanned them avidly. Then, shaking her head as if in baffled disappointment, she rose. She came close to the giant Cimmerian, and laid her slender hands on his arching breast. Her dark eyes, like wet black jewels in the starlight, gazed up into his.

"You are a man! Help me! Totrasmek must die! Slay him for me!"

"And put my neck into a Turanian noose?" he grunted.

"Nay!" The slender arms, strong as pliant steel, were around his corded neck. Her supple body throbbed against his. "The Hyrkanians have no love for Totrasmek. The priests of Set fear him. He is a mongrel, who rules men by fear and superstition. I worship Set, and the Turanians bow to Erlik, but Totrasmek sacrifices to Hanuman the accursed! The Turanian lords fear his black arts and his power over the hybrid population, and they hate him. Even Jungir Khan and his mistress Nafertari fear and hate him. If he were slain in his temple at night, they would not seek his slayer very closely."

"And what of his magic?" rumbled the Cimmerian.

"You are a fighting-man," she answered. "To risk your life is part of your profession."

"For a price," he admitted.

"There will be a price!" she breathed, rising on tiptoes, to gaze into his eyes.

The nearness of her vibrant body drove a flame through his veins. The perfume of her breath mounted to his brain. But as his arms closed about her supple figure she avoided them with a lithe movement, saying: "Wait! First serve me in this matter."

112

"Name your price." He spoke with some difficulty.

"Pick up my lover," she directed, and the Cimmerian stooped and swung the tall form easily to his broad shoulder. At the moment he felt as if he could have toppled over Jungir Khan's palace with equal ease. The girl murmured an endearment to the unconscious man, and there was no hypocrisy in her attitude. She obviously loved Alafdhal sincerely. Whatever business arrangement she made with Conan would have no bearing on her relationship with Alafdhal. Women are more practical about these things than men.

"Follow me!" She hurried along the street, while the Cimmerian strode easily after her, in no way discomforted by his limp burden. He kept a wary eye out for black shadows skulking under arches, but saw nothing suspicious. Doubtless the men of Darfar were all gathered at the roasting-pit. The girl turned down a narrow side street, and presently knocked cautiously at an arched door.

Almost instantly a wicket opened in the upper panel, and a black face glanced out. She bent close to the opening, whispering swiftly. Bolts creaked in their sockets, and the door opened. A giant black man stood framed against the soft glow of a copper lamp. A quick glance showed Conan the man was not from Darfar. His teeth were unfiled and his kinky hair was cropped close to his skull. He was from the Wadai.

At a word from Zabibi, Conan gave the limp body into the black's arms, and saw the young officer laid on a velvet divan. He showed no signs of returning consciousness. The blow that had rendered him senseless might have felled an ox. Zabibi bent over him for an instant, her fingers nervously twining and twisting. Then she straightened and beckoned the Cimmerian.

The door closed softly, the locks clicked behind them, and the closing wicket shut off the glow of the lamps. In the starlight of the street Zabibi took Conan's hand. Her own hand trembled a little.

"You will not fail me?"

He shook his maned head, massive against the stars.

"Then follow me to Hanuman's shrine, and the gods have mercy on our souls!"

Along the silent streets they moved like phantoms of antiquity. They went in silence. Perhaps the girl was thinking of her lover lying senseless on the divan under the copper lamps; or was shrinking with fear of what lay ahead of them in the demon-haunted shrine of Hanuman. The barbarian was thinking only of the woman moving so supplely beside him. The perfume of her scented hair was in his nostrils, the sensuous aura of her presence filled his brain and left room for no other thoughts.

Once they heard the clank of brass-shod feet, and drew into the shadows of a gloomy arch while a squad of Pelishtim watchmen swung past. There were fifteen of them; they marched in close formation, pikes at the ready, and the rearmost men had their broad brass shields slung on their backs, to protect them from a knife-stroke from behind. The skulking menace of the black man-eaters was a threat even to armed men.

As soon as the clang of their sandals had receded up the street, Conan and the girl emerged from their hiding-place and hurried on. A few moments later they saw the squat, flat-topped edifice they sought looming ahead of them.

The temple of Hanuman stood alone in the midst of a broad square, which lay silent and deserted beneath the stars. A marble wall surrounded the shrine, with a broad opening directly before the portico. This opening had no gate or any sort of barrier.

"Why don't the blacks seek their prey here?" muttered Conan. "There's nothing to keep them out of the temple."

He could feel the trembling of Zabibi's body as she pressed close to him.

"They fear Totrasmek, as all in Zamboula fear him, even Jungir Khan and Nafertari. Come! Come quickly, before my courage flows from me like water!"

The girl's fear was evident, but she did not falter. Conan drew his sword and strode ahead of her as they advanced through the open gateway. He knew the hideous habits of the priests of the East, and was aware that an invader of Hanuman's shrine might expect to encounter almost any sort of nightmare horror. He knew there was a good chance that neither he nor the girl would ever leave the shrine alive, but he had risked his life too many times before to devote much thought to that consideration.

They entered a court paved with marble which gleamed whitely in the starlight. A short flight of broad marble steps led up to the pillared portico. The great bronze doors stood wide open as they had stood for centuries. But no worshippers burnt incense within. In the day men and women might come timidly into the shrine and place offerings to the ape-god on the black altar. At night the people shunned the temple of Hanuman as hares shun the lair of the serpent.

Burning censers bathed the interior in a soft weird glow that created an illusion of unreality. Near the rear wall, behind the black stone altar, sat the god with his gaze fixed for ever on the open door, through which for centuries his victims had come, dragged by chains of roses. A faint groove ran from the sill to the altar, and when Conan's foot felt it, he stepped away as quickly as if he had trodden upon a snake. That groove had been worn by the faltering feet of the multitude of those who had died screaming on that grim altar.

Bestial in the uncertain light Hanuman leered with his carven mask. He sat, not as an ape would crouch, but cross-legged as a man would sit, but his aspect was no less simian for that reason. He was carved from black marble, but his eyes were rubies, which glowed red and lustful as the coals of hell's deepest pits. His great hands lay upon his lap, palms upward, taloned fingers spread and grasping. In the gross emphasis of his attributes, in the leer of his satyr-countenance, was reflected the abominable cynicism of the degenerate cult which deified him.

The girl moved around the image, making toward the back wall, and when her sleek flank brushed against a carven knee, she shrank aside and shuddered as if a reptile had touched her. There was a space of several feet between the broad back of the idol and the marble wall with its frieze of gold leaves. On either hand, flanking the idol, an ivory door under a gold arch was set in the wall.

"Those doors open into each end of a hair-pin shaped corridor," she said hurriedly. "Once I was in the interior of the shrine—once!" She shivered and twitched her slim shoulders at a memory both terrifying and obscene. "The corridor is bent like a horseshoe, with each horn opening into this room. Totrasmek's chambers are enclosed within the curve of the corridor and open into it. But there is a secret door in this wall which opens directly into an inner chamber—"

She began to run her hands over the smooth surface, where no crack or crevice showed. Conan stood beside her, sword in hand, glancing warily about him. The silence, the emptiness of the shrine, with imagination picturing what might lie behind that wall, made him feel like a wild beast nosing a trap.

"Ah!" The girl had found a hidden spring at last; a square opening gaped blackly in the wall. Then: "Set!" she screamed, and even as Conan leaped toward her, he saw that a great misshapen hand had fastened itself in her hair. She was snatched off her feet and jerked head-first through the opening. Conan, grabbing ineffectually at her, felt his fingers slip from a naked limb, and in an instant she had vanished and the wall showed blank as before. Only from beyond it came briefly the muffled sounds of a struggle, a scream, faintly heard, and a low laugh that made Conan's blood congeal in his veins.

3. Black Hands Gripping

WITH AN OATH the Cimmerian smote the wall a terrific blow with the pommel of his sword, and the marble cracked and chipped. But the hidden door did not give way, and reason told him that doubtless it had been bolted on the other side of the wall. Turning, he sprang across the chamber to one of the ivory doors.

He lifted his sword to shatter the panels, but on a venture tried the door first with his left hand. It swung open easily, and he glared into a long corridor that curved away into dimness under the weird light of censers similar to those in the shrine. A heavy gold bolt showed on the jamb of the door, and he touched it lightly with his finger tips. The faint warmness of the metal could have been detected only by a man whose faculties were akin to those of a wolf. That bolt had been touched—and therefore drawn—within the last few seconds. The affair was taking on more and more of the aspect of a baited trap. He might have known Totrasmek would know when anyone entered the temple.

To enter the corridor would undoubtedly be to walk into whatever trap the priest had set for him. But Conan did not hesitate. Somewhere in that dim-lit interior Zabibi was a captive, and, from what he knew of the characteristics of Hanuman's priests, he was sure that she needed help badly. Conan stalked into the corridor with a pantherish tread, poised to strike right or left.

On his left, ivory, arched doors opened into the corridor, and he tried each in turn. All were locked. He had gone perhaps seventy-five feet when the corridor bent sharply to the left, describing the curve the girl had mentioned. A door opened into this curve, and it gave under his hand.

He was looking into a broad, square chamber, somewhat more clearly lighted than the corridor. Its walls were of white marble, the floor of ivory, the ceiling of fretted silver. He saw divans of rich satin, gold-worked footstools of ivory, a disk-shaped table of some massive, metal-like substance. On one of the divans a man was reclining, looking toward the door. He laughed as he met the Cimmerian's startled glare.

This man was naked except for a loin-cloth and high-strapped sandals. He was brown-skinned, with close-cropped black hair and restless black eyes that set off a broad, arrogant face. In girth and breadth he was enormous, with huge limbs on which the great muscles swelled and rippled at each slightest movement. His hands were the largest Conan had ever seen. The assurance of gigantic physical strength colored his every action and inflection.

"Why not enter, barbarian?" he called mockingly, with an exaggerated gesture of invitation.

Conan's eyes began to smolder ominously, but he trod warily into the chamber, his sword ready.

"Who the devil are you?" he growled.

"I am Baal-pteor," the man answered. "Once, long ago and in another land, I had another name. But this is a good name, and why Totrasmek gave it to me, any temple wench can tell you."

"So you're his dog!" grunted Conan. "Well, curse your brown hide, Baal-pteor, where's the wench you jerked through the wall?"

"My master entertains her!" laughed Baal-pteor. "Listen!"

From beyond a door opposite the one by which Conan had entered there sounded a woman's scream,

119

faint and muffled in the distance.

"Blast your soul!" Conan took a stride toward the door, then wheeled with his skin tingling. Baal-pteor was laughing at him, and that laugh was edged with menace that made the hackles rise on Conan's neck and sent a red wave of murder-lust driving across his vision.

He started toward Baal-pteor, the knuckles on his sword-hand showing white. With a swift motion the brown man threw something at him—a shining crystal sphere that glistened in the weird light.

Conan dodged instinctively, but, miraculously, the globe stopped short in midair, a few feet from his face. It did not fall to the floor. It hung suspended, as if by invisible filaments, some five feet above the floor. And as he glared in amazement, it began to rotate with growing speed. And as it revolved it grew, expanded, became nebulous. It filled the chamber. It enveloped him. It blotted out furniture, walls, the smiling countenance of Baal-pteor. He was lost in the midst of a blinding bluish blur of whirling speed. Terrific winds screamed past Conan, tugging, tearing at him, striving to wrench him from his feet, to drag him into the vortex that spun madly before him.

With a choking cry Conan lurched backward, reeled, felt the solid wall against his back. At the contact the illusion ceased to be. The whirling, titanic sphere vanished like a bursting bubble. Conan reeled upright in the silver-ceilinged room, with a gray mist coiling about his feet, and saw Baal-pteor lolling on the divan, shaking with silent laughter.

"Son of a slut!" Conan lunged at him. But the mist swirled up from the floor, blotting out that giant brown form. Groping in a rolling cloud that blinded him, Conan felt a rending sensation of dislocation—and then room and mist and brown man were gone together. He was standing alone among the high reeds of a marshy fen, and a buffalo was lunging at him, head down. He leaped aside from the ripping simitar-curved horns, and drove his sword in behind the foreleg, through ribs and heart. And then it was not a buffalo dying there in the mud, but the brown-skinned Baal-pteor. With a curse Conan struck off his head; and the head soared from the ground and snapped beast-like tusks into his throat. For all his mighty strength he could not tear it loose—he was choking—strangling; then there was a rush and roar through space, the dislocating shock of an immeasurable impact, and he was back in the chamber with Baal-pteor, whose head was once more set firmly on his shoulders, and who laughed silently at him from the divan.

"Mesmerism!" muttered Conan, crouching and digging his toes hard against the marble.

His eyes blazed. This brown dog was playing with him, making sport of him! But this mummery, this child's play of mists and shadows of thought, it could not harm him. He had but to leap and strike and the brown acolyte would be a mangled corpse under his heel. This time he would not be fooled by shadows of illusion—but he was.

A blood-curdling snarl sounded behind him, and he wheeled and struck in a flash at the panther crouching to spring on him from the metal-colored table. Even as he struck, the apparition vanished and his blade clashed deafeningly on the adamantine surface. Instantly he sensed something abnormal. The blade stuck to the table! He wrenched at it savagely. It did not give. This was no mesmeristic trick. The table was a giant magnet. He gripped the hilt with both hands, when a voice at his shoulder brought him about, to face the brown man, who had at last risen from the divan.

Slightly taller than Conan, and much heavier, Baal-pteor loomed before him, a daunting image of muscular development. His mighty arms were unnaturally long, and his great hands opened and closed, twitching convulsively. Conan released the hilt of his imprisoned sword and fell silent, watching his enemy through slitted lids.

"Your head, Cimmerian!" taunted Baal-pteor. "I shall take it with my bare hands, twisting it from your shoulders as the head of a fowl is twisted! Thus the sons of Kosala offer sacrifice to Yajur. Barbarian, you look upon a strangler of Yota-pong. I was chosen by the priests of Yajur in my infancy, and throughout childhood, boyhood and youth I was trained in the art of slaying with the naked hands—for only thus are the sacrifices enacted. Yajur loves blood, and we waste not a drop from the victim's veins. When I was a child they gave me infants to throttle; when I was a boy I strangled young girls; as a youth, women, old men and young boys. Not until I reached my full manhood was I given a strong man to slay on the altar of Yota-pong.

"For years I offered the sacrifices to Yajur. Hundreds of necks have snapped between these fingers—" he worked them before the Cimmerian's angry eyes. "Why I fled from Yota-pong to become Totrasmek's servant is no concern of yours. In a moment you will be beyond curiosity. The priests of Kosala, the stranglers of Yajur, are strong beyond the belief of men. And I was stronger than any. With my hands, barbarian, I shall break your neck!"

And like the stroke of twin cobras, the great hands closed on Conan's throat. The Cimmerian made no attempt to dodge or fend them away, but his own hands darted to the Kosalan's bull-neck. Baal-pteor's black eyes widened as he felt the thick cords of muscles that protected the barbarian's throat. With a snarl he exerted his inhuman strength, and knots and lumps and ropes of thews rose along his massive arms. And then a choking gasp burst from him as Conan's fingers locked on his throat. For an instant they stood there like statues, their faces masks of effort, veins beginning to stand out purply on their temples. Conan's thin lips drew back from his teeth in a grinning snarl. Baalpteor's eyes were distended; in them grew an awful surprize and the glimmer of fear. Both men stood motionless as images, except for the expanding of their muscles on rigid arms and braced legs, but strength beyond common conception was warring there— strength that might have uprooted trees and crushed the skulls of bullocks.

The wind whistled suddenly from between Baalpteor's parted teeth. His face was growing purple. Fear flooded his eyes. His thews seemed ready to burst from his arms and shoulders, yet the muscles of the Cimmerian's thick neck did not give; they felt like masses of woven iron cords under his desperate fingers. But his own flesh was giving way under the iron fingers of the Cimmerian which ground deeper and deeper into the yielding throat-muscles, crushing them in upon jugular and windpipe.

The statuesque immobility of the group gave way to sudden, frenzied motion, as the Kosalan began to wrench and heave, seeking to throw himself backward. He let go of Conan's throat and grasped his wrists, trying to tear away those inexorable fingers.

With a sudden lunge Conan bore him backward until the small of his back crashed against the table. And still farther over its edge Conan bent him, back and back, until his spine was ready to snap.

Conan's low laugh was merciless as the ring of steel.

"You fool!" he all but whispered. "I think you never saw a man from the West before. Did you deem yourself strong, because you were able to twist the heads off civilized folk, poor weaklings with muscles like rotten string? Hell! Break the neck of a wild Cimmerian bull before you call yourself strong. I did that, before I was a full-grown man—like this!"

And with a savage wrench he twisted Baal-pteor's head around until the ghastly face leered over the left shoulder, and the vertebrae snapped like a rotten branch.

Conan hurled the flopping corpse to the floor, turned to the sword again and gripped the hilt with both hands, bracing his feet against the floor. Blood trickled down his broad breast from the wounds Baal-pteor's finger nails had torn in the skin of his neck. His black hair was damp, sweat ran down his face, and his chest heaved. For all his vocal scorn of Baal-pteor's strength, he had almost met his match in the inhuman Kosalan. But without pausing to catch his breath, he exerted all his strength in a mighty wrench that tore the sword from the magnet where it clung.

Another instant and he had pushed open the door from behind which the scream had sounded, and was looking down a long straight corridor, lined with ivory doors. The other end was masked by a rich velvet curtain, and from beyond that curtain came the devilish strains of such music as Conan had never heard, not even in nightmares. It made the short hairs bristle on the back of his neck. Mingled with it was the panting, hysterical sobbing of a woman. Grasping his sword firmly, he glided down the corridor.

4. Dance, Girl, Dance!

WHEN ZABIBI WAS jerked head-first through the
aperture which opened in the wall behind the idol, her
first, dizzy, disconnected thought was that her time had
come. She instinctively shut her eyes and waited for the
blow to fall. But instead she felt herself dumped
unceremoniously onto the smooth marble floor, which
bruised her knees and hip. Opening her eyes she stared
fearfully around her, just as a muffled impact sounded
from beyond the wall. She saw a brown-skinned giant
in a loin-cloth standing over her, and, across the
chamber into which she had come, a man sat on a
divan, with his back to a rich black velvet curtain, a
broad, fleshy man, with fat white hands and snaky
eyes. And her flesh crawled, for this man was
Totrasmek, the priest of Hanuman, who for years had
spun his slimy webs of power throughout the city of
Zamboula.

"The barbarian seeks to batter his way through the
wall," said Totrasmek sardonically, "but the bolt will
hold."

The girl saw that a heavy golden bolt had been shot
across the hidden door, which was plainly discernible
from this side of the wall. The bolt and its sockets
would have resisted the charge of an elephant.

"Go open one of the doors for him, Baal-pteor,"
ordered Totrasmek. "Slay him in the square chamber
at the other end of the corridor."

The Kosalan salaamed and departed by the way of a
door in the side wall of the chamber. Zabibi rose,
staring fearfully at the priest, whose eyes ran avidly
over her splendid figure. To this she was indifferent. A
dancer of Zamboula was accustomed to nakedness.

But the cruelty in his eyes started her limbs to quivering.

"Again you come to me in my retreat, beautiful one," he purred with cynical hypocrisy. "It is an unexpected honor. You seemed to enjoy your former visit so little, that I dared not hope for you to repeat it. Yet I did all in my power to provide you with an interesting experience."

For a Zamboula dancer to blush would be an impossibility, but a smolder of anger mingled with the fear in Zabibi's dilated eyes.

"Fat pig! You know I did not come here for love of you."

"No," laughed Totrasmek, "you came like a fool, creeping through the night with a stupid barbarian to cut my throat. Why should you seek my life?"

"You know why!" she cried, knowing the futility of trying to dissemble.

"You are thinking of your lover," he laughed. "The fact that you are here seeking my life shows that he quaffed the drug I gave you. Well, did you not ask for it? And did I not send what you asked for, out of the love I bear you?"

"I asked you for a drug that would make him slumber harmlessly for a few hours," she said bitterly. "And you—you sent your servant with a drug that drove him mad! I was a fool ever to trust you. I might have known your protestations of friendship were lies, to disguise your hate and spite."

"Why did you wish your lover to sleep?" he retorted. "So you could steal from him the only thing he would never give you—the ring with the jewel men call the Star of Khorala—the star stolen from the queen of Ophir, who would pay a roomful of gold for its return. He would not give it to you willingly, because he knew

126

that it holds a magic which, when properly controlled, will enslave the hearts of any of the opposite sex. You wished to steal it from him, fearing that his magicians would discover the key to that magic and he would forget you in his conquests of the queens of the world. You would sell it back to the queen of Ophir, who understands its power and would use it to enslave men, as she did before it was stolen."

"And why did *you* want it?" she demanded sulkily.

"I understand its powers. It would increase the power of my arts."

"Well," she snapped, "you have it now!"

"*I* have the Star of Khorala? Nay, you err."

"Why bother to lie?" she retorted bitterly. "He had it on his finger when he drove me into the streets. He did not have it when I found him again. Your servant must have been watching the house, and have taken it from him, after I escaped him. To the devil with it! I want my lover back sane and whole. You have the ring; you have punished us both. Why do you not restore his mind to him? Can you?"

"I could," he assured her, in evident enjoyment of her distress. He drew a phial from among his robes. "This contains the juice of the golden lotus. If your lover drank it he would be sane again. Yes, I will be merciful. You have both thwarted and flouted me, not once but many times; he has constantly opposed my wishes. But I will be merciful. Come and take the phial from my hand."

She stared at Totrasmek, trembling with eagerness to seize it, but fearing it was but some cruel jest. She advanced timidly, with a hand extended, and he laughed heartlessly and drew back out of her reach. Even as her lips parted to curse him, some instinct snatched her eyes upward. From the gilded ceiling four

127

jade-hued vessels were falling. She dodged, but they did not strike her. They crashed to the floor about her, forming the four corners of a square. And she screamed, and screamed again. For out of each ruin reared the hooded head of a cobra, and one struck at her bare leg. Her convulsive movement to evade it brought her within reach of the one on the other side and again she had to shift like lightning to avoid the flash of its hideous head.

She was caught in a frightful trap. All four serpents were swaying and striking at foot, ankle, calf, knee, thigh, hip, whatever portion of her voluptuous body chanced to be nearest to them, and she could not spring over them or pass between them to safety. She could only whirl and spring aside and twist her body to avoid the strokes, and each time she moved to dodge one snake, the motion brought her within range of another, so that she had to keep shifting with the speed of light. She could move only a short space in any direction, and the fearful hooded crests were menacing her every second. Only a dancer of Zamboula could have lived in that grisly square.

She became, herself, a blur of bewildering motion. The heads missed her by hair's breadths, but they missed, as she pitted her twinkling feet, flickering limbs and perfect eye against the blinding speed of the scaly demons her enemy had conjured out of thin air.

Somewhere a thin whining music struck up, mingling with the hissing of the serpents, like an evil night-wind blowing through the empty sockets of a skull. Even in the flying speed of her urgent haste she realized that the darting of the serpents was no longer at random. They obeyed the grisly piping of the eery music. They struck with a horrible rhythm, and perforce her swaying, writhing, spinning body attuned

128

itself to their rhythm. Her frantic motions melted into the measures of a dance compared to which the most obscene tarantella of Zamora would have seemed sane and restrained. Sick with shame and terror Zabibi heard the hateful mirth of her merciless tormenter.

"The Dance of the Cobras, my lovely one!" laughed Totrasmek. "So maidens danced in the sacrifice to Hanuman centuries ago—but never with such beauty and suppleness. Dance, girl, dance! How long can you avoid the fangs of the Poison People? Minutes? Hours? You will weary at last. Your swift, sure feet will stumble, your legs falter, your hips slow in their rotations. Then the fangs will begin to sink deep into your ivory flesh—"

Behind him the curtain shook as if struck by a gust of wind, and Totrasmek screamed. His eyes dilated and his hands caught convulsively at the length of bright steel which jutted suddenly from his breast.

The music broke off short. The girl swayed dizzily in her dance, crying out in dreadful anticipation of the flickering fangs—and then only four wisps of harmless blue smoke curled up from the floor about her, as Totrasmek sprawled head-long from the divan.

Conan came from behind the curtain, wiping his broad blade. Looking through the hangings he had seen the girl dancing desperately between four swaying spirals of smoke, but he had guessed that their appearance was very different to her. He knew he had killed Totrasmek.

Zabibi sank down on the floor, panting, but even as Conan started toward her, she staggered up again, though her legs trembled with exhaustion.

"The phial!" she gasped. "The phial!"

Totrasmek still grasped it in his stiffening hand. Ruthlessly she tore it from his locked fingers, and then began frantically to ransack his garments.

"What the devil are you looking for?" Conan demanded.

"A ring—he stole it from Alafdhal. He must have, while my lover walked in madness through the streets. Set's devils!"

She had convinced herself that it was not on the person of Totrasmek. She began to cast about the chamber, tearing up divan-covers and hangings, and upsetting vessels.

She paused and raked a damp lock of hair out of her eyes.

"I forgot Baal-pteor!"

"He's in hell with his neck broken," Conan assured her.

She expressed vindictive gratification at the news, but an instant later swore expressively.

"We can't stay here. It's not many hours until dawn. Lesser priests are likely to visit the temple at any hour of the night, and if we're discovered here with his corpse, the people will tear us to pieces. The Turanians could not save us."

She lifted the bolt on the secret door, and a few moments later they were in the streets and hurrying away from the silent square where brooded the age-old shrine of Hanuman.

In a winding street a short distance away Conan halted and checked his companion with a heavy hand on her naked shoulder.

"Don't forget there was a price—"

"I have not forgotten!" She twisted free. "But we must go to—to Alafdhal first!"

A few minutes later the black slave let them through the wicket door. The young Turanian lay upon the divan, his arms and legs bound with heavy velvet ropes.

His eyes were open, but they were like those of a mad dog, and foam was thick on his lips. Zabibi shuddered.

"Force his jaws open!" she commanded, and Conan's iron fingers accomplished the task.

Zabibi emptied the phial down the maniac's gullet. The effect was like magic. Instantly he became quiet. The glare faded from his eyes; he stared up at the girl in a puzzled way, but with recognition and intelligence. Then he fell into a normal slumber.

"When he awakes he will be quite sane," she whispered, motioning to the silent slave.

With a deep bow he gave into her hands a small leathern bag, and drew about her shoulders a silken cloak. Her manner had subtly changed when she beckoned Conan to follow her out of the chamber.

In an arch that opened on the street, she turned to him, drawing herself up with a new regality.

"I must now tell you the truth," she said. "I am not Zabibi. I am Nafertari. And *he* is not Alafdhal, a poor captain of the guardsmen. He is Jungir Khan, satrap of Zamboula."

Conan made no comment; his scarred dark countenance was immobile.

"I lied to you because I dared not divulge the truth to anyone," she said. "We were alone when Jungir Khan went mad. None knew of it but myself. Had it been known that the satrap of Zamboula was a madman, there would have been instant revolt and rioting, even as Totrasmek planned, who plotted our destruction.

"You see now how impossible is the reward for which you hoped. The satrap's mistress is not—cannot be for you. But you shall not go unrewarded. Here is a sack of gold."

She gave him the bag she had received from the slave.

"Go, now, and when the sun is up come to the palace. I will have Jungir Khan make you captain of his guard. But you will take your orders from me, secretly. Your first duty will be to march a squad to the shrine of Hanuman, ostensibly to search for clues of the priest's slayer; in reality to search for the Star of Khorala. It must be hidden there somewhere. When you find it, bring it to me. You have my leave to go now."

He nodded, still silent, and strode away. The girl, watching the swing of his broad shoulders, was piqued to note that there was nothing in his bearing to show that he was in any way chagrined or abashed.

When he had rounded a corner, he glanced back, and then changed his direction and quickened his pace. A few moments later he was in the quarter of the city containing the Horse Market. There he smote on a door until from the window above a bearded head was thrust to demand the reason for the disturbance.

"A horse," demanded Conan. "The swiftest steed you have."

"I open no gates at this time of night," grumbled the horse-trader.

Conan rattled his coins.

"Dog's son knave! Don't you see I'm white, and alone? Come down, before I smash your door!"

Presently, on a bay stallion, Conan was riding toward the house of Aram Baksh.

He turned off the road into the alley that lay between the tavern compound and the date-palm garden, but he did not pause at the gate. He rode on to the northeast corner of the wall, then turned and rode along the north wall, to halt within a few paces of the northwest angle. No trees grew near the wall, but there were some low bushes. To one of these he tied his horse, and was about to climb into the saddle again, when he heard a low muttering of voices beyond the corner of the wall.

Drawing his foot from the stirrup he stole to the angle and peered around it. Three men were moving down the road toward the palm groves, and from their slouching gait he knew they were negroes. They halted at his low call, bunching themselves as he strode toward them, his sword in his hand. Their eyes gleamed whitely in the starlight. Their brutish lust shone in their ebony faces, but they knew their three cudgels could not prevail against his sword, just as he knew it.

"Where are you going?" he challenged.

"To bid our brothers put out the fire in the pit beyond the groves," was the sullen, guttural reply. "Aram Baksh promised us a man, but he lied. We found one of our brothers dead in the trap-chamber. We go hungry this night."

"I think not," smiled Conan. "Aram Baksh will give you a man. Do you see that door?"

He pointed to a small, iron-bound portal set in the midst of the western wall.

"Wait there. Aram Baksh will give you a man."

Backing warily away until he was out of reach of a sudden bludgeon blow, he turned and melted around the northwest angle of the wall. Reaching his horse he paused to ascertain that the blacks were not sneaking after him, and then he climbed into the saddle and stood upright on it, quieting the uneasy steed with a low word. He reached up, grasped the coping of the wall and drew himself up and over. There he studied the grounds for an instant. The tavern was built in the southwest corner of the enclosure, the remaining space of which was occupied by groves and gardens. He saw no one in the grounds. The tavern was dark and silent, and he knew all the doors and windows were barred and bolted.

Conan knew that Aram Baksh slept in a chamber that opened into a cypress-bordered path that led to the door in the western wall. Like a shadow he glided among the trees and a few moments later he rapped lightly on the chamber door.

"What is it?" asked a rumbling voice within.

"Aram Baksh!" hissed Conan. "The blacks are stealing over the wall!"

Almost instantly the door opened, framing the tavern-keeper, naked but for his shirt, with a dagger in his hand.

He craned his neck to stare into the Cimmerian's face.

"What tale is this—*you*!"

Conan's vengeful fingers strangled the yell in his throat. They went to the floor together and Conan wrenched the dagger from his enemy's hand. The blade glinted in the starlight, and blood spurted. Aram Baksh made hideous noises, gasping and gagging on a mouthful of blood. Conan dragged him to his feet and again the dagger slashed, and most of the curly beard fell to the floor.

Still gripping his captive's throat—for a man can scream incoherently even with his tongue slit—Conan dragged him out of the dark chamber and down the cypress-shadowed path, to the iron-bound door in the outer wall. With one hand he lifted the bolt and threw the door open, disclosing the three shadowy figures which waited like black vultures outside. Into their eager arms Conan thrust the innkeeper.

A horrible, blood-choked scream rose from the Zamboulan's throat, but there was no response from the silent tavern. The people there were used to screams outside the wall. Aram Baksh fought like a wild man,

134

his distended eyes turned frantically on the Cimmerian's face. He found no mercy there. Conan was thinking of the scores of wretches who owed their bloody doom to this man's greed.

In glee the negroes dragged him down the road, mocking his frenzied gibberings. How could they recognize Aram Baksh in this half-naked, blood-stained figure, with the grotesquely shorn beard and unintelligible babblings? The sounds of the struggle came back to Conan, standing beside the gate, even after the clump of figures had vanished among the palms.

Closing the door behind him, Conan returned to his horse, mounted and turned westward, toward the open desert, swinging wide to skirt the sinister belt of palm groves. As he rode, he drew from his belt a ring in which gleamed a jewel that snared the starlight in a shimmering iridescence. He held it up to admire it, turning it this way and that. The compact bag of gold pieces clinked gently at his saddle-bow, like a promise of the greater riches to come.

"I wonder what she'd say if she knew I recognized her as Nafertari and him as Jungir Khan the instant I saw them," he mused. "I knew the Star of Khorala, too. There'll be a fine scene if she ever guesses that I slipped it off his finger while I was tying him with his sword-belt. But they'll never catch me, with the start I'm getting."

He glanced back at the shadowy palm groves, among which a red glare was mounting. A chanting rose to the night, vibrating with savage exultation. And another sound mingled with it, a mad, incoherent screaming, a frenzied gibbering in which no words could be distinguished. The noise followed Conan as he rode westward beneath the paling stars.

Red Nails

1. *The Skull on the Crag*

THE WOMAN ON the horse reined in her weary steed. It stood with its legs wide-braced, its head drooping, as if it found even the weight of the gold-tassled, red-leather bridle too heavy. The woman drew a booted foot out of the silver stirrup and swung down from the gilt-worked saddle. She made the reins fast to the fork of a sapling, and turned about, hands on her hips, to survey her surroundings.

They were not inviting. Giant trees hemmed in the small pool where her horse had just drunk. Clumps of undergrowth limited the vision that quested under the somber twilight of the lofty arches formed by intertwining branches. The woman shivered with a twitch of her magnificent shoulders, and then cursed.

She was tall, full-bosomed and large-limbed, with compact shoulders. Her whole figure reflected an unusual strength, without detracting from the femininity of her appearance. She was all woman, in spite of her bearing and her garments. The latter were incongruous, in view of her present environs. Instead of a skirt she wore short, wide-legged silk breeches, which ceased a hand's breadth short of her knees, and were upheld by a wide silken sash worn as a girdle. Flaring-topped boots of soft leather came almost to her knees, and a low-necked, wide-collared, wide-sleeved silk shirt completed her costume. On one shapely hip she wore a straight double-edged sword, and on the other a long dirk. Her unruly golden hair, cut square at her shoulders, was confined by a band of crimson satin.

Against the background of somber, primitive forest she posed with an unconscious picturesqueness, bizarre and out of place. She should have been posed against a background of sea-clouds, painted masts and wheeling gulls. There was the color of the sea in her wide eyes. And that was as it should have been, because this was Valeria of the Red Brotherhood, whose deeds are celebrated in song and ballad wherever seafarers gather.

She strove to pierce the sullen green roof of the arched branches and see the sky which presumably lay about it, but presently gave it up with a muttered oath.

Leaving her horse tied she strode off toward the east, glancing back toward the pool from time to time in order to fix her route in her mind. The silence of the forest depressed her. No birds sang in the lofty boughs, nor did any rustling in the bushes indicate the presence of any small animals. For leagues she had traveled in a realm of brooding stillness, broken only by the sounds of her own flight.

She had slaked her thirst at the pool, but she felt the gnawings of hunger and began looking about for some of the fruit on which she had sustained herself since exhausting the food she had brought in her saddle-bags.

Ahead of her, presently, she saw an outcropping of dark, flint-like rock that sloped upward into what looked like a rugged crag rising among the trees. Its summit was lost to view amidst a cloud of encircling leaves. Perhaps its peak rose above the tree-tops, and from it she could see what lay beyond—if, indeed, anything lay beyond but more of this apparently illimitable forest through which she had ridden for so many days.

A narrow ridge formed a natural ramp that led up the steep face of the crag. After she had ascended some fifty feet she came to the belt of leaves that surrounded the rock. The trunks of the trees did not crowd close to the crag, but the ends of their lower branches extended about it, veiling it with their foliage. She groped on in leafy obscurity, not able to see either above or below her; but presently she glimpsed blue sky, and a moment later came out in the clear, hot sunlight and saw the forest roof stretching away under her feet.

She was standing on a broad shelf which was about even with the tree-tops, and from it rose a spire-like jut that was the ultimate peak of the crag she had climbed. But something else caught her attention at the moment. Her foot had struck something in the litter of blown dead leaves which carpeted the shelf. She kicked them aside and looked down on the skeleton of a man. She ran an experienced eye over the bleached frame, but saw no broken bones nor any sign of violence. The man must have died a natural death; though why he should have climbed a tall crag to die she could not imagine.

She scrambled up to the summit of the spire and looked toward the horizons. The forest roof—which looked like a floor from her vantage-point—was just as impenetrable as from below. She could not even see the pool by which she had left her horse. She glanced northward, in the direction from which she had come. She saw only the rolling green ocean stretching away and away, with only a vague blue line in the distance to hint of the hill-range she had crossed days before, to plunge into this leafy waste.

West and east the view was the same; though the blue hill-line was lacking in those directions. But when she turned her eyes southward she stiffened and caught her breath. A mile away in that direction the forest thinned out and ceased abruptly, giving way to a cactus-dotted plain. And in the midst of that plain rose the walls and towers of a city. Valeria swore in amazement. This passed belief. She would not have

141

been surprized to sight human habitations of another sort—the beehive-shaped huts of the black people, or the cliff-dwellings of the mysterious brown race which legends declared inhabited some country of this unexplored region. But it was a startling experience to come upon a walled city here so many long weeks' march from the nearest outposts of any sort of civilization.

Her hands tiring from clinging to the spire-like pinnacle, she let herself down on the shelf, frowning in indecision. She had come far—from the camp of the mercenaries by the border town of Sukhmet amidst the level grasslands, where desperate adventurers of many races guard the Stygian frontier against the raids that come up like a red wave from Darfar. Her flight had been blind, into a country of which she was wholly ignorant. And now she wavered between an urge to ride directly to that city in the plain, and the instinct of caution which prompted her to skirt it widely and continue her solitary flight.

Her thoughts were scattered by the rustling of the leaves below her. She wheeled cat-like, snatched at her sword; and then she froze motionless, staring wide-eyed at the man before her.

He was almost a giant in stature, muscles rippling smoothly under his skin which the sun had burned brown. His garb was similar to hers, except that he wore a broad leather belt instead of a girdle. Broadsword and poniard hung from this belt.

"Conan, the Cimmerian!" ejaculated the woman. "What are *you* doing on my trail?"

He grinned hardly, and his fierce blue eyes burned with a light any woman could understand as they ran over her magnificent figure, lingering on the swell of her splendid breasts beneath the light shirt, and the clear white flesh displayed between breeches and boot-tops.

"Don't you know?" he laughed. "Haven't I made my admiration for you plain ever since I first saw you?"

"A stallion could have made it no plainer," she answered disdainfully. "But I never expected to encounter you so far from the ale-barrels and meat-pots of Sukhmet. Did you really follow me from Zarallo's camp, or were you whipped forth for a rogue?"

He laughed at her insolence and flexed his mighty biceps.

"You know Zarallo didn't have enough knaves to whip me out of camp," he grinned. "Of course I followed you. Lucky thing for you, too, wench! When you knifed that Stygian officer, you forfeited Zarallo's favor and protection, and you outlawed yourself with the Stygians."

"I know it," she replied sullenly. "But what else could I do? You know what my provocation was."

"Sure," he agreed. "If I'd been there, I'd have knifed him myself. But if a woman must live in the war-camps of men, she can expect such things."

Valeria stamped her booted foot and swore.

"Why won't men let me live a man's life?"

"That's obvious!" Again his eager eyes devoured her. "But you were wise to run away. The Stygians would have had you skinned. That officer's brother followed you; faster than you thought, I don't doubt. He wasn't far behind you when I caught up with him. His horse was better than yours. He'd have caught you and cut your throat within a few more miles."

"Well?" she demanded.

"Well what?" He seemed puzzled.

"What of the Stygian?"

"Why, what do you suppose?" he returned impatiently. "I killed him, of course, and left his carcass for the vultures. That delayed me, though, and I almost lost your trail when you crossed the rocky spurs of the hills. Otherwise I'd have caught up with you long ago."

"And now you think you'll drag me back to Zarallo's camp?" she sneered.

"Don't talk like a fool," he grunted. "Come, girl, don't be such a spitfire. I'm not like that Stygian you knifed, and you know it."

"A penniless vagabond," she taunted.

He laughed at her.

"What do you call yourself? You haven't enough money to buy a new seat for your breeches. Your disdain doesn't deceive me. You know I've commanded bigger ships and more men than you ever did in your life. As for being penniless—what rover isn't, most of the time? I've squandered enough gold in the sea-ports of the world to fill a galleon. You know that, too."

"Where are the fine ships and the bold lads you commanded, now?" she sneered.

"At the bottom of the sea, mostly," he replied cheerfully. "The Zingarans sank my last ship off the Shemite shore—that's why I joined Zarallo's Free Companions. But I saw I'd been stung when we marched to the Darfar border. The pay was poor and the wine was sour, and I don't like black women. And that's the only kind that came to our camp at Sukhmet—rings in their noses and their teeth filed— bah! Why did you join Zarallo? Sukhmet's a long way from salt water."

"Red Ortho wanted to make me his mistress," she answered sullenly. "I jumped overboard one night and swam ashore when we were anchored off the Kushite coast. Off Zabhela, it was. There a Shemite trader told me that Zarallo had brought his Free Companies south to guard the Darfar border. No better employment offered. I joined an east-bound caravan and eventually came to Sukhmet."

"It was madness to plunge southward as you did," commented Conan, "but it was wise, too, for Zarallo's patrols never thought to look for you in this direction. Only the brother of the man you killed happened to strike your trail."

"And now what do you intend doing?" she demanded.

"Turn west," he answered. "I've been this far south, but not this far east. Many days' traveling to the west will bring us to the open savannas, where the black tribes graze their cattle. I have friends among them. We'll get to the coast and find a ship. I'm sick of the jungle."

"Then be on your way," she advised. "I have other plans."

"Don't be a fool!" He showed irritation for the first time. "You can't keep on wandering through this forest."

"I can if I choose."

"But what do you intend doing?"

"That's none of your affair," she snapped.

"Yes, it is," he answered calmly. "Do you think I've followed you this far, to turn around and ride off empty-handed? Be sensible, wench. I'm not going to harm you."

He stepped toward her, and she sprang back, whipping out her sword.

"Keep back, you barbarian dog! I'll spit you like a roast pig!"

He halted, reluctantly, and demanded: "Do you want me to take that toy away from you and spank you with it?"

"Words! Nothing but words!" she mocked, lights like the gleam of the sun on blue water dancing in her reckless eyes.

He knew it was the truth. No living man could disarm Valeria of the Brotherhood with his bare hands. He scowled, his sensations a tangle of conflicting emotions. He was angry, yet he was amused and filled with admiration for her spirit. He burned with eagerness to seize that splendid figure and crush it in his iron arms, yet he greatly desired not to hurt the girl. He was torn between a desire to shake her soundly, and a desire to caress her. He knew if he came any nearer her sword would be sheathed in his heart. He had seen Valeria kill too many men in border forays and tavern brawls to have any illusions about her. He knew she was as quick and ferocious as a tigress. He could draw his broadsword and disarm her, beat the blade out of her hand, but the thought of drawing a sword on a woman, even without intent of injury, was extremely repugnant to him.

"Blast your soul, you hussy!" he exclaimed in exasperation. "I'm going to take off your—"

He started toward her, his angry passion making him reckless, and she poised herself for a deadly thrust. Then came a startling interruption to a scene at once ludicrous and perilous.

"What's that?"

It was Valeria who exclaimed, but they both started violently, and Conan wheeled like a cat, his great sword flashing into his hand. Back in the forest had burst forth an appalling medley of screams—the screams of horses in terror and agony. Mingled with their screams there came the snap of splintering bones.

"Lions are slaying the horses!" cried Valeria.

"Lions, nothing!" snorted Conan, his eyes blazing. "Did you hear a lion roar? Neither did I! Listen at those bones snap—not even a lion could make that much noise killing a horse."

He hurried down the natural ramp and she followed, their personal feud forgotten in the adventurers' instinct to unite against common peril. The screams had ceased when they worked their way downward through the green veil of leaves that brushed the rock.

"I found your horse tied by the pool back there," he muttered, treading so noiselessly that she no longer wondered how he had surprized her on the crag. "I tied mine beside it and followed the tracks of your boots. Watch, now!"

They had emerged from the belt of leaves, and stared down into the lower reaches of the forest. Above them the green roof spread its dusky canopy. Below them the sunlight filtered in just enough to make a jade-tinted twilight. The giant trunks of trees less than a hundred yards away looked dim and ghostly.

"The horses should be beyond that thicket, over there," whispered Conan, and his voice might have been a breeze moving through the branches. "Listen!"

Valeria had already heard, and a chill crept through her veins; so she unconsciously laid her white hand on her companion's muscular brown arm. From beyond the thicket came the noisy crunching of bones and the loud rending of flesh, together with the grinding, slobbering sounds of a horrible feast.

"Lions wouldn't make that noise," whispered Conan. "Something's eating our horses, but it's not a lion—Crom!"

The noise stopped suddenly, and Conan swore

softly. A suddenly risen breeze was blowing from them directly toward the spot where the unseen slayer was hidden.

"Here it comes!" muttered Conan, half lifting his sword.

The thicket was violently agitated, and Valeria clutched Conan's arm hard. Ignorant of jungle-lore, she yet knew that no animal she had ever seen could have shaken the tall brush like that.

"It must be as big as an elephant," muttered Conan, echoing her thought. "What the devil—" His voice trailed away in stunned silence.

Through the thicket was thrust a head of nightmare and lunacy. Grinning jaws bared rows of dripping yellow tusks; above the yawning mouth wrinkled a saurian-like snout. Huge eyes, like those of a python a thousand times magnified, stared unwinkingly at the petrified humans clinging to the rock above it. Blood smeared the scaly, flabby lips and dripped from the huge mouth.

The head, bigger than that of a crocodile, was further extended on a long scaled neck on which stood up rows of serrated spikes, and after it, crushing down the briars and saplings, waddled the body of a titan, a gigantic, barrel-bellied torso on absurdly short legs. The whitish belly almost raked the ground, while the serrated back-bone rose higher than Conan could have reached on tiptoe. A long spiked tail, like that of a gargantuan scorpion, trailed out behind.

"Back up the crag, quick!" snapped Conan, thrusting the girl behind him. "I don't think he can climb, but he can stand on his hind-legs and reach us—"

With a snapping and rending of bushes and saplings the monster came hurtling through the thickets, and they fled up the rock before him like leaves blown before a wind. As Valeria plunged into the leafy screen a backward glance showed her the titan rearing up fearsomely on his massive hinder legs, even as Conan had predicted. The sight sent panic racing through her. As he reared, the beast seemed more gigantic than ever; his snouted head towered among the trees. Then Conan's iron hand closed on her wrist and she was jerked headlong into the blinding welter of the leaves, and out again into the hot sunshine above, just as the monster fell forward with his front feet on the crag with an impact that made the rock vibrate.

Behind the fugitives the huge head crashed through the twigs, and they looked down for a horrifying instant at the nightmare visage framed among the green leaves, eyes flaming, jaws gaping. Then the giant tusks clashed together futilely, and after that the head was withdrawn, vanishing from their sight as if it had sunk in a pool.

Peering down through broken branches that scraped the rock, they saw it squatting on its haunches at the foot of the crag, staring unblinkingly up at them.

Valeria shuddered.

"How long do you suppose he'll crouch there?"

Conan kicked the skull on the leaf-strewn shelf.

"That fellow must have climbed up here to escape him, or one like him. He must have died of starvation. There are no bones broken. That thing must be a dragon, such as the black people speak of in their legends. If so, it won't leave here until we're both dead."

Valeria looked at him blankly, her resentment forgotten. She fought down a surging of panic. She had proved her reckless courage a thousand times in wild battles on sea and land, on the blood-slippery decks of burning war-ships, in the storming of walled cities, and on the trampled sandy beaches where the desperate men of the Red Brotherhood bathed their knives in one another's blood in their fights for leadership. But the prospect now confronting her congealed her blood. A cutlas stroke in the heat of battle was nothing; but to sit idle and helpless on a bare rock until she perished of starvation, besieged by a monstrous survival of an elder age—the thought sent panic throbbing through her brain.

"He must leave to eat and drink," she said helplessly.

"He won't have to go far to do either," Conan pointed out. "He's just gorged on horse-meat, and like a real snake, he can go for a long time without eating or drinking again. But he doesn't sleep after eating, like a real snake, it seems. Anyway, he can't climb this crag."

Conan spoke imperturbably. He was a barbarian, and the terrible patience of the wilderness and its children was as much a part of him as his lusts and rages. He could endure a situation like this with a coolness impossible to a civilized person.

"Can't we get into the trees and get away, traveling like apes through the branches?" she asked desperately.

He shook his head. "I thought of that. The branches that touch the crag down there are too light. They'd break with our weight. Besides, I have an idea that devil could tear up any tree around here by its roots."

"Well, are we going to sit here on our rumps until we starve, like that?" she cried furiously, kicking the skull clattering across the ledge. "I won't do it! I'll go down there and cut his damned head off—"

Conan had seated himself on a rocky projection at the foot of the spire. He looked up with a glint of admiration at her blazing eyes and tense, quivering figure, but, realizing that she was in just the mood for any madness, he let none of his admiration sound in his voice.

"Sit down," he grunted, catching her by her wrist and pulling her down on his knee. She was too surprized to resist as he took her sword from her hand and shoved it back in its sheath. "Sit still and calm down. You'd only break your steel on his scales. He'd gobble you up at one gulp, or smash you like an egg with that spiked tail of his. We'll get out of this jam some way, but we shan't do it by getting chewed up and swallowed."

She made no reply, nor did she seek to repulse his arm from about her waist. She was frightened, and the sensation was new to Valeria of the Red Brotherhood. So she sat on her companion's—or captor's—knee with a docility that would have amazed Zarallo, who had anathematized her as a she-devil out of hell's seraglio.

Conan played idly with her curly yellow locks, seemingly intent only upon his conquest. Neither the skeleton at his feet nor the monster crouching below disturbed his mind or dulled the edge of his interest.

The girl's restless eyes, roving the leaves below them, discovered splashes of color among the green. It was fruit, large, darkly crimson globes suspended from the boughs of a tree whose broad leaves were a peculiarly rich and vivid green. She became aware of both thirst and hunger, though thirst had not assailed her until she knew she could not descend from the crag to find food and water.

"We need not starve," she said. "There is fruit we can reach."

Conan glanced where she pointed.

"If we ate that we wouldn't need the bite of a dragon," he grunted. "That's what the black people of Kush call the Apples of Derketa. Derketa is the Queen of the Dead. Drink a little of the juice, or spill it on your flesh, and you'd be dead before you could tumble to the foot of this crag."

"Oh!"

She lapsed into dismayed silence. There seemed no way out of their predicament, she reflected gloomily. She saw no way of escape, and Conan seemed to be concerned only with her supple waist and curly tresses. If he was trying to formulate a plan of escape he did not show it.

"If you'll take your hands off me long enough to climb up on that peak," she said presently, "you'll see something that will surprize you."

He cast her a questioning glance, then obeyed with a shrug of his massive shoulders. Clinging to the spire-like pinnacle, he stared out over the forest roof.

He stood a long moment in silence, posed like a bronze statue on the rock.

"It's a walled city, right enough," he muttered presently. "Was that where you were going, when you tried to send me off alone to the coast?"

"I saw it before you came. I knew nothing of it when I left Sukhmet."

"Who'd have thought to find a city here? I don't believe the Stygians ever penetrated this far. Could black people build a city like that? I see no herds on the plain, no signs of cultivation, or people moving about."

"How could you hope to see all that, at this distance?" she demanded.

He shrugged his shoulders and dropped down on the shelf.

"Well, the folk of the city can't help us just now. And they might not, if they could. The people of the Black Countries are generally hostile to strangers. Probably stick us full of spears—"

He stopped short and stood silent, as if he had

forgotten what he was saying, frowning down at the crimson spheres gleaming among the leaves.

"Spears!" he muttered. "What a blasted fool I am not to have thought of that before! That shows what a pretty woman does to a man's mind."

"What are you talking about?" she inquired.

Without answering her question, he descended to the belt of leaves and looked down through them. The great brute squatted below, watching the crag with the frightful patience of the reptile folk. So might one of his breed have glared up at their troglodyte ancestors, treed on a high-flung rock, in the dim dawn ages. Conan cursed him without heat, and began cutting branches, reaching out and severing them as far from the end as he could reach. The agitation of the leaves made the monster restless. He rose from his haunches and lashed his hideous tail, snapping off saplings as if they had been toothpicks. Conan watched him warily from the corner of his eye, and just as Valeria believed the dragon was about to hurl himself up the crag again, the Cimmerian drew back and climbed up to the ledge with the branches he had cut. There were three of these, slender shafts about seven feet long, but not larger than his thumb. He had also cut several strands of tough, thin vine.

"Branches too light for spear-hafts, and creepers no thicker than cords," he remarked, indicating the foliage about the crag. "It won't hold our weight—but there's strength in union. That's what the Aquilonian renegades used to tell us Cimmerians when they came into the hills to raise an army to invade their own country. But we always fight by clans and tribes."

"What the devil has that got to do with those sticks?" she demanded.

"You wait and see."

Gathering the sticks in a compact bundle, he wedged his poniard hilt between them at one end. Then with the vines he bound them together, and when he had completed his task, he had a spear of no small strength, with a sturdy shaft seven feet in length.

"What good will that do?" she demanded. "You told me that a blade couldn't pierce his scales—"

"He hasn't got scales all over him," answered Conan. "There's more than one way of skinning a panther."

Moving down to the edge of the leaves, he reached the spear up and carefully thrust the blade through one of the Apples of Derketa, drawing aside to avoid the darkly purple drops that dripped from the pierced fruit. Presently he withdrew the blade and showed her the blue steel stained a dull purplish crimson.

"I don't know whether it will do the job or not," quoth he. "There's enough poison there to kill an elephant, but—well, we'll see."

Valeria was close behind him as he let himself down among the leaves. Cautiously holding the poisoned pike away from him, he thrust his head through the branches and addressed the monster.

"What are you waiting down there for, you misbegotten offspring of questionable parents?" was one of his more printable queries. "Stick your ugly head up here again, you long-necked brute—or do you want me to come down there and kick you loose from your illegitimate spine?"

There was more of it—some of it couched in eloquence that made Valeria stare, in spite of her profane education among the seafarers. And it had its effect on the monster. Just as the incessant yapping of a dog worries and enrages more constitutionally silent animals, so the clamorous voice of a man rouses fear in some bestial bosoms and insane rage in others.

Suddenly and with appalling quickness, the mastodonic brute reared up on its mighty hind legs and elongated its neck and body in a furious effort to reach this vociferous pigmy whose clamor was disturbing the primeval silence of its ancient realm.

But Conan had judged his distance with precision. Some five feet below him the mighty head crashed terribly but futilely through the leaves. And as the monstrous mouth gaped like that of a great snake, Conan drove his spear into the red angle of the jawbone hinge. He struck downward with all the strength of both arms, driving the long poniard blade to the hilt in flesh, sinew and bone.

Instantly the jaws clashed convulsively together, severing the triple-pieced shaft and almost precipitating Conan from his perch. He would have fallen but for the girl behind him, who caught his sword-belt in a desperate grasp. He clutched at a rocky projection, and grinned his thanks back at her.

Down on the ground the monster was wallowing like a dog with pepper in its eyes. He shook his head from side to side, pawed at it, and opened his mouth repeatedly to its widest extent. Presently he got a huge front foot on the stump of the shaft and managed to tear the blade out. Then he threw up his head, jaws wide and spouting blood, and glared up at the crag with such concentrated and intelligent fury that Valeria trembled and drew her sword. The scales along his back and flanks turned from rusty brown to a dull lurid red. Most horribly the monster's silence was broken. The sounds that issued from his blood-streaming jaws did not sound like anything that could have been produced by an earthly creation.

With harsh, grating roars, the dragon hurled himself at the crag that was the citadel of his enemies. Again and again his mighty head crashed upward through the branches, snapping vainly on empty air. He hurled his full ponderous weight against the rock until it vibrated from base to crest. And rearing upright he gripped it with his front legs like a man and tried to tear it up by the roots, as if it had been a tree.

This exhibition of primordial fury chilled the blood in Valeria's veins, but Conan was too close to the primitive himself to feel anything but a comprehending interest. To the barbarian, no such gulf existed between himself and other men, and the animals, as existed in the conception of Valeria. The monster below them, to Conan, was merely a form of life differing from himself mainly in physical shape. He attributed to it characteristics similar to his own, and saw in its wrath a counterpart of his rages, in its roars and bellowings merely reptilian equivalents to the curses he had bestowed upon it. Feeling a kinship with all wild things, even dragons, it was impossible for him to experience the sick horror which assailed Valeria at the sight of the brute's ferocity.

He sat watching it tranquilly, and pointed out the various changes that were taking place in its voice and actions.

"The poison's taking hold," he said with conviction

"I don't believe it." To Valeria it seemed preposterous to suppose that anything, however lethal, could have any effect on that mountain of muscle and fury

"There's pain in his voice," declared Conan. "First he was merely angry because of the stinging in his jaw Now he feels the bite of the poison. Look! He's staggering. He'll be blind in a few more minutes. Wha did I tell you?"

For suddenly the dragon had lurched about and went crashing off through the bushes.

"Is he running away?" inquired Valeria uneasily.

"He's making for the pool!" Conan sprang up, galvanized into swift activity. "The poison makes him thirsty. Come on! He'll be blind in a few moments, but he can smell his way back to the foot of the crag, and if our scent's here still, he'll sit there until he dies. And others of his kind may come at his cries. Let's go!"

"Down there?" Valeria was aghast.

"Sure! We'll make for the city! They may cut our heads off there, but it's our only chance. We may run into a thousand more dragons on the way, but it's sure death to stay here. If we wait until he dies, we may have a dozen more to deal with. After me, in a hurry!"

He went down the ramp as swiftly as an ape, pausing only to aid his less agile companion, who, until she saw the Cimmerian climb, had fancied herself the equal of any man in the rigging of a ship or on the sheer face of a cliff.

They descended into the gloom below the branches and slid to the ground silently, though Valeria felt as if the pounding of her heart must surely be heard from far away. A noisy gurgling and lapping beyond the dense thicket indicated that the dragon was drinking at the pool.

"As soon as his belly is full he'll be back," muttered Conan. "It may take hours for the poison to kill him—if it does at all."

Somewhere beyond the forest the sun was sinking to the horizon. The forest was a misty twilight place of black shadows and dim vistas. Conan gripped Valeria's wrist and glided away from the foot of the crag. He made less noise than a breeze blowing among the tree-trunks, but Valeria felt as if her soft boots were betraying their flight to all the forest.

"I don't think he can follow a trail," muttered

Conan. "But if a wind blew our body-scent to him, he could smell us out."

"Mitra grant that the wind blow not!" Valeria breathed.

Her face was a pallid oval in the gloom. She gripped her sword in her free hand, but the feel of the shagreen-bound hilt inspired only a feeling of helplessness in her.

They were still some distance from the edge of the forest when they heard a snapping and crashing behind them. Valeria bit her lip to check a cry.

"He's on our trail!" she whispered fiercely.

Conan shook his head.

"He didn't smell us at the rock, and he's blundering about through the forest trying to pick up our scent. Come on! It's the city or nothing now! He could tear down any tree we'd climb. If only the wind stays down—"

They stole on until the trees began to thin out ahead of them. Behind them the forest was a black impenetrable ocean of shadows. The ominous crackling still sounded behind them, as the dragon blundered in his erratic course.

"There's the plain ahead," breathed Valeria. "A little more and we'll—"

"Crom!" swore Conan.

"Mitra!" whispered Valeria.

Out of the south a wind had sprung up.

It blew over them directly into the black forest behind them. Instantly a horrible roar shook the woods. The aimless snapping and crackling of the bushes changed to a sustained crashing as the dragon came like a hurricane straight toward the spot from which the scent of his enemies was wafted.

"Run!" snarled Conan, his eyes blazing like those of a trapped wolf. "It's all we can do!"

Sailor's boots are not made for sprinting, and the life of a pirate does not train one for a runner. Within a hundred yards Valeria was panting and reeling in her gait, and behind them the crashing gave way to a rolling thunder as the monster broke out of the thickets and into the more open ground.

Conan's iron arm about the woman's waist half lifted her; her feet scarcely touched the earth as she was borne along at a speed she could never have attained herself. If he could keep out of the beast's way for a bit, perhaps that betraying wind would shift—but the wind held, and a quick glance over his shoulder showed Conan that the monster was almost upon them, coming like a war-galley in front of a hurricane. He thrust Valeria from him with a force that sent her reeling a dozen feet to fall in a crumpled heap at the foot of the nearest tree, and the Cimmerian wheeled in the path of the thundering titan.

Convinced that his death was upon him, the Cimmerian acted according to his instinct, and hurled himself full at the awful face that was bearing down on him. He leaped, slashing like a wildcat, felt his sword cut deep into the scales that sheathed the mighty snout—and then a terrific impact knocked him rolling and tumbling for fifty feet with all the wind and half the life battered out of him.

How the stunned Cimmerian regained his feet, not even he could have ever told. But the only thought that filled his brain was of the woman lying dazed and helpless almost in the path of the hurtling fiend, and before the breath came whistling back into his gullet he was standing over her with his sword in his hand.

She lay where he had thrown her, but she was struggling to a sitting posture. Neither tearing tusks nor trampling feet had touched her. It had been a shoulder or front leg that struck Conan, and the blind monster rushed on, forgetting the victims whose scent it had been following, in the sudden agony of its death throes. Headlong on its course it thundered until its low-hung head crashed into a gigantic tree in its path. The impact tore the tree up by the roots and must have dashed the brains from the misshapen skull. Tree and monster fell together, and the dazed humans saw the branches and leaves shaken by the convulsions of the creature they covered—and then grow quiet.

Conan lifted Valeria to her feet and together they started away at a reeling run. A few moments later they emerged into the still twilight of the treeless plain.

Conan paused an instant and glanced back at the ebon fastness behind them. Not a leaf stirred, nor a bird chirped. It stood as silent as it must have stood before Man was created.

"Come on," muttered Conan, taking his companion's hand. "It's touch and go now. If more dragons come out of the woods after us—"

He did not have to finish the sentence.

The city looked very far away across the plain, farther than it had looked from the crag. Valeria's heart hammered until she felt as if it would strangle her. At every step she expected to hear the crashing of the bushes and see another colossal nightmare bearing down upon them. But nothing disturbed the silence of the thickets.

With the first mile between them and the woods, Valeria breathed more easily. Her buoyant self-confidence began to thaw out again. The sun had set and darkness was gathering over the plain, lightened a little by the stars that made stunted ghosts out of the cactus growths.

"No cattle, no plowed fields," muttered Conan.

"How do these people live?"

"Perhaps the cattle are in pens for the night," suggested Valeria, "and the fields and grazing pastures are on the other side of the city."

"Maybe," he grunted. "I didn't see any from the crag, though."

The moon came up behind the city, etching walls and towers blackly in the yellow glow. Valeria shivered. Black against the moon the strange city had a somber, sinister look.

Perhaps something of the same feeling occurred to Conan, for he stopped, glanced about him, and grunted: "We stop here. No use coming to their gates in the night. They probably wouldn't let us in. Besides, we need rest, and we don't know how they'll receive us. A few hours' sleep will put us in better shape to fight or run."

He led the way to a bed of cactus which grew in a circle—a phenomenon common to the southern desert. With his sword he chopped an opening, and motioned Valeria to enter.

"We'll be safe from snakes here, anyhow."

She glanced fearfully back toward the black line that indicated the forest some six miles away.

"Suppose a dragon comes out of the woods?"

"We'll keep watch," he answered, though he made no suggestion as to what they would do in such an event. He was staring at the city, a few miles away. Not a light shone from spire or tower. A great black mass of mystery, it reared cryptically against the moonlit sky.

"Lie down and sleep. I'll keep the first watch."

She hesitated, glancing at him uncertainly, but he sat down cross-legged in the opening, facing toward the plain, his sword across his knees, his back to her. Without further comment she lay down on the sand inside the spiky circle.

"Wake me when the moon is at its zenith," she directed.

He did not reply nor look toward her. Her last impression, as she sank into slumber, was of his muscular figure, immobile as a statue hewn out of bronze, outlined against the low-hanging stars.

2. *By the Blaze of the Fire Jewels*

VALERIA AWOKE WITH a start, to the realization that a gray dawn was stealing over the plain.

She sat up, rubbing her eyes. Conan squatted beside the cactus, cutting off the thick pears and dexterously twitching out the spikes.

"You didn't awake me," she accused. "You let me sleep all night!"

"You were tired," he answered. "Your posterior must have been sore, too, after that long ride. You pirates aren't used to horseback."

"What about yourself?" she retorted.

"I was a *kozak* before I was a pirate," he answered. "They live in the saddle. I snatch naps like a panther watching beside the trail for a deer to come by. My ears keep watch while my eyes sleep."

And indeed the giant barbarian seemed as much refreshed as if he had slept the whole night on a golden bed. Having removed the thorns, and peeled off the tough skin, he handed the girl a thick, juicy cactus leaf.

"Skin your teeth in that pear. It's food and drink to a desert man. I was a chief of the Zuagirs once—desert men who live by plundering the caravans."

"Is there anything you haven't been?" inquired the girl, half in derision and half in fascination.

"I've never been king of an Hyborian kingdom," he grinned, taking an enormous mouthful of cactus. "But I've dreamed of being even that. I may be too, some day. Why shouldn't I?"

She shook her head in wonder at his calm audacity, and fell to devouring her pear. She found it not unpleasing to the palate, and full of cool and thirst-satisfying juice. Finishing his meal, Conan wiped his hands in the sand, rose, ran his fingers through his thick black mane, hitched at his sword-belt and said:

"Well, let's go. If the people in that city are going to cut our throats they may as well do it now, before the heat of the day begins."

His grim humor was unconscious, but Valeria reflected that it might be prophetic. She too hitched her sword-belt as she rose. Her terrors of the night were past. The roaring dragons of the distant forest were like a dim dream. There was a swagger in her stride as she moved off beside the Cimmerian. Whatever perils lay ahead of them, their foes would be men. And Valeria of the Red Brotherhood had never seen the face of the man she feared.

Conan glanced down at her as she strode along beside him with her swinging stride that matched his own.

"You walk more like a hillman than a sailor," he said. "You must be an Aquilonian. The suns of Darfar never burnt your white skin brown. Many a princess would envy you."

"I am from Aquilonia," she replied. His compliments no longer irritated her. His evident admiration pleased her. For another man to have kept her watch while she slept would have angered her; she had always fiercely resented any man's attempting to shield or protect her because of her sex. But she found a secret pleasure in the fact that this man had done so. And he had not taken advantage of her fright and the weakness resulting from it. After all, she reflected, her companion was no common man.

The sun rose behind the city, turning the towers to a sinister crimson.

"Black last night against the moon," grunted Conan, his eyes clouding with the abysmal superstition of the barbarian. "Blood-red as a threat of blood against the sun this dawn. I do not like this city."

But they went on, and as they went Conan pointed out the fact that no road ran to the city from the north.

"No cattle have trampled the plain on this side of the city," said he. "No plowshare has touched the earth for years, maybe centuries. But look: once this plain was cultivated."

Valeria saw the ancient irrigation ditches he indicated, half filled in places, and overgrown with cactus. She frowned with perplexity as her eyes swept over the plain that stretched on all sides of the city to the forest edge, which marched in a vast, dim ring. Vision did not extend beyond that ring.

She looked uneasily at the city. No helmets or spearheads gleamed on battlements, no trumpets sounded, no challenge rang from the towers. A silence as absolute as that of the forest brooded over the walls and minarets.

The sun was high above the eastern horizon when they stood before the great gate in the northern wall, in the shadow of the lofty rampart. Rust flecked the iron bracings of the mighty bronze portal. Spiderwebs glistened thickly on hinge and sill and bolted panel.

"It hasn't been opened for years!" exclaimed Valeria.

"A dead city," grunted Conan. "That's why the ditches were broken and the plain untouched."

"But who built it? Who dwelt here? Where did they go? Why did they abandon it?"

"Who can say? Maybe an exiled clan of Stygians built it. Maybe not. It doesn't look like Stygian architecture. Maybe the people were wiped out by enemies, or a plague exterminated them."

"In that case their treasures may still be gathering

dust and cobwebs in there," suggested Valeria, the acquisitive instincts of her profession waking in her; prodded, too, by feminine curiosity. "Can we open the gate? Let's go in and explore a bit."

Conan eyed the heavy portal dubiously, but placed his massive shoulder against it and thrust with all the power of his muscular calves and thighs. With a rasping screech of rusty hinges the gate moved ponderously inward, and Conan straightened and drew his sword. Valeria stared over his shoulder, and made a sound indicative of surprize.

They were not looking into an open street or court as one would have expected. The opened gate, or door, gave directly into a long, broad hall which ran away and away until its vista grew indistinct in the distance. It was of heroic proportions, and the floor of a curious red stone, cut in square tiles, that seemed to smolder as if with the reflection of flames. The walls were of a shiny green material.

"Jade, or I'm a Shemite!" swore Conan.

"Not in such quantity!" protested Valeria.

"I've looted enough from the Khitan caravans to know what I'm talking about," he asserted. "That's jade!"

The vaulted ceiling was of lapis lazuli, adorned with clusters of great green stones that gleamed with a poisonous radiance.

"Green fire-stones," growled Conan. "That's what the people of Punt call them. They're supposed to be the petrified eyes of those prehistoric snakes the ancients called Golden Serpents. They glow like a cat's eyes in the dark. At night this hall would be lighted by them, but it would be a hellishly weird illumination. Let's look around. We might find a cache of jewels."

"Shut the door," advised Valeria. "I'd hate to have to

outrun a dragon down this hall."

Conan grinned, and replied: "I don't believe the dragons ever leave the forest."

But he complied, and pointed out the broken bolt on the inner side.

"I thought I heard something snap when I shoved against it. That bolt's freshly broken. Rust has eaten nearly through it. If the people ran away, why should it have been bolted on the inside?"

"They undoubtedly left by another door," suggested Valeria.

She wondered how many centuries had passed since the light of outer day had filtered into that great hall through the open door. Sunlight was finding its way somehow into the hall, and they quickly saw the source. High up in the vaulted ceiling skylights were set in slot-like openings—translucent sheets of some crystalline substance. In the splotches of shadow between them, the green jewels winked like the eyes of angry cats. Beneath their feet the dully lurid floor smoldered with changing hues and colors of flame. It was like treading the floors of hell with evil stars blinking overhead.

Three balustraded galleries ran along on each side of the hall, one above the other.

"A four-storied house," grunted Conan, "and this hall extends to the roof. It's long as a street. I seem to see a door at the other end."

Valeria shrugged her white shoulders.

"Your eyes are better than mine, then, though I'm accounted sharp-eyed among the sea-rovers."

They turned into an open door at random, and traversed a series of empty chambers, floored like the hall, and with walls of the same green jade, or of marble or ivory or chalcedony, adorned with friezes of bronze, gold or silver. In the ceilings the green fire-gems were set, and their light was as ghostly and illusive as Conan had predicted. Under the witch-fire glow the intruders moved like specters.

Some of the chambers lacked this illumination, and their doorways showed black as the mouth of the Pit. These Conan and Valeria avoided, keeping always to the lighted chambers.

Cobwebs hung in the corners, but there was no perceptible accumulation of dust on the floor, or on the tables and seats of marble, jade or carnelian which occupied the chambers. Here and there were rugs of that silk known as Khitan which is practically indestructible. Nowhere did they find any windows, or doors opening into streets or courts. Each door merely opened into another chamber or hall.

"Why don't we come to a street?" grumbled Valeria. "This place or whatever we're in must be as big as the king of Turan's seraglio."

"They must not have perished of plague," said Conan, meditating upon the mystery of the empty city. "Otherwise we'd find skeletons. Maybe it became haunted, and everybody got up and left. Maybe—"

"Maybe, hell!" broke in Valeria rudely. "We'll never know. Look at these friezes. They portray men. What race do they belong to?"

Conan scanned them and shook his head.

"I never saw people exactly like them. But there's the smack of the East about them—Vendhya, maybe, or Kosala."

"Were you a king in Kosala?" she asked, masking her keen curiosity with derision.

"No. But I was a war-chief of the Afghulis who live in the Himelian mountains above the borders of Vendhya. These people favor the Kosalans. But why should Kosalans be building a city this far to west?"

The figures portrayed were those of slender, olive-skinned men and women, with finely chiseled, exotic features. They wore filmy robes and many delicate jeweled ornaments, and were depicted mostly in attitudes of feasting, dancing or love-making.

"Easterners, all right," grunted Conan, "but from where I don't know. They must have lived a disgustingly peaceful life, though, or they'd have scenes of wars and fights. Let's go up that stair."

It was an ivory spiral that wound up from the chamber in which they were standing. They mounted three flights and came into a broad chamber on the fourth floor, which seemed to be the highest tier in the building. Skylights in the ceiling illuminated the room, in which light the fire-gems winked pallidly. Glancing through the doors they saw, except on one side, a series of similarly lighted chambers. This other door opened upon a balustraded gallery that overhung a hall much smaller than the one they had recently explored on the lower floor.

"Hell!" Valeria sat down disgustedly on a jade bench. "The people who deserted this city must have taken all their treasures with them. I'm tired of wandering through these bare rooms at random."

"All these upper chambers seem to be lighted," said Conan. "I wish we could find a window that overlooked the city. Let's have a look through that door over there."

"You have a look," advised Valeria. "I'm going to sit here and rest my feet."

Conan disappeared through the door opposite that one opening upon the gallery, and Valeria leaned back with her hands clasped behind her head, and thrust her booted legs out in front of her. These silent rooms and halls with their gleaming green clusters of ornaments and burning crimson floors were beginning to depress her. She wished they could find their way out of the maze into which they had wandered and emerge into a street. She wondered idly what furtive, dark feet had glided over those flaming floors in past centuries, how many deeds of cruelty and mystery those winking ceiling-gems had blazed down upon.

It was a faint noise that brought her out of her reflections. She was on her feet with her sword in her hand before she realized what had disturbed her. Conan had not returned, and she knew it was not he that she had heard.

The sound had come from somewhere beyond the door that opened on to the gallery. Soundlessly in her soft leather boots she glided through it, crept across the balcony and peered down between the heavy balustrades.

A man was stealing along the hall.

The sight of a human being in this supposedly deserted city was a startling shock. Crouching down behind the stone balusters, with every nerve tingling, Valeria glared down at the stealthy figure.

The man in no way resembled the figures depicted on the friezes. He was slightly above middle height, very dark, though not negroid. He was naked but for a scanty silk clout that only partly covered his muscular hips, and a leather girdle, a hand's breath broad, about his lean waist. His long black hair hung in lank strands about his shoulders, giving him a wild appearance. He was gaunt, but knots and cords of muscles stood out on his arms and legs, without that fleshy padding that presents a pleasing symmetry of contour. He was built with an economy that was almost repellent.

Yet it was not so much his physical appearance as his

attitude that impressed the woman who watched him. He slunk along, stooped in a semi-crouch, his head turning from side to side. He grasped a wide-tipped blade in his right hand, and she saw it shake with the intensity of the emotion that gripped him. He was afraid, trembling in the grip of some dire terror. When he turned his head she caught the blaze of wild eyes among the lank strands of black hair.

He did not see her. On tiptoe he glided across the hall and vanished through an open door. A moment later she heard a choking cry, and then silence fell again.

Consumed with curiosity, Valeria glided along the gallery until she came to a door above the one through which the man had passed. It opened into another, smaller gallery that encircled a large chamber.

This chamber was on the third floor, and its ceiling was not so high as that of the hall. It was lighted only by the fire-stones, and their weird green glow left the spaces under the balcony in shadows.

Valeria's eyes widened. The man she had seen was still in the chamber.

He lay face down on a dark crimson carpet in the middle of the room. His body was limp, his arms spread wide. His curved sword lay near him.

She wondered why he should lie there so motionless. Then her eyes narrowed as she stared down at the rug on which he lay. Beneath and about him the fabric showed a slightly different color, a deeper, brighter crimson.

Shivering slightly, she crouched down closer behind the balustrade, intently scanning the shadows under the overhanging gallery. They gave up no secret.

Suddenly another figure entered the grim drama. He was a man similar to the first, and he came in by a door opposite that which gave upon the hall.

171

His eyes glared at the sight of the man on the floor, and he spoke something in a staccato voice that sounded like "Chicmec!" The other did not move.

The man stepped quickly across the floor, bent, gripped the fallen man's shoulder and turned him over. A choking cry escaped him as the head fell back limply, disclosing a throat that had been severed from ear to ear.

The man let the corpse fall back upon the blood-stained carpet, and sprang to his feet, shaking like a wind-blown leaf. His face was an ashy mask of fear. But with one knee flexed for flight, he froze suddenly, became as immobile as an image, staring across the chamber with dilated eyes.

In the shadows beneath the balcony a ghostly light began to glow and grow, a light that was not part of the fire-stone gleam. Valeria felt her hair stir as she watched it; for, dimly visible in the throbbing radiance, there floated a human skull, and it was from this skull—human yet appallingly misshapen—that the spectral light seemed to emanate. It hung there like a disembodied head, conjured out of night and the shadows, growing more and more distinct; human, and yet not human as she knew humanity.

The man stood motionless, an embodiment of paralyzed horror, staring fixedly at the apparition. The thing moved out from the wall and a grotesque shadow moved with it. Slowly the shadow became visible as a man-like figure whose naked torso and limbs shone whitely, with the hue of bleached bones. The bare skull on its shoulders grinned eyelessly, in the midst of its unholy nimbus, and the man confronting it seemed unable to take his eyes from it. He stood still, his sword dangling from nerveless fingers, on his face the expression of a man bound by the spells of a mesmerist.

172

Valeria realized that it was not fear alone that paralyzed him. Some hellish quality of that throbbing glow had robbed him of his power to think and act. She herself, safely above the scene, felt the subtle impact of a nameless emanation that was a threat to sanity.

The horror swept toward its victim and he moved at last, but only to drop his sword and sink to his knees, covering his eyes with his hands. Dumbly he awaited the stroke of the blade that now gleamed in the apparition's hand as it reared above him like Death triumphant over mankind.

Valeria acted according to the first impulse of her wayward nature. With one tigerish movement she was over the balustrade and dropping to the floor behind the awful shape. It wheeled at the thud of her soft boots on the floor, but even as it turned, her keen blade lashed down, and a fierce exultation swept her as she felt the edge cleave solid flesh and mortal bone.

The apparition cried out gurglingly and went down, severed through shoulder, breast-bone and spine, and as it fell the burning skull rolled clear, revealing a lank mop of black hair and a dark face twisted in the convulsions of death. Beneath the horrific masquerade there was a human being, a man similar to the one kneeling supinely on the floor.

The latter looked up at the sound of the blow and the cry, and now he glared in wild-eyed amazement at the white-skinned woman who stood over the corpse with a dripping sword in her hand.

He staggered up, yammering as if the sight had almost unseated his reason. She was amazed to realize that she understood him. He was gibbering in the Stygian tongue, though in a dialect unfamiliar to her.

"Who are you? Whence come you? What do you in Xuchotl?" Then rushing on, without waiting for her to reply: "But you are a friend—goddess or devil, it makes no difference! You have slain the Burning Skull! It was but a man beneath it, after all! We deemed it a demon *they* conjured up out of the catacombs! *Listen!*"

He stopped short in his ravings and stiffened, straining his ears with painful intensity. The girl heard nothing.

"We must hasten!" he whispered. "*They* are west of the Great Hall! They may be all around us here! They may be creeping upon us even now!"

He seized her wrist in a convulsive grasp she found hard to break.

"Whom do you mean by 'they'?" she demanded.

He stared at her uncomprehendingly for an instant, as if he found her ignorance hard to understand.

"They?" he stammered vaguely. "Why—why, the people of Xotalanc! The clan of the man you slew. They who dwell by the eastern gate."

"You mean to say this city is inhabited?" she exclaimed.

"Aye! Aye!" He was writhing in the impatience of apprehension. "Come away! Come quick! We must return to Tecuhltli!"

"Where is that?" she demanded.

"The quarter by the western gate!" He had her wrist again and was pulling her toward the door through which he had first come. Great beads of perspiration dripped from his dark forehead, and his eyes blazed with terror.

"Wait a minute!" she growled, flinging off his hand. "Keep your hands off me, or I'll split your skull. What's all this about? Who are you? Where would you take me?"

He took a firm grip on himself, casting glances to all sides, and began speaking so fast his words tripped over each other.

"My name is Techotl. I am of Tecuhltli. I and this man who lies with his throat cut came into the Halls of Silence to try and ambush some of the Xotalancas. But we became separated and I returned here to find him with his gullet slit. The Burning Skull did it, I know, just as he would have slain me had you not killed him. But perhaps he was not alone. Others may be stealing from Xotalanc! The gods themselves blench at the fate of those they take alive!"

At the thought he shook as with an ague and his dark skin grew ashy. Valeria frowned puzzledly at him. She sensed intelligence behind this rigmarole, but it was meaningless to her.

She turned toward the skull, which still glowed and pulsed on the floor, and was reaching a booted toe tentatively toward it, when the man who called himself Techotl sprang forward with a cry.

"Do not touch it! Do not even look at it! Madness and death lurk in it. The wizards of Xotalanc understand its secret—they found it in the catacombs, where lie the bones of terrible kings who ruled in Xuchotl in the black centuries of the past. To gaze upon it freezes the blood and withers the brain of a man who understands not its mystery. To touch it causes madness and destruction."

She scowled at him uncertainly. He was not a reassuring figure, with his lean, muscle-knotted frame, and snaky locks. In his eyes, behind the glow of terror, lurked a weird light she had never seen in the eyes of a man wholly sane. Yet he seemed sincere in his protestations.

"Come!" he begged, reaching for her hand, and then recoiling as he remembered her warning. "You are a stranger. How you came here I do not know, but if you were a goddess or a demon, come to aid Tecuhltli, you would know all the things you have asked me. You must be from beyond the great forest, whence our ancestors came. But you are our friend, or you would not have slain my enemy. Come quickly, before the Xotalancas find us and slay us!"

From his repellent, impassioned face she glanced to the sinister skull, smoldering and glowing on the floor near the dead man. It was like a skull seen in a dream, undeniably human, yet with disturbing distortions and malformations of contour and outline. In life the wearer of that skull must have presented an alien and monstrous aspect. Life? It seemed to possess some sort of life of its own. Its jaws yawned at her and snapped together. Its radiance grew brighter, more vivid, yet the impression of nightmare grew too; it was a dream; all life was a dream—it was Techotl's urgent voice which snapped Valeria back from the dim gulfs whither she was drifting.

"Do not look at the skull! Do not look at the skull!" It was a far cry from across unreckoned voids.

Valeria shook herself like a lion shaking his mane. Her vision cleared. Techotl was chattering: "In life it housed the awful brain of a king of magicians! It holds still the life and fire of magic drawn from outer spaces!"

With a curse Valeria leaped, lithe as a panther, and the skull crashed to flaming bits under her swinging sword. Somewhere in the room, or in the void, or in the dim reaches of her consciousness, an inhuman voice cried out in pain and rage.

Techotl's hand was plucking at her arm and he was gibbering: "You have broken it! You have destroyed it! Not all the black arts of Xotalanc can rebuild it! Come away! Come away quickly, now!"

"But I can't go," she protested. "I have a friend

somewhere near by—"

The flare of his eyes cut her short as he stared past her with an expression grown ghastly. She wheeled just as four men rushed through as many doors, converging on the pair in the center of the chamber.

They were like the others she had seen, the same knotted muscles bulging on otherwise gaunt limbs, the same lank blue-black hair, the same mad glare in their wide eyes. They were armed and clad like Techotl, but on the breast of each was painted a white skull.

There were no challenges or war-cries. Like blood-mad tigers the men of Xotalanc sprang at the throats of their enemies. Techotl met them with the fury of desperation, ducked the swipe of a wide-headed blade, and grappled with the wielder, and bore him to the floor where they rolled and wrestled in murderous silence.

The other three swarmed on Valeria, their weird eyes red as the eyes of mad dogs.

She killed the first who came within reach before he could strike a blow, her long straight blade splitting his skull even as his own sword lifted for a stroke. She side-stepped a thrust, even as she parried a slash. Her eyes danced and her lips smiled without mercy. Again she was Valeria of the Red Brotherhood, and the hum of her steel was like a bridal song in her ears.

Her sword darted past a blade that sought to parry, and sheathed six inches of its point in a leather-guarded midriff. The man gasped agonizedly and went to his knees, but his tall mate lunged in, in ferocious silence, raining blow on blow so furiously that Valeria had no opportunity to counter. She stepped back coolly, parrying the strokes and watching for her chance to thrust home. He could not long keep up that flailing whirlwind. His arm would tire, his wind would fail; he would weaken, falter, and then her blade would slide smoothly into his heart. A sidelong glance showed her Techotl kneeling on the breast of his antagonist and striving to break the other's hold on his wrist and to drive home a dagger.

Sweat beaded the forehead of the man facing her, and his eyes were like burning coals. Smite as he would, he could not break past nor beat down her guard. His breath came in gusty gulps, his blows began to fall erratically. She stepped back to draw him out—and felt her thighs locked in an iron grip. She had forgotten the wounded man on the floor.

Crouching on his knees, he held her with both arms locked about her legs, and his mate croaked in triumph and began working his way around to come at her from the left side. Valeria wrenched and tore savagely, but in vain. She could free herself of this clinging menace with a downward flick of her sword, but in that instant the curved blade of the tall warrior would crash through her skull. The wounded man began to worry at her bare thigh with his teeth like a wild beast.

She reached down with her left hand and gripped his long hair, forcing his head back so that his white teeth and rolling eyes gleamed up at her. The tall Xotalanc cried out fiercely and leaped in, smiting with all the fury of his arm. Awkwardly she parried the stroke, and it beat the flat of her blade down on her head so that she saw sparks flash before her eyes, and staggered. Up went the sword again, with a low, beast-like cry of triumph—and then a giant form loomed behind the Xotalanc and steel flashed like a jet of blue lightning. The cry of the warrior broke short and he went down like an ox beneath the pole-ax, his brains gushing from his skull that had been split to the throat.

"Conan!" gasped Valeria. In a gust of passion she

turned on the Xotalanc whose long hair she still gripped in her left hand. "Dog of hell!" Her blade swished as it cut the air in an upswinging arc with a blur in the middle, and the headless body slumped down, spurting blood. She hurled the severed head across the room.

"What the devil's going on here?" Conan bestrode the corpse of the man he had killed, broadsword in hand, glaring about him in amazement.

Techotl was rising from the twitching figure of the last Xotalanc, shaking red drops from his dagger. He was bleeding from the stab deep in the thigh. He stared at Conan with dilated eyes.

"What is all this?" Conan demanded again, not yet recovered from the stunning surprize of finding Valeria engaged in a savage battle with these fantastic figures in a city he had thought empty and uninhabited. Returning from an aimless exploration of the upper chambers to find Valeria missing from the room where he had left her, he had followed the sounds of strife that burst on his dumfounded ears.

"Five dead dogs!" exclaimed Techotl, his flaming eyes reflecting a ghastly exultation. "Five slain! Five crimson nails for the black pillar! The gods of blood be thanked!"

He lifted quivering hands on high, and then, with the face of a fiend, he spat on the corpses and stamped on their faces, dancing in his ghoulish glee. His recent allies eyed him in amazement, and Conan asked, in the Aquilonian tongue: "Who is this madman?"

Valeria shrugged her shoulders.

"He says his name's Techotl. From his babblings I gather that his people live at one end of this crazy city, and these others at the other end. Maybe we'd better go with him. He seems friendly, and it's easy to see that the other clan isn't."

Techotl had ceased his dancing and was listening again, his head tilted sidewise, dog-like, triumph struggling with fear in his repellent countenance.

"Come away, now!" he whispered. "We have done enough! Five dead dogs! My people will welcome you! They will honor you! But come! It is far to Tecuhltli. At any moment the Xotalancs may come on us in numbers too great even for your swords."

"Lead the way," grunted Conan.

Techotl instantly mounted a stair leading up to the gallery, beckoning them to follow him, which they did, moving rapidly to keep on his heels. Having reached the gallery, he plunged into a door that opened toward the west, and hurried through chamber after chamber, each lighted by skylights or green fire-jewels.

"What sort of a place can this be?" muttered Valeria under her breath.

"Crom knows!" answered Conan. "I've seen *his* kind before, though. They live on the shores of Lake Zuad, near the border of Kush. They're a sort of mongrel Stygians, mixed with another race that wandered into Stygia from the east some centuries ago and were absorbed by them. They're called Tlazitlans. I'm willing to bet it wasn't they who built this city, though."

Techotl's fear did not seem to diminish as they drew away from the chamber where the dead men lay. He kept twisting his head on his shoulder to listen for sounds of pursuit, and stared with burning intensity into every doorway they passed.

Valeria shivered in spite of herself. She feared no man. But the weird floor beneath her feet, the uncanny jewels over her head, dividing the lurking shadows among them, the stealth and terror of their guide, impressed her with a nameless apprehension, a sensation of lurking, inhuman peril.

"They may be between us and Tecuhltli!" he whispered once. "We must beware lest they be lying in wait!"

"Why don't we get out of this infernal palace, and take to the streets?" demanded Valeria.

"There are no streets in Xuchotl," he answered. "No squares nor open courts. The whole city is built like one giant palace under one great roof. The nearest approach to a street is the Great Hall which traverses the city from the north gate to the south gate. The only doors opening into the outer world are the city gates, through which no living man has passed for fifty years."

"How long have you dwelt here?" asked Conan.

"I was born in the castle of Tecuhltli thirty-five years ago. I have never set foot outside the city. For the love of the gods, let us go silently! These halls may be full of lurking devils. Olmec shall tell you all when we reach Tecuhltli."

So in silence they glided on with the green fire-stones blinking overhead and the flaming floors smoldering under their feet, and it seemed to Valeria as if they fled through hell, guided by a dark-faced lank-haired goblin.

Yet it was Conan who halted them as they were crossing an unusually wide chamber. His wilderness-bred ears were keener even than the ears of Techotl, whetted though these were by a lifetime of warfare in those silent corridors.

"You think some of your enemies may be ahead of us, lying in ambush?"

"They prowl through these rooms at all hours," answered Techotl, "as do we. The halls and chambers between Tecuhltli and Xotalanc are a disputed region, owned by no man. We call it the Halls of Silence. Why do you ask?"

"Because men are in the chambers ahead of us," answered Conan. "I heard steel clink against stone."

Again a shaking seized Techotl, and he clenched his teeth to keep them from chattering.

"Perhaps they are your friends," suggested Valeria.

"We dare not chance it," he panted, and moved with frenzied activity. He turned aside and glided through a doorway on the left which led into a chamber from which an ivory staircase wound down into darkness.

"This leads to an unlighted corridor below us!" he hissed, great beads of perspiration standing out on his brow. "They may be lurking there, too. It may all be a trick to draw us into it. But we must take the chance that they have laid their ambush in the rooms above. Come swiftly, now!"

Softly as phantoms they descended the stair and came to the mouth of a corridor black as night. They crouched there for a moment, listening, and then melted into it. As they moved along, Valeria's flesh crawled between her shoulders in momentary expectation of a sword-thrust in the dark. But for Conan's iron fingers gripping her arm she had no physical cognizance of her companions. Neither made as much noise as a cat would have made. The darkness was absolute. One hand, outstretched, touched a wall, and occasionally she felt a door under her fingers. The hallway seemed interminable.

Suddenly they were galvanized by a sound behind them. Valeria's flesh crawled anew, for she recognized it as the soft opening of a door. Men had come into the corridor behind them. Even with the thought she stumbled over something that felt like a human skull. It rolled across the floor with an appalling clatter.

"Run!" yelped Techotl, a note of hysteria in his voice, and was away down the corridor like a flying ghost.

Again Valeria felt Conan's hand bearing her up and sweeping her along as they raced after their guide. Conan could see in the dark no better than she, but he possessed a sort of instinct that made his course unerring. Without his support and guidance she would have fallen or stumbled against the wall. Down the corridor they sped, while the swift patter of flying feet drew closer and closer, and then suddenly Techotl panted: "Here is the stair! After me, quick! Oh, quick!"

His hand came out of the dark and caught Valeria's wrist as she stumbled blindly on the steps. She felt herself half dragged, half lifted up the winding stair, while Conan released her and turned on the steps, his ears and instincts telling him their foes were hard at their backs. *And the sounds were not all those of human feet.*

Something came writhing up the steps, something that slithered and rustled and brought a chill in the air with it. Conan lashed down with his great sword and felt the blade shear through something that might have been flesh and bone, and cut deep into the stair beneath. Something touched his foot that chilled like the touch of frost, and then the darkness beneath him was disturbed by a frightful thrashing and lashing, and a man cried out in agony.

The next moment Conan was racing up the winding staircase, and through a door that stood open at the head.

Valeria and Techotl were already through, and Techotl slammed the door and shot a bolt across it— the first Conan had seen since they left the outer gate.

Then he turned and ran across the well-lighted

chamber into which they had come, and as they passed through the farther door, Conan glanced back and saw the door groaning and straining under heavy pressure violently applied from the other side.

Though Techotl did not abate either his speed or his caution, he seemed more confident now. He had the air of a man who has come into familiar territory, within call of friends.

But Conan renewed his terror by asking: "What was that thing that I fought on the stair?"

"The men of Xotalanc," answered Techotl, without looking back. "I told you the halls were full of them."

"This wasn't a man," grunted Conan. "It was something that crawled, and it was as cold as ice to the touch. I think I cut it asunder. It fell back on the men who were following us, and must have killed one of them in its death throes."

Techotl's head jerked back, his face ashy again. Convulsively he quickened his pace.

"It was the Crawler! A monster *they* have brought out of the catacombs to aid them! What it is, we do not know, but we have found our people hideously slain by it. In Set's name, hasten! If they put it on our trail, it will follow us to the very doors of Tecuhltli!"

"I doubt it," grunted Conan. "That was a shrewd cut I dealt it on the stair."

"Hasten! Hasten!" groaned Techotl.

They ran through a series of green-lit chambers, traversed a broad hall, and halted before a giant bronze door.

Techotl said: "This is Tecuhltli!"

3. The People of the Feud

TECHOTL SMOTE ON the bronze door with his clenched hand, and then turned sidewise, so that he could watch back along the hall.

"Men have been smitten down before this door, when they thought they were safe," he said.

"Why don't they open the door?" asked Conan.

"They are looking at us through the Eye," answered Techotl. "They are puzzled at the sight of you." He lifted his voice and called: "Open the door, Xecelan! It is I, Techotl, with friends from the great world beyond the forest!—They will open," he assured his allies.

"They'd better do it in a hurry, then," said Conan grimly. "I hear something crawling along the floor beyond the hall."

Techotl went ashy again and attacked the door with his fists, screaming: "Open, you fools, open! The Crawler is at our heels!"

Even as he beat and shouted, the great bronze door swung noiselessly back, revealing a heavy chain across the entrance, over which spearheads bristled and fierce countenances regarded them intently for an instant. Then the chain was dropped and Techotl grasped the arms of his friends in a nervous frenzy and fairly dragged them over the threshold. A glance over his shoulder just as the door was closing showed Conan the long dim vista of the hall, and dimly framed at the other end an ophidian shape that writhed slowly and painfully into view, flowing in a dull-hued length from a chamber door, its hideous blood-stained head wagging drunkenly. Then the closing door shut off the view.

Inside the square chamber into which they had come

185

heavy bolts were drawn across the door, and the chain locked into place. The door was made to stand the battering of a siege. Four men stood on guard, of the same lank-haired, dark-skinned breed as Techotl, with spears in their hands and swords at their hips. In the wall near the door there was a complicated contrivance of mirrors which Conan guessed was the Eye Techotl had mentioned, so arranged that a narrow, crystal-paned slot in the wall could be looked through from within without being discernible from without. The four guardsmen stared at the strangers with wonder, but asked no question, nor did Techotl vouchsafe any information. He moved with easy confidence now, as if he had shed his cloak of indecision and fear the instant he crossed the threshold.

"Come!" he urged his new-found friends, but Conan glanced toward the door.

"What about those fellows who were following us? Won't they try to storm that door?"

Techotl shook his head.

"They know they cannot break down the Door of the Eagle. They will flee back to Xotalanc, with their crawling fiend. Come! I will take you to the rulers of Tecuhltli."

One of the four guards opened the door opposite the one by which they had entered, and they passed through into a hallway which, like most of the rooms on that level, was lighted by both the slot-like skylights and the clusters of winking fire-gems. But unlike the other rooms they had traversed, this hall showed evidences of occupation. Velvet tapestries adorned the glossy jade walls, rich rugs were on the crimson floors, and the ivory seats, benches and divans were littered with satin cushions.

The hall ended in an ornate door, before which

stood no guard. Without ceremony Techotl thrust the door open and ushered his friends into a broad chamber, where some thirty dark-skinned men and women lounging on satin-covered couches sprang up with exclamations of amazement.

The men, all except one, were of the same type as Techotl, and the women were equally dark and strange-eyed, though not unbeautiful in a weird dark way. They wore sandals, golden breast-plates, and scanty silk skirts supported by gem-crusted girdles, and their black manes, cut square at their naked shoulders, were bound with silver circlets.

On a wide ivory seat on a jade dais sat a man and a woman who differed subtly from the others. He was a giant, with an enormous sweep of breast and the shoulders of a bull. Unlike the others, he was bearded, with a thick, blue-black beard which fell almost to his broad girdle. He wore a robe of purple silk which reflected changing sheens of color with his every movement, and one wide sleeve, drawn back to his elbow, revealed a forearm massive with corded muscles. The band which confined his blue-black locks was set with glittering jewels.

The woman beside him sprang to her feet with a startled exclamation as the strangers entered, and her eyes, passing over Conan, fixed themselves with burning intensity on Valeria. She was tall and lithe, by far the most beautiful woman in the room. She was clad more scantily even than the others; for instead of a skirt she wore merely a broad strip of gilt-worked purple cloth fastened to the middle of her girdle which fell below her knees. Another strip at the back of her girdle completed that part of her costume, which she wore with a cynical indifference. Her breast-plates and the circlet about her temples were adorned with gems.

In her eyes alone of all the dark-skinned people there lurked no brooding gleam of madness. She spoke no word after her first exclamation; she stood tensely, her hands clenched, staring at Valeria.

The man on the ivory seat had not risen.

"Prince Olmec," spoke Techotl, bowing low, with arms outspread and the palms of his hands turned upward, "I bring allies from the world beyond the forest. In the Chamber of Tezcoti the Burning Skull slew Chicmec, my companion—"

"The Burning Skull!" It was a shuddering whisper of fear from the people of Tecuhltli.

"Aye! Then came I, and found Chicmec lying with his throat cut. Before I could flee, the Burning Skull came upon me, and when I looked upon it my blood became as ice and the marrow of my bones melted. I could neither fight nor run. I could only await the stroke. Then came this white-skinned woman and struck him down with her sword; and lo, it was only a dog of Xotalanc with white paint upon his skin and the living skull of an ancient wizard upon his head! Now that skull lies in many pieces, and the dog who wore it is a dead man!"

An indescribably fierce exultation edged the last sentence, and was echoed in the low, savage exclamations from the crowding listeners.

"But wait!" exclaimed Techotl. "There is more! While I talked with the woman, four Xotalancs came upon us! One I slew—there is the stab in my thigh to prove how desperate was the fight. Two the woman killed. But we were hard pressed when this man came into the fray and split the skull of the fourth! Aye! Five crimson nails there are to be driven into the pillar of vengeance!"

He pointed at a black column of ebony which stood

188

behind the dais. Hundreds of red dots scarred its polished surface—the bright scarlet heads of heavy copper nails driven into the black wood.

"Five red nails for five Xotalanca lives!" exulted Techotl, and the horrible exultation in the faces of the listeners made them inhuman.

"Who are these people?" asked Olmec, and his voice was like the low, deep rumble of a distant bull. None of the people of Xuchotl spoke loudly. It was as if they had absorbed into their souls the silence of the empty halls and deserted chambers.

"I am Conan, a Cimmerian," answered the barbarian briefly. "This woman is Valeria of the Red Brotherhood, an Aquilonian pirate. We are deserters from an army on the Darfar border, far to the north, and are trying to reach the coast."

The woman on the dais spoke loudly, her words tripping in her haste.

"You can never reach the coast! There is no escape from Xuchotl! You will spend the rest of your lives in this city!"

"What do you mean?" growled Conan, clapping his hand to his hilt and stepping about so as to face both the dais and the rest of the room. "Are you telling us we're prisoners?"

"She did not mean that," interposed Olmec. "We are your friends. We would not restrain you against your will. But I fear other circumstances will make it impossible for you to leave Xuchotl."

His eyes flickered to Valeria, and he lowered them quickly.

"This woman is Tascela," he said. "She is a princess of Tecuhltli. But let food and drink be brought our guests. Doubtless they are hungry, and weary from their long travels."

He indicated an ivory table, and after an exchange of glances, the adventurers seated themselves. The Cimmerian was suspicious. His fierce blue eyes roved about the chamber, and he kept his sword close to his hand. But an invitation to eat and drink never found him backward. His eyes kept wandering to Tascela, but the princess had eyes only for his white-skinned companion.

Techotl, who had bound a strip of silk about his wounded thigh, placed himself at the table to attend to the wants of his friends, seeming to consider it a privilege and honor to see after their needs. He inspected the food and drink the others brought in gold vessels and dishes, and tasted each before he placed it before his guests. While they ate, Olmec sat in silence on his ivory seat, watching them from under his broad black brows. Tascela sat beside him, chin cupped in her hands and her elbows resting on her knees. Her dark, enigmatic eyes, burning with a mysterous light, never left Valeria's supple figure. Behind her seat a sullen handsome girl waved an ostrich-plume fan with a slow rhythm.

The food was fruit of an exotic kind unfamiliar to the wanderers, but very palatable, and the drink was a light crimson wine that carried a heady tang.

"You have come from afar," said Olmec at last. "I have read the books of our fathers. Aquilonia lies beyond the lands of the Stygians and the Shemites, beyond Argos and Zingara; and Cimmeria lies beyond Aquilonia."

"We have each a roving foot," answered Conan carelessly.

"How you won through the forest is a wonder to me," quoth Olmec. "In bygone days a thousand fighting-men scarcely were able to carve a road through its perils."

"We encountered a bench-legged monstrosity about the size of a mastodon," said Conan casually, holding out his wine goblet which Techotl filled with evident pleasure. "But when we'd killed it we had no further trouble."

The wine vessel slipped from Techotl's hand to crash on the floor. His dusky skin went ashy. Olmec started to his feet, an image of stunned amazement, and a low gasp of awe or terror breathed up from the others. Some slipped to their knees as if their legs would not support them. Only Tascela seemed not to have heard. Conan glared about him bewilderedly.

"What's the matter? What are you gaping about?"

"You—you slew the dragon-god?"

"God? I killed a dragon. Why not? It was trying to gobble us up."

"But dragons are immortal!" exclaimed Olmec. "They slay each other, but no man ever killed a dragon! The thousand fighting-men of our ancestors who fought their way to Xuchotl could not prevail against them! Their swords broke like twigs against their scales!"

"If your ancestors had thought to dip their spears in the poisonous juice of Derketa's Apples," quoth Conan, with his mouth full, "and jab them in the eyes or mouth or somewhere like that, they'd have seen that dragons are not more immortal than any other chunk of beef. The carcass lies at the edge of the trees, just within the forest. If you don't believe me, go and look for yourself."

Olmec shook his head, not in disbelief but in wonder.

"It was because of the dragons that our ancestors took refuge in Xuchotl," said he. "They dared not pass through the plain and plunge into the forest beyond. Scores of them were seized and devoured by the monsters before they could reach the city."

"Then your ancestors didn't build Xuchotl?" asked Valeria.

"It was ancient when they first came into the land. How long it had stood here, not even its degenerate inhabitants knew."

"Your people came from Lake Zuad?" questioned Conan.

"Aye. More than half a century ago a tribe of the Tlazitlans rebelled against the Stygian king, and, being defeated in battle, fled southward. For many weeks they wandered over grasslands, desert and hills, and at last they came into the great forest, a thousand fighting-men with their women and children.

"It was in the forest that the dragons fell upon them, and tore many to pieces; so the people fled in a frenzy of fear before them, and at last came into the plain and saw the city of Xuchotl in the midst of it.

"They camped before the city, not daring to leave the plain, for the night was made hideous with the noise of the battling monsters throughout the forest. They made war incessantly upon one another. Yet they came not into the plain.

"The people of the city shut their gates and shot arrows at our people from the walls. The Tlazitlans were imprisoned on the plain, as if the ring of the forest had been a great wall; for to venture into the woods would have been madness.

"That night there came secretly to their camp a slave from the city, one of their own blood, who with a band of exploring soldiers had wandered into the forest long before, when he was a young man. The dragons had devoured all his companions, but he had been taken into the city to dwell in servitude. His name was Tolkemec." A flame lighted the dark eyes at mention of the name, and some of the people muttered obscenely and spat. "He promised to open the gates to the warriors. He asked only that all captives taken be delivered into his hands.

"At dawn he opened the gates. The warriors swarmed in and the halls of Xuchotl ran red. Only a few hundred folk dwelt there, decaying remnants of a once great race. Tolkemec said they came from the east, long ago, from Old Kosala, when the ancestors of those who now dwell in Kosala came up from the south and drove forth the original inhabitants of the land. They wandered far westward and finally found this forest-girdled plain, inhabited then by a tribe of black people.

"These they enslaved and set to building a city. From the hills to the east they brought jade and marble and lapis lazuli, and gold, silver and copper. Herds of elephants provided them with ivory. When their city was completed, they slew all the black slaves. And their magicians made a terrible magic to guard the city; for by their necromantic arts they re-created the dragons which had once dwelt in this lost land, and whose monstrous bones they found in the forest. Those bones they clothed in flesh and life, and the living beasts walked the earth as they walked it when Time was young. But the wizards wove a spell that kept them in the forest and they came not into the plain.

"So for many centuries the people of Xuchotl dwelt in their city, cultivating the fertile plain, until their wise men learned how to grow fruit within the city—fruit which is not planted in soil, but obtains its nourishment out of the air—and then they let the irrigation ditches run dry, and dwelt more and more in luxurious sloth, until decay seized them. They were a dying race when our ancestors broke through the forest and came into the plain. Their wizards had died, and the people had forgot their ancient necromancy. They could fight neither by sorcery nor the sword.

"Well, our fathers slew the people of Xuchotl, all except a hundred which were given living into the hands of Tolkemec, who had been their slave; and for many days and nights the halls re-echoed to their screams under the agony of his tortures.

"So the Tlazitlans dwelt here, for a while in peace, ruled by the brothers Tecuhltli and Xotalanc, and by Tolkemec. Tolkemec took a girl of the tribe to wife, and because he had opened the gates, and because he knew many of the arts of the Xuchotlans, he shared the rule of the tribe with the brothers who had led the rebellion and the flight.

"For a few years, then, they dwelt at peace within the city, doing little but eating, drinking and making love, and raising children. There was no necessity to till the plain, for Tolkemec taught them how to cultivate the air-devouring fruits. Besides, the slaying of the Xuchotlans broke the spell that held the dragons in the forest, and they came nightly and bellowed about the gates of the city. The plain ran red with the blood of their eternal warfare, and it was then that—" He bit his tongue in the midst of the sentence, then presently continued, but Valeria and Conan felt that he had checked an admission he had considered unwise.

"Five years they dwelt in peace. Then"—Olmec's eyes rested briefly on the silent woman at his side— "Xotalanc took a woman to wife, a woman whom both Tecuhltli and old Tolkemec desired. In his madness, Tecuhltli stole her from her husband. Aye, she went willingly enough. Tolkemec, to spite Xotalanc, aided Tecuhltli. Xotalanc demanded that she be given back

194

to him, and the council of the tribe decided that the matter should be left to the woman. She chose to remain with Tecuhltli. In wrath Xotalanc sought to take her back by force, and the retainers of the brothers came to blows in the Great Hall.

"There was much bitterness. Blood was shed on both sides. The quarrel became a feud, the feud an open war. From the welter three factions emerged—Tecuhltli, Xotalanc, and Tolkemec. Already, in the days of peace, they had divided the city between them. Tecuhltli dwelt in the western quarter of the city, Xotalanc in the eastern, and Tolkemec with his family by the southern gate.

"Anger and resentment and jealousy blossomed into bloodshed and rape and murder. Once the sword was drawn there was no turning back; for blood called for blood, and vengeance followed swift on the heels of atrocity. Tecuhltli fought with Xotalanc, and Tolkemec aided first one and then the other, betraying each faction as it fitted his purposes. Tecuhltli and his people withdrew into the quarter of the western gate, where we now sit. Xuchotl is built in the shape of an oval. Tecuhltli, which took its name from its prince, occupies the western end of the oval. The people blocked up all doors connecting the quarter with the rest of the city, except one on each floor, which could be defended easily. They went into the pits below the city and built a wall cutting off the western end of the catacombs, where lie the bodies of the ancient Xuchotlans, and of those Tlazitlans slain in the feud. They dwelt as in a besieged castle, making sorties and forays on their enemies.

"The people of Xotalanc likewise fortified the eastern quarter of the city, and Tolkemec did likewise with the quarter by the southern gate. The central part of the city was left bare and uninhabited. Those empty halls and chambers became a battleground, and a region of brooding terror.

"Tolkemec warred on both clans. He was a fiend in the form of a human, worse than Xotalanc. He knew many secrets of the city he never told the others. From the crypts of the catacombs he plundered the dead of their grisly secrets—secrets of ancient kings and wizards, long forgotten by the degenerate Xuchotlans our ancestors slew. But all his magic did not aid him the night we of Tecuhltli stormed his castle and butchered all his people. Tolkemec we tortured for many days."

His voice sank to a caressing slur, and a far-away look grew in his eyes, as if he looked back over the years to a scene which caused him intense pleasure.

"Aye, we kept the life in him until he screamed for death as for a bride. At last we took him living from the torture chamber and cast him into a dungeon for the rats to gnaw as he died. From that dungeon, somehow, he managed to escape, and dragged himself into the catacombs. There without doubt he died, for the only way out of the catacombs beneath Tecuhltli is through Tecuhltli, and he never emerged by that way. His bones were never found, and the superstitious among our people swear that his ghost haunts the crypts to this day, wailing among the bones of the dead. Twelve years ago we butchered the people of Tolkemec, but the feud raged on between Tecuhltli and Xotalanc, as it will rage until the last man, the last woman is dead.

"It was fifty years ago that Tecuhltli stole the wife of Xotalanc. Half a century the feud has endured. I was born in it. All in this chamber, except Tascela, were born in it. We expect to die in it.

"We are a dying race, even as those Xuchotlans our ancestors slew. When the feud began there were hundreds in each faction. Now we of Tecuhltli number only these you see before you, and the men who guard the four doors: forty in all. How many Xotalancas there are we do not know, but I doubt if they are much more numerous than we. For fifteen years no children have been born to us, and we have seen none among the Xotalancas.

"We are dying, but before we die we will slay as many of the men of Xotalanc as the gods permit."

And with his weird eyes blazing, Olmec spoke long of that grisly feud, fought out in silent chambers and dim halls under the blaze of the green fire-jewels, on floors smoldering with the flames of hell and splashed with deeper crimson from severed veins. In that long butchery a whole generation had perished. Xotalanc was dead, long ago, slain in a grim battle on an ivory stair. Tecuhltli was dead, flayed alive by the maddened Xotalancas who had captured him.

Without emotion Olmec told of hideous battles fought in black corridors, of ambushes on twisting stairs, and red butcheries. With a redder, more abysmal gleam in his deep dark eyes he told of men and women flayed alive, mutilated and dismembered, of captives howling under tortures so ghastly that even the barbarous Cimmerian grunted. No wonder Techotl had trembled with the terror of capture. Yet he had gone forth to slay if he could, driven by hate that was stronger than his fear. Olmec spoke further, of dark and mysterious matters, of black magic and wizardry conjured out of the black night of the catacombs, of weird creatures invoked out of darkness for horrible allies. In these things the Xotalancas had the advantage, for it was in the eastern catacombs where lay the bones of the greatest wizards of the ancient Xuchotlans, with their immemorial secrets.

Valeria listened with morbid fascination. The feud had become a terrible elemental power driving the people of Xuchotl inexorably on to doom and extinction. It filled their whole lives. They were born in it, and they expected to die in it. They never left their barricaded castle except to steal forth into the Halls of Silence that lay between the opposing fortresses, to slay and be slain. Sometimes the raiders returned with frantic captives, or with grim tokens of victory in fight. Sometimes they did not return at all, or returned only as severed limbs cast down before the bolted bronze doors. It was a ghastly, unreal nightmare existence these people lived, shut off from the rest of the world, caught together like rabid rats in the same trap, butchering one another through the years, crouching and creeping through the sunless corridors to maim and torture and murder.

While Olmec talked, Valeria felt the blazing eyes of Tascela fixed upon her. The princess seemed not to hear what Olmec was saying. Her expression, as he narrated victories or defeats, did not mirror the wild rage or fiendish exultation that alternated on the faces of the other Tecuhltli. The feud that was an obsession to her clansmen seemed meaningless to her. Valeria found her indifferent callousness more repugnant than Olmec's naked ferocity.

"And we can never leave the city," said Olmec. "For fifty years no one has left it except those—" Again he checked himself.

"Even without the peril of the dragons," he continued, "we who were born and raised in the city would not dare leave it. We have never set foot outside the walls. We are not accustomed to the open sky and the naked sun. No; we were born in Xuchotl, and in Xuchotl we shall die."

"Well," said Conan, "with your leave we'll take our chances with the dragons. This feud is none of our business. If you'll show us to the west gate we'll be on our way."

Tascela's hands clenched, and she started to speak, but Olmec interrupted her: "It is nearly nightfall. If you wander forth into the plain by night, you will certainly fall prey to the dragons."

"We crossed it last night, and slept in the open without seeing any," returned Conan.

Tascela smiled mirthlessly. "You dare not leave Xuchotl!"

Conan glared at her with instinctive antagonism; she was not looking at him, but at the woman opposite him.

"I think they dare," retorted Olmec. "But look you, Conan and Valeria, the gods must have sent you to us, to cast victory into the laps of the Tecuhltli! You are professional fighters—why not fight for us? We have wealth in abundance—precious jewels are as common in Xuchotl as cobblestones are in the cities of the world. Some the Xuchotlans brought with them from Kosala. Some, like the firestones, they found in the hills to the east. Aid us to wipe out the Xotalancas, and we will give you all the jewels you can carry."

"And will you help us destroy the dragons?" asked Valeria. "With bows and poisoned arrows thirty men could slay all the dragons in the forest."

"Aye!" replied Olmec promptly. "We have forgotten the use of the bow, in years of hand-to-hand fighting, but we can learn again."

"What do you say?" Valeria inquired of Conan.

"We're both penniless vagabonds," he grinned hardily. "I'd as soon kill Xotalancas as anybody."

"Then you agree?" exclaimed Olmec, while Techotl

fairly hugged himself with delight.

"Aye. And now suppose you show us chambers where we can sleep, so we can be fresh tomorrow for the beginning of the slaying."

Olmec nodded, and waved a hand, and Techotl and a woman led the adventurers into a corridor which led through a door off to the left of the jade dais. A glance back showed Valeria Olmec sitting on his throne, chin on knotted fist, staring after them. His eyes burned with a weird flame. Tascela leaned back in her seat, whispering to the sullen-faced maid, Yasala, who leaned over her shoulder, her ear to the princess' moving lips.

The hallway was not so broad as most they had traversed, but it was long. Presently the woman halted, opened a door, and drew aside for Valeria to enter.

"Wait a minute," growled Conan. "Where do I sleep?"

Techotl pointed to a chamber across the hallway, but one door farther down. Conan hesitated, and seemed inclined to raise an objection, but Valeria smiled spitefully at him and shut the door in his face. He muttered something uncomplimentary about women in general, and strode off down the corridor after Techotl.

In the ornate chamber where he was to sleep, he glanced up at the slot-like skylights. Some were wide enough to admit the body of a slender man, supposing the glass were broken.

"Why don't the Xotalancas come over the roofs and shatter those skylights?" he asked.

"They cannot be broken," answered Techotl. "Besides, the roofs would be hard to clamber over. They are mostly spires and domes and steep ridges."

He volunteered more information about the "castle"

200

of Tecuhltli. Like the rest of the city it contained four stories, or tiers of chambers, with towers jutting up from the roof. Each tier was named; indeed, the people of Xuchotl had a name for each chamber, hall and stair in the city, as people of more normal cities designate streets and quarters. In Tecuhltli the floors were named The Eagle's Tier, The Ape's Tier, The Tiger's Tier and The Serpent's Tier, in the order as enumerated, The Eagle's Tier being the highest, or fourth, floor.

"Who is Tascela?" asked Conan. "Olmec's wife?"

Techotl shuddered and glanced furtively about him before answering.

"No. She is—Tascela! She was the wife of Xotalanc—the woman Tecuhltli stole, to start the feud."

"What are you talking about?" demanded Conan. "That woman is beautiful and young. Are you trying to tell me that she was a wife fifty years ago?"

"Aye! I swear it! She was a full-grown woman when the Tlazitlans journeyed from Lake Zuad. It was because the king of Stygia desired her for a concubine that Xotalanc and his brother rebelled and fled into the wilderness. She is a witch, who possesses the secret of perpetual youth."

"What's that?" asked Conan.

Techotl shuddered again.

"Ask me not! I dare not speak. It is too grisly, even for Xuchotl!"

And touching his finger to his lips, he glided from the chamber.

4. Scent of Black Lotus

VALERIA UNBUCKLED HER sword-belt and laid it with the sheathed weapon on the couch where she meant to sleep. She noted that the doors were supplied with bolts, and asked where they led.

"Those lead into adjoining chambers," answered the woman, indicating the doors on right and left. "That one"—pointing to a copper-bound door opposite that which opened into the corridor—"leads to a corridor which runs to a stair that descends into the catacombs. Do not fear; naught can harm you here."

"Who spoke of fear?" snapped Valeria. "I just like to know what sort of harbor I'm dropping anchor in. No, I don't want you to sleep at the foot of my couch. I'm not accustomed to being waited on—not by women, anyway. You have my leave to go."

Alone in the room, the pirate shot the bolts on all the doors, kicked off her boots and stretched luxuriously out on the couch. She imagined Conan similarly situated across the corridor, but her feminine vanity prompted her to visualize him as scowling and muttering with chagrin as he cast himself on his solitary couch, and she grinned with gleeful malice as she prepared herself for slumber.

Outside, night had fallen. In the halls of Xuchotl the green fire-jewels blazed like the eyes of prehistoric cats. Somewhere among the dark towers a night wind moaned like a restless spirit. Through the dim passages stealthy figures began stealing, like disembodied shadows.

Valeria awoke suddenly on her couch. In the dusky emerald glow of the fire-gems she saw a shadowy figure bending over her. For a bemused instant the apparition seemed part of the dream she had been dreaming. She had seemed to lie on the couch in the chamber as she was actually lying, while over her pulsed and throbbed a gigantic black blossom so enormous that it hid the ceiling. Its exotic perfume pervaded her being, inducing a delicious, sensuous languor that was something more and less than sleep. She was sinking into scented billows of insensible bliss, when something touched her face. So supersensitive were her drugged senses, that the light touch was like a dislocating impact, jolting her rudely into full wakefulness. Then it was that she saw, not a gargantuan blossom, but a dark-skinned woman standing above her.

With the realization came anger and instant action. The woman turned lithely, but before she could run Valeria was on her feet and had caught her arm. She fought like a wildcat for an instant, and then subsided as she felt herself crushed by the superior strength of her captor. The pirate wrenched the woman around to face her, caught her chin with her free hand and forced her captive to meet her gaze. It was the sullen Yasala, Tascela's maid.

"What the devil were you doing bending over me? What's that in your hand?"

The woman made no reply, but sought to cast away the object. Valeria twisted her arm around in front of her, and the thing fell to the floor—a great black exotic blossom on a jade-green stem, large as a woman's head, to be sure, but tiny beside the exaggerated vision she had seen.

"The black lotus!" said Valeria between her teeth. "The blossom whose scent brings deep sleep. You were trying to drug me! If you hadn't accidentally touched my face with the petals, you'd have—why did you do it? What's your game?"

Yasala maintained a sulky silence, and with an oath Valeria whirled her around, forced her to her knees and twisted her arm up behind her back.

"Tell me, or I'll tear your arm out of its socket!"

Yasala squirmed in anguish as her arm was forced excruciatingly up between her shoulder-blades, but a violent shaking of her head was the only answer she made.

"Slut!" Valeria cast her from her to sprawl on the floor. The pirate glared at the prostrate figure with blazing eyes. Fear and the memory of Tascela's burning eyes stirred in her, rousing all her tigerish instincts of self-preservation. These people were decadent; any sort of perversity might be expected to be encountered among them. But Valeria sensed here something that moved behind the scenes, some secret terror fouler than common degeneracy. Fear and revulsion of this weird city swept her. These people were neither sane nor normal; she began to doubt if they were even human. Madness smoldered in the eyes of them all—all except the cruel, cryptic eyes of Tascela, which held secrets and mysteries more abysmal than madness.

She lifted her head and listened intently. The halls of Xuchotl were as silent as if it were in reality a dead city. The green jewels bathed the chamber in a nightmare glow, in which the eyes of the woman on the floor glittered eerily up at her. A thrill of panic throbbed through Valeria, driving the last vestige of mercy from her fierce soul.

"Why did you try to drug me?" she muttered, grasping the woman's black hair, and forcing her head back to glare into her sullen, long-lashed eyes. "Did Tascela send you?"

No answer. Valeria cursed venomously and slapped

the woman first on one cheek and then the other. The blows resounded through the room, but Yasala made no outcry.

"Why don't you scream?" demanded Valeria savagely. "Do you fear someone will hear you? Whom do you fear? Tascela? Olmec? Conan?"

Yasala made no reply. She crouched, watching her captor with eyes baleful as those of a basilisk. Stubborn silence always fans anger. Valeria turned and tore a handful of cords from a nearby hanging.

"You sulky slut!" she said between her teeth. "I'm going to strip you stark naked and tie you across that couch and whip you until you tell me what you were doing here, and who sent you!"

Yasala made no verbal protest, nor did she offer any resistance, as Valeria carried out the first part of her threat with a fury that her captive's obstinacy only sharpened. Then for a space there was no sound in the chamber except the whistle and crackle of hard-woven silken cords on naked flesh. Yasala could not move her fast-bound hands or feet. Her body writhed and quivered under the chastisement, her head swayed from side to side in rhythm with the blows. Her teeth were sunk into her lower lip and a trickle of blood began as the punishment continued. But she did not cry out.

The pliant cords made no great sound as they encountered the quivering body of the captive; only a sharp crackling snap, but each cord left a red streak across Yasala's dark flesh. Valeria inflicted the punishment with all the strength of her war-hardened arm, with all the mercilessness acquired during a life where pain and torment were daily happenings, and with all the cynical ingenuity which only a woman displays toward a woman. Yasala suffered more,

205

physically and mentally, than she would have suffered under a lash wielded by a man, however strong.

It was the application of this feminine cynicism which at last tamed Yasala.

A low whimper escaped from her lips, and Valeria paused, arm lifted, and raked back a damp yellow lock. "Well, are you going to talk?" she demanded. "I can keep this up all night, if necessary!"

"Mercy!" whispered the woman. "I will tell."

Valeria cut the cords from her wrists and ankles, and pulled to her feet. Yasala sank down on the couch, half reclining on one bare hip, supporting herself on her arm, and writhing at the contact of her smarting flesh with the couch. She was trembling in every limb.

"Wine!" she begged, dry-lipped, indicating with a quivering hand a gold vessel on an ivory table. "Let me drink. I am weak with pain. Then I will tell you all."

Valeria picked up the vessel, and Yasala rose unsteadily to receive it. She took it, raised it toward her lips—then dashed the contents full into the Aquilonian's face. Valeria reeled backward, shaking and clawing the stinging liquid out of her eyes. Through a smarting mist she saw Yasala dart across the room, fling back a bolt, throw open the copper-bound door and run down the hall. The pirate was after her instantly, sword out and murder in her heart.

But Yasala had the start, and she ran with the nervous agility of a woman who has just been whipped to the point of hysterical frenzy. She rounded a corner in the corridor, yards ahead of Valeria, and when the pirate turned it, she saw only an empty hall, and at the other end a door that gaped blackly. A damp moldy scent reeked up from it, and Valeria shivered. That must be the door that led to the catacombs. Yasala had taken refuge among the dead.

Valeria advanced to the door and looked down a flight of stone steps that vanished quickly into utter blackness. Evidently it was a shaft that led straight to the pits below the city, without opening upon any of the lower floors. She shivered slightly at the thought of the thousands of corpses lying in their stone crypts down there, wrapped in their moldering cloths. She had no intention of groping her way down those stone steps. Yasala doubtless knew every turn and twist of the subterranean tunnels.

She was turning back, baffled and furious, when a sobbing cry welled up from the blackness. It seemed to come from a great depth, but human words were faintly distinguishable, and the voice was that of a woman. "Oh, help! Help, in Set's name! Ahhh!" It trailed away, and Valeria thought she caught the echo of a ghostly tittering.

Valeria felt her skin crawl. What had happened to Yasala down there in the thick blackness? There was no doubt that it had been she who had cried out. But what peril could have befallen her? Was a Xotalanca lurking down there? Olmec had assured them that the catacombs below Tecuhltli were walled off from the rest, too securely for their enemies to break through. Besides, that tittering had not sounded like a human being at all.

Valeria hurried back down the corridor, not stopping to close the door that opened on the stair. Regaining her chamber, she closed the door and shot the bolt behind her. She pulled on her boots and buckled her sword-belt about her. She was determined to make her way to Conan's room and urge him, if he still lived, to join her in an attempt to fight their way out of that city of devils.

But even as she reached the door that opened into the corridor, a long-drawn scream of agony rang through the halls, followed by the stamp of running feet and the loud clangor of swords.

5. Twenty Red Nails

TWO WARRIORS LOUNGED in the guardroom on the floor known as the Tier of the Eagle. Their attitude was casual, though habitually alert. An attack on the great bronze door from without was always a possibility, but for many years no such assault had been attempted on either side.

"The strangers are strong allies," said one. "Olmec will move against the enemy tomorrow, I believe."

He spoke as a soldier in a war might have spoken. In the miniature world of Xuchotl each handful of feudists was an army, and the empty halls between the castles was the country over which they campaigned.

The other meditated for a space.

"Suppose with their aid we destroy Xotalanc," he said. "What then, Xatmec?"

"Why," returned Xatmec, "we will drive red nails for them all. The captives we will burn and flay and quarter."

"But afterward?" pursued the other. "After we have slain them all? Will it not seem strange, to have no foes to fight? All my life I have fought and hated the Xotalancas. With the feud ended, what is left?"

Xatmec shrugged his shoulders. His thoughts had never gone beyond the destruction of their foes. They could not go beyond that.

Suddenly both men stiffened at a noise outside the door.

"To the door, Xatmec!" hissed the last speaker. "I shall look through the Eye—"

Xatmec, sword in hand, leaned against the bronze door, straining his ear to hear through the metal. His mate looked into the mirror. He started convulsively. Men were clustered thickly outside the door; grim,

dark-faced men with swords gripped in their teeth—
and their fingers thrust into their ears. One who wore a
feathered head-dress had a set of pipes which he set to
his lips, and even as the Tecuhltli started to shout a
warning, the pipes began to skirl.

The cry died in the guard's throat as the thin, weird
piping penetrated the metal door and smote on his ears.
Xatmec leaned frozen against the door, as if paralyzed
in that position. His face was that of a wooden image,
his expression one of horrified listening. The other
guard, farther removed from the source of the sound,
yet sensed the horror of what was taking place, the
grisly threat that lay in that demoniac fifing. He felt the
weird strains plucking like unseen fingers at the tissues
of his brain, filling him with alien emotions and
impulses of madness. But with a soul-tearing effort he
broke the spell, and shrieked a warning in a voice he did
not recognize as his own.

But even as he cried out, the music changed to an
unbearable shrilling that was like a knife in the ear-
drums. Xatmec screamed in sudden agony, and all the
sanity went out of his face like a flame blown out in a
wind. Like a madman he ripped loose the chain, tore
open the door and rushed out into the hall, sword lifted
before his mate could stop him. A dozen blades struck
him down, and over his mangled body the Xotalancas
surged into the guardroom, with a long-drawn, blood-
mad yell that sent the unwonted echoes reverberating.

His brain reeling from the shock of it all, the
remaining guard leaped to meet them with goring
spear. The horror of the sorcery he had just witnessed
was submerged in the stunning realization that the
enemy were in Tecuhltli. And as his spearhead ripped
through a dark-skinned belly he knew no more, for a
swinging sword crushed his skull, even as wild-eyed

warriors came pouring in from the chambers behind the guardroom.

It was the yelling of men and the clanging of steel that brought Conan bounding from his couch, wide awake and broadsword in hand. In an instant he had reached the door and flung it open, and was glaring out into the corridor just as Techotl rushed up it, eyes blazing madly.

"The Xotalancas!" he screamed, in a voice hardly human. *They are within the door!*

Conan ran down the corridor, even as Valeria emerged from her chamber.

"What the devil is it?" she called.

"Techotl says the Xotalancas are in," he answered hurriedly. "That racket sounds like it."

With the Tecuhltli on their heels they burst into the throneroom and were confronted by a scene beyond the most frantic dream of blood and fury. Twenty men and women, their black hair streaming, and the white skulls gleaming on their breasts, were locked in combat with the people of Tecuhltli. The women on both sides fought as madly as the men, and already the room and the hall beyond were strewn with corpses.

Olmec, naked but for a breech-clout, was fighting before his throne, and as the adventurers entered, Tascela ran from an inner chamber with a sword in her hand.

Xatmec and his mate were dead, so there was none to tell the Tecuhltli how their foes had found their way into their citadel. Nor was there any to say what had prompted that mad attempt. But the losses of the Xotalancas had been greater, their position more desperate, than the Tecuhltli had known. The maiming of their scaly ally, the destruction of the Burning Skull, and the news, gasped by a dying man, that mysterious

211

white-skin allies had joined their enemies, had driven them to the frenzy of desperation and the wild determination to die dealing death to their ancient foes.

The Tecuhltli, recovering from the first stunning shock of the surprize that had swept them back into the throneroom and littered the floor with their corpses, fought back with an equally desperate fury, while the door-guards from the lower floors came racing to hurl themselves into the fray. It was the death-fight of rabid wolves, blind, panting, merciless. Back and forth it surged, from door to dais, blades whickering and striking into flesh, blood spurting, feet stamping the crimson floor where redder pools were forming. Ivory tables crashed over, seats were splintered, velvet hangings torn down were stained red. It was the bloody climax of a bloody half-century, and every man there sensed it.

But the conclusion was inevitable. The Tecuhltli outnumbered the invaders almost two to one, and they were heartened by that fact and by the entrance into the mêlée of their light-skinned allies.

These crashed into the fray with the devastating effect of a hurricane plowing through a grove of saplings. In sheer strength no three Tlazitlans were a match for Conan, and in spite of his weight he was quicker on his feet than any of them. He moved through the whirling, eddying mass with the surety and destructiveness of a gray wolf amidst a pack of alley curs, and he strode over a wake of crumpled figures.

Valeria fought beside him, her lips smiling and her eyes blazing. She was stronger than the average man, and far quicker and more ferocious. Her sword was like a living thing in her hand. Where Conan beat down opposition by the sheer weight and power of his blows, breaking spears, splitting skulls and cleaving bosoms to the breastbone, Valeria brought into action a finesse of swordplay that dazzled and bewildered her antagonists before it slew them. Again and again a warrior, heaving high his heavy blade, found her point in his jugular before he could strike. Conan, towering above the field, strode through the welter smiting right and left, but Valeria moved like an illusive phantom, constantly shifting, and thrusting and slashing as she shifted. Swords missed her again and again as the wielders flailed the empty air and died with her point in their hearts or throats, and her mocking laughter in their ears.

Neither sex nor condition was considered by the maddened combatants. The five women of the Xotalancas were down with their throats cut before Conan and Valeria entered the fray, and when a man or woman went down under the stamping feet, there was always a knife ready for the helpless throat, or a sandaled foot eager to crush the prostrate skull.

From wall to wall, from door to door rolled the waves of combat, spilling over into adjoining chambers. And presently only Tecuhltli and their white-skinned allies stood upright in the great throneroom. The survivors stared bleakly and blankly at each other, like survivors after Judgment Day or the destruction of the world. On legs wide-braced, hands gripping notched and dripping swords, blood trickling down their arms, they stared at one another across the mangled corpses of friends and foes. They had no breath left to shout, but a bestial mad howling rose from their lips. It was not a human cry of triumph. It was the howling of a rabid wolf-pack stalking among the bodies of its victims.

Conan caught Valeria's arm and turned her about. "You've got a stab in the calf of your leg," he growled.

She glanced down, for the first time aware of a stinging in the muscles of her leg. Some dying man on the floor had fleshed his dagger with his last effort.

"You look like a butcher yourself," she laughed.

He shook a red shower from his hands.

"Not mine. Oh, a scratch here and there. Nothing to bother about. But that calf ought to be bandaged."

Olmec came through the litter, looking like a ghoul with his naked massive shoulders splashed with blood, and his black beard dabbled in crimson. His eyes were red, like the reflection of flame on black water.

"We have won!" he croaked dazedly. "The feud is ended! The dogs of Xotalanc lie dead! Oh, for a captive to flay alive! Yet it is good to look upon their dead faces. Twenty dead dogs! Twenty red nails for the black column!"

"You'd best see to your wounded," grunted Conan, turning away from him. "Here, girl, let me see that leg."

"Wait a minute!" she shook him off impatiently. The fire of fighting still burned brightly in her soul. "How do we know these are all of them? These might have come on a raid of their own."

"They would not split the clan on a foray like this," said Olmec, shaking his head, and regaining some of his ordinary intelligence. Without his purple robe the man seemed less like a prince than some repellent beast of prey. "I will stake my head upon it that we have slain them all. There were less of them than I dreamed, and they must have been desperate. But how came they in Tecuhltli?"

Tascela came forward, wiping her sword on her naked thigh, and holding in her other hand an object she had taken from the body of the feathered leader of the Xotalancas.

"The pipes of madness," she said. "A warrior tells me that Xatmec opened the door to the Xotalancas and was cut down as they stormed into the guardroom. This warrior came to the guardroom from the inner hall just in time to see it happen and to hear the last of a weird strain of music which froze his very soul. Tolkemec used to talk of these pipes, which the Xuchotlans swore were hidden somewhere in the catacombs with the bones of the ancient wizard who used them in his lifetime. Somehow the dogs of Xotalanc found them and learned their secret."

"Somebody ought to go to Xotalanc and see if any remain alive," said Conan. "I'll go if somebody will guide me."

Olmec glanced at the remnants of his people. There were only twenty left alive, and of these several lay groaning on the floor. Tascela was the only one of the Tecuhltli who had escaped without a wound. The princess was untouched, though she had fought as savagely as any.

"Who will go with Conan to Xotalanc?" asked Olmec.

Techotl limped forward. The wound in his thigh had started bleeding afresh, and he had another gash across his ribs.

"I will go!"

"No, you won't," vetoed Conan. "And you're not going either, Valeria. In a little while that leg will be getting stiff."

"I will go," volunteered a warrior, who was knotting a bandage about a slashed forearm.

"Very well, Yanath. Go with the Cimmerian. And you, too, Topal." Olmec indicated another man whose

215

injuries were slight. "But first aid us to lift the badly wounded on these couches where we may bandage their hurts."

This was done quickly. As they stooped to pick up a woman who had been stunned by a war-club, Olmec's beard brushed Topal's ear. Conan thought the prince muttered something to the warrior, but he could not be sure. A few moments later he was leading his companions down the hall.

Conan glanced back as he went out the door, at that shambles where the dead lay on the smoldering floor, blood-stained dark limbs knotted in attitudes of fierce muscular effort, dark faces frozen in masks of hate, glassy eyes glaring up at the green fire-jewels which bathed the ghastly scene in a dusky emerald witchlight. Among the dead the living moved aimlessly, like people moving in a trance. Conan heard Olmec call a woman and direct her to bandage Valeria's leg. The pirate followed the woman into an adjoining chamber, already beginning to limp slightly.

Warily the two Tecuhltli led Conan along the hall beyond the bronze door, and through chamber after chamber shimmering in the green fire. They saw no one, heard no sound. After they crossed the Great Hall which bisected the city from north to south, their caution was increased by the realization of their nearness to enemy territory. But chambers and halls lay empty to their wary gaze, and they came at last along a broad dim hallway and halted before a bronze door similar to the Eagle Door of Tecuhltli. Gingerly they tried it, and it opened silently under their fingers. Awed, they stared into the green-lit chambers beyond. For fifty years no Tecuhltli had entered those halls save as a prisoner going to a hideous doom. To go to

Xotalanc had been the ultimate horror that could befall a man of the western castle. The terror of it had stalked through their dreams since earliest childhood. To Yanath and Topal that bronze door was like the portal of hell.

They cringed back, unreasoning horror in their eyes, and Conan pushed past them and strode into Xotalanc.

Timidly they followed him. As each man set foot over the threshold he stared and glared wildly about him. But only their quick, hurried breathing disturbed the silence.

They had come into a square guardroom, like that behind the Eagle Door of Tecuhltli, and, similarly, a hall ran away from it to a broad chamber that was a counterpart of Olmec's throneroom.

Conan glanced down the hall with its rugs and divans and hangings, and stood listening intently. He heard no noise, and the rooms had an empty feel. He did not believe there were any Xotalancas left alive in Xuchotl.

"Come on," he muttered, and started down the hall.

He had not gone far when he was aware that only Yanath was following him. He wheeled back to see Topal standing in an attitude of horror, one arm out as if to fend off some threatening peril, his distended eyes fixed with hypnotic intensity on something protruding from behind a divan.

"What the devil?" Then Conan saw what Topal was staring at, and he felt a faint twitching of the skin between his giant shoulders. A monstrous head protruded from behind the divan, a reptilian head, broad as the head of a crocodile, with down-curving fangs that projected over the lower jaw. But there was an unnatural limpness about the thing, and the hideous eyes were glazed.

217

Conan peered behind the couch. It was a great serpent which lay there limp in death, but such a serpent as he had never seen in his wanderings. The reek and chill of the deep black earth were about it, and its color was an indeterminable hue which changed with each new angle from which he surveyed it. A great wound in the neck showed what had caused its death.

"It is the Crawler!" whispered Yanath.

"It's the thing I slashed on the stair," grunted Conan. "After it trailed us to the Eagle Door, it dragged itself here to die. How could the Xotalancas control such a brute?"

The Tecuhltli shivered and shook their heads.

"They brought it up from the black tunnels *below* the catacombs. They discovered secrets unknown to Tecuhltli."

"Well, it's dead, and if they'd had any more of them, they'd have brought them along when they came to Tecuhltli. Come on."

They crowded close at his heels as he strode down the hall and thrust on the silver-worked door at the other end.

"If we don't find anybody on this floor," he said, "we'll descend into the lower floors. We'll explore Xotalanc from the roof to the catacombs. If Xotalanc is like Tecuhltli, all the rooms and halls in this tier will be lighted—what the devil!"

They had come into the broad throne-chamber, so similar to that one in Tecuhltli. There were the same jade dais and ivory seat, the same divans, rugs and hangings on the walls. No black, red-scarred column stood behind the throne-dais, but evidences of the grim feud were not lacking.

Ranged along the wall behind the dais were rows of glass-covered shelves. And on those shelves hundreds of human heads, perfectly preserved, stared at the startled watchers with emotionless eyes, as they had stared for only the gods knew how many months and years.

Topal muttered a curse, but Yanath stood silent, the mad light growing in his wide eyes. Conan frowned, knowing that Tlazitlan sanity was hung on a hair-trigger.

Suddenly Yanath pointed to the ghastly relics with a twitching finger.

"There is my brother's head!" he murmured. "And there is my father's younger brother! And there beyond them is my sister's eldest son!"

Suddenly he began to weep, dry-eyed, with harsh, loud sobs that shook his frame. He did not take his eyes from the heads. His sobs grew shriller, changed to frightful, high-pitched laughter, and that in turn became an unbearable screaming. Yanath was stark mad.

Conan laid a hand on his shoulder, and as if the touch had released all the frenzy in his soul, Yanath screamed and whirled, striking at the Cimmerian with his sword. Conan parried the blow, and Topal tried to catch Yanath's arm. But the madman avoided him and with froth flying from his lips, he drove his sword deep into Topal's body. Topal sank down with a groan, and Yanath whirled for an instant like a crazy dervish; then he ran at the shelves and began hacking at the glass with his sword, screeching blasphemously.

Conan sprang at him from behind, trying to catch him unaware and disarm him, but the madman wheeled and lunged at him, screaming like a lost soul. Realizing that the warrior was hopelessly insane, the Cimmerian side-stepped, and as the maniac went past, he swung a cut that severed the shoulder-bone and breast, and dropped the man dead beside his dying victim.

Conan bent over Topal, seeing that the man was at his last gasp. It was useless to seek to stanch the blood gushing from the horrible wound.

"You're done for, Topal," grunted Conan. "Any word you want to send to your people?"

"Bend closer," gasped Topal, and Conan complied—and an instant later caught the man's wrist as Topal struck at his breast with a dagger.

"Crom!" swore Conan. "Are you mad, too?"

"Olmec ordered it!" gasped the dying man. "I know not why. As we lifted the wounded upon the couches he whispered to me, bidding me to slay you as we returned to Tecuhltli—" And with the name of his clan on his lips, Topal died.

Conan scowled down at him in puzzlement. This whole affair had an aspect of lunacy. Was Olmec mad, too? Were all the Tecuhltli madder than he had realized? With a shrug of his shoulders he strode down the hall and out of the bronze door, leaving the dead Tecuhltli lying before the staring dead eyes of their kinsmen's heads.

Conan needed no guide back through the labyrinth they had traversed. His primitive instinct of direction led him unerringly along the route they had come. He traversed it as warily as he had before, his sword in his hand, and his eyes fiercely searching each shadowed nook and corner; for it was his former allies he feared now, not the ghosts of the slain Xotalancas.

He had crossed the Great Hall and entered the chambers beyond when he heard something moving ahead of him—something which gasped and panted, and moved with a strange, floundering, scrambling noise. A moment later Conan saw a man crawling over the flaming floor toward him—a man whose progress left a broad bloody smear on the smoldering surface. It was Techotl and his eyes were already glazing; from a deep gash in his breast blood gushed steadily between the fingers of his clutching hand. With the other he clawed and hitched himself along.

"Conan," he cried chokingly, "Conan! Olmec has taken the yellow-haired woman!"

"So that's why he told Topal to kill me!" murmured Conan, dropping to his knee beside the man, who his experienced eye told him was dying. "Olmec isn't so mad as I thought."

Techotl's groping fingers plucked at Conan's arm. In the cold, loveless and altogether hideous life of the Tecuhltli his admiration and affection for the invaders from the outer world formed a warm, human oasis, constituted a tie that connected him with a more natural humanity that was totally lacking in his fellows, whose only emotions were hate, lust and the urge of sadistic cruelty.

"I sought to oppose him," gurgled Techotl, blood bubbling frothily to his lips. "But he struck me down. He thought he had slain me, but I crawled away. Ah, Set, how far I have crawled in my own blood! Beware, Conan! Olmec may have set an ambush for your return! Slay Olmec! He is a beast. Take Valeria and flee! Fear not to traverse the forest. Olmec and Tascela lied about the dragons. They slew each other years ago, all save the strongest. For a dozen years there has been only one dragon. If you have slain him, there is naught in the forest to harm you. He was the god Olmec worshipped; and Olmec fed human sacrifices to him, the very old and the very young, bound and hurled from the wall. Hasten! Olmec has taken Valeria to the Chamber of the—"

His head slumped down and he was dead before it came to rest on the floor.

Conan sprang up, his eyes like live coals. So that was Olmec's game, having first used the strangers to destroy his foes! He should have known that something of the sort would be going on in that black-bearded degenerate's mind.

The Cimmerian started toward Tecuhltli with reckless speed. Rapidly he reckoned the numbers of his former allies. Only twenty-one, counting Olmec, had survived that fiendish battle in the throneroom. Three had died since, which left seventeen enemies with which to reckon. In his rage Conan felt capable of accounting for the whole clan single-handed.

But the innate craft of the wilderness rose to guide his berserk rage. He remembered Techotl's warning of an ambush. It was quite probable that the prince would make such provisions, on the chance that Topal might have failed to carry out his order. Olmec would be expecting him to return by the same route he had followed in going to Xotalanc.

Conan glanced up at a skylight under which he was passing and caught the blurred glimmer of stars. They had not yet begun to pale for dawn. The events of the night had been crowded into a comparatively short space of time.

He turned aside from his direct course and descended a winding staircase to the floor below. He did not know where the door was to be found that let into the castle on that level, but he knew he could find it. How he was to force the locks he did not know; he believed that the doors of Tecuhltli would all be locked and bolted, if for no other reason than the habits of half a century. But there was nothing else but to attempt it.

Sword in hand, he hurried noiselessly on through a

maze of green-lit or shadowy rooms and halls. He knew he must be near Tecuhltli, when a sound brought him up short. He recognized it for what it was—a human being trying to cry out through a stifling gag. It came from somewhere ahead of him, and to the left. In those deathly-still chambers a small sound carried a long way.

Conan turned aside and went seeking after the sound, which continued to be repeated. Presently he was glaring through a doorway upon a weird scene. In the room into which he was looking a low rack-like frame of iron lay on the floor, and a giant figure was bound prostrate upon it. His head rested on a bed of iron spikes, which were already crimson-pointed with blood where they had pierced his scalp. A peculiar harness-like contrivance was fastened about his head, though in such a manner that the leather band did not protect his scalp from the spikes. This harness was connected by a slender chain to the mechanism that upheld a huge iron ball which was suspended above the captive's hairy breast. As long as the man could force himself to remain motionless the iron ball hung in its place. But when the pain of the iron points caused him to lift his head, the ball lurched downward a few inches. Presently his aching neck muscles would no longer support his head in its unnatural position and it would fall back on the spikes again. It was obvious that eventually the ball would crush him to a pulp, slowly and inexorably. The victim was gagged, and above the gag his great black ox-eyes rolled wildly toward the man in the doorway, who stood in silent amazement. The man on the rack was Olmec, prince of Tecuhltli.

6. *The Eyes of Tascela*

"WHY DID YOU bring me into this chamber to bandage my legs?" demanded Valeria. "Couldn't you have done it just as well in the throneroom?"

She sat on a couch with her wounded leg extended upon it, and the Tecuhltli woman had just bound it with silk bandages. Valeria's red-stained sword lay on the couch beside her.

She frowned as she spoke. The woman had done her task silently and efficiently, but Valeria liked neither the lingering, caressing touch of her slim fingers nor the expression in her eyes.

"They have taken the rest of the wounded into the other chambers," answered the woman in the soft speech of the Tecuhltli women, which somehow did not suggest either softness or gentleness in the speakers. A little while before, Valeria had seen this same woman stab a Xotalanca woman through the breast and stamp the eyeballs out of a wounded Xotalanca man.

"They will be carrying the corpses of the dead down into the catacombs," she added, "lest the ghosts escape into the chambers and dwell there."

"Do you believe in ghosts?" asked Valeria.

"I know the ghost of Tolkemec dwells in the catacombs," she answered with a shiver. "Once I saw it, as I crouched in a crypt among the bones of a dead queen. It passed by in the form of an ancient man with flowing white beard and locks, and luminous eyes that blazed in the darkness. It was Tolkemec; I saw him living when I was a child and he was being tortured."

Her voice sank to a fearful whisper: "Olmec laughs, but I *know* Tolkemec's ghost dwells in the catacombs! They say it is rats which gnaw the flesh from the bones of the newly dead —but ghosts eat flesh. Who knows but that—"

She glanced up quickly as a shadow fell across the couch. Valeria looked up to see Olmec gazing down at her. The prince had cleansed his hands, torso and beard of the blood that had splashed them; but he had not donned his robe, and his great dark-skinned hairless body and limbs renewed the impression of strength bestial in its nature. His deep black eyes burned with a more elemental light, and there was the suggestion of a twitching in the fingers that tugged at his thick blue-black beard.

He stared fixedly at the woman, and she rose and glided from the chamber. As she passed through the door she cast a look over her shoulder at Valeria, a glance full of cynical derision and obscene mockery.

"She has done a clumsy job," criticized the prince, coming to the divan and bending over the bandage. "Let me see—"

With a quickness amazing in one of his bulk he snatched her sword and threw it across the chamber. His next move was to catch her in his giant arms.

Quick and unexpected as the move was, she almost matched it; for even as he grabbed her, her dirk was in her hand and she stabbed murderously at his throat. More by luck than skill he caught her wrist, and then began a savage wrestling-match. She fought him with fists, feet, knees, teeth and nails, with all the strength of her magnificent body and all the knowledge of hand-to-hand fighting she had acquired in her years of roving and fighting on sea and land. It availed her nothing against his brute strength. She lost her dirk in the first moment of contact, and thereafter found herself powerless to inflict any appreciable pain on her giant attacker.

225

The blaze in his weird black eyes did not alter, and their expression filled her with fury, fanned by the sardonic smile that seemed carved upon his bearded lips. Those eyes and that smile contained all the cruel cynicism that seethes below the surface of a sophisticated and degenerate race, and for the first time in her life Valeria experienced fear of a man. It was like struggling against some huge elemental force; his iron arms thwarted her efforts with an ease that sent panic racing through her limbs. He seemed impervious to any pain she could inflict. Only once, when she sank her white teeth savagely into his wrist so that the blood started, did he react. And that was to buffet her brutally upon the side of the head with his open hand, so that stars flashed before her eyes and her head rolled on her shoulders.

Her shirt had been torn open in the struggle, and with cynical cruelty he rasped his thick beard across her bare breasts, bringing the blood to suffuse the fair skin, and fetching a cry of pain and outraged fury from her. Her convulsive resistance was useless; she was crushed down on a couch, disarmed and panting, her eyes blazing up at him like the eyes of a trapped tigress.

A moment later he was hurrying from the chamber, carrying her in his arms. She made no resistance, but the smoldering of her eyes showed that she was unconquered in spirit, at least. She had not cried out. She knew that Conan was not within call, and it did not occur to her that any in Tecuhltli would oppose their prince. But she noticed that Olmec went stealthily, with his head on one side as if listening for sounds of pursuit, and he did not return to the throne-chamber. He carried her through a door that stood opposite that through which he had entered, crossed another room and began stealing down a hall. As she became convinced that he feared some opposition to the abduction, she threw back her head and screamed at the top of her lusty voice.

She was rewarded by a slap that half stunned her, and Olmec quickened his pace to a shambling run.

But her cry had been echoed, and twisting her head about, Valeria, through the tears and stars that partly blinded her, saw Techotl limping after them.

Olmec turned with a snarl, shifting the woman to an uncomfortable and certainly undignified position under one huge arm, where he held her writhing and kicking vainly, like a child.

"Olmec!" protested Techotl. "You cannot be such a dog as to do this thing! She is Conan's woman! She helped us slay the Xotalancas, and –"

Without a word Olmec balled his free hand into a huge fist and stretched the wounded warrior senseless at his feet. Stooping, and hindered not at all by the struggles and imprecations of his captive, he drew Techotl's sword from its sheath and stabbed the warrior in the breast. Then casting aside the weapon he fled on along the corridor. He did not see a woman's dark face peer cautiously after him from behind a hanging. It vanished, and presently Techotl groaned and stirred, rose dazedly and staggered drunkenly away, calling Conan's name.

Olmec hurried on down the corridor, and descended a winding ivory staircase. He crossed several corridors and halted at last in a broad chamber whose doors were veiled with heavy tapestries, with one exception—a heavy bronze door similar to the Door of the Eagle on the upper floor.

He was moved to rumble, pointing to it: "That is one of the outer doors of Tecuhltli. For the first time in fifty years it is unguarded. We need not guard it now, for

Xotalanc is no more."

"Thanks to Conan and me, you bloody rogue!" sneered Valeria, trembling with fury and the shame of physical coercion. "You treacherous dog! Conan will cut your throat for this!"

Olmec did not bother to voice his belief that Conan's own gullet had already been severed according to his whispered command. He was too utterly cynical to be at all interested in her thoughts or opinions. His flame-lit eyes devoured her, dwelling burningly on the generous expanses of clear white flesh exposed where her shirt and breeches had been torn in the struggle.

"Forget Conan," he said thickly. "Olmec is lord of Xuchotl. Xotalanc is no more. There will be no more fighting. We shall spend our lives in drinking and love-making. First let us drink!"

He seated himself on an ivory table and pulled her down on his knees, like a dark-skinned satyr with a white nymph in his arms. Ignoring her un-nymphlike profanity, he held her helpless with one great arm about her waist while the other reached across the table and secured a vessel of wine.

"Drink!" he commanded, forcing it to her lips, as she writhed her head away.

The liquor slopped over, stinging her lips, splashing down on her naked breasts.

"Your guest does not like your wine, Olmec," spoke a cool, sardonic voice.

Olmec stiffened; fear grew in his flaming eyes. Slowly he swung his great head about and stared at Tascela who posed negligently in the curtained doorway, one hand on her smooth hip. Valeria twisted herself about in his iron grip, and when she met the burning eyes of Tascela, a chill tingled along her supple spine. New experiences were flooding Valeria's proud soul that night. Recently she had learned to fear a man; now she knew what it was to fear a woman.

Olmec sat motionless, a gray pallor growing under his swarthy skin. Tascela brought her other hand from behind her and displayed a small gold vessel.

"I feared she would not like your wine, Olmec," purred the princess, "so I brought some of mine, some I brought with me long ago from the shores of Lake Zuad—do you understand, Olmec?"

Beads of sweat stood out suddenly on Olmec's brow. His muscles relaxed, and Valeria broke away and put the table between them. But though reason told her to dart from the room, some fascination she could not understand held her rigid, watching the scene.

Tascela came toward the seated prince with a swaying, undulating walk that was mockery in itself. Her voice was soft, slurringly caressing, but her eyes gleamed. Her slim fingers stroked his beard lightly.

"You are selfish, Olmec," she crooned, smiling. "You would keep our handsome guest to yourself, though you knew I wished to entertain her. You are much at fault, Olmec!"

The mask dropped for an instant; her eyes flashed, her face was contorted and with an appalling show of strength her hand locked convulsively in his beard and tore out a great handful. This evidence of unnatural strength was no more terrifying than the momentary baring of the hellish fury that raged under her bland exterior.

Olmec lurched up with a roar, and stood swaying like a bear, his mighty hands clenching and unclenching.

"Slut!" His booming voice filled the room. "Witch! She-devil! Tecuhltli should have slain you fifty years ago! Begone! I have endured too much from you! This white-skinned wench is mine! Get hence before I slay you!"

The princess laughed and dashed the blood-stained strands into his face. Her laughter was less merciful than the ring of flint on steel.

"Once you spoke otherwise, Olmec," she taunted. "Once, in your youth, you spoke words of love. Aye, you were my lover once, years ago, and because you loved me, you slept in my arms beneath the enchanted lotus—and thereby put into my hands the chains that enslaved you. You know you cannot withstand me. You know I have but to gaze into your eyes, with the mystic power a priest of Stygia taught me, long ago, and you are powerless. You remember the night beneath the black lotus that waved above us, stirred by no worldly breeze; you scent again the unearthly perfumes that stole and rose like a cloud about you to enslave you. You cannot fight against me. You are my slave as you were that night—as you shall be so long as you shall live, Olmec of Xuchotl!"

Her voice had sunk to a murmur like the rippling of a stream running through starlit darkness. She leaned close to the prince and spread her long tapering fingers upon his giant breast. His eyes glazed, his great hands fell limply to his sides.

With a smile of cruel malice, Tascela lifted the vessel and placed it to his lips.

"Drink!"

Mechanically the prince obeyed. And instantly the glaze passed from his eyes and they were flooded with fury, comprehension and an awful fear. His mouth gaped, but no sound issued. For an instant he reeled on buckling knees, and then fell in a sodden heap on the floor.

His fall jolted Valeria out of her paralysis. She

turned and sprang toward the door, but with a movement that would have shamed a leaping panther, Tascela was before her. Valeria struck at her with her clenched fist, and all the power of her supple body behind the blow. It would have stretched a man senseless on the floor. But with a lithe twist of her torso, Tascela avoided the blow and caught the pirate's wrist. The next instant Valeria's left hand was imprisoned, and holding her wrists together with one hand, Tascela calmly bound them with a cord she drew from her girdle. Valeria thought she had tasted the ultimate in humiliation already that night, but her shame at being manhandled by Olmec was nothing to the sensations that now shook her supple frame. Valeria had always been inclined to despise the other members of her sex; and it was overwhelming to encounter another woman who could handle her like a child. She scarcely resisted at all when Tascela forced her into a chair and drawing her bound wrists down between her knees, fastened them to the chair.

Casually stepping over Olmec, Tascela walked to the bronze door and shot the bolt and threw it open, revealing a hallway without.

"Opening upon this hall," she remarked, speaking to her feminine captive for the first time, "there is a chamber which in old times was used as a torture room. When we retired into Tecuhltli, we brought most of the apparatus with us, but there was one piece too heavy to move. It is still in working order. I think it will be quite convenient now."

An understanding flame of terror rose in Olmec's eyes. Tascela strode back to him, bent and gripped him by the hair.

"He is only paralyzed temporarily," she remarked conversationally. "He can hear, think, and feel—aye,

231

he can feel very well indeed!"

With which sinister observation she started toward the door, dragging the giant bulk with an ease that made the pirate's eyes dilate. She passed into the hall and moved down it without hesitation, presently disappearing with her captive into a chamber that opened into it, and whence shortly thereafter issued the clank of iron.

Valeria swore softly and tugged vainly, with her legs braced against the chair. The cords that confined her were apparently unbreakable.

Tascela presently returned alone; behind her a muffled groaning issued from the chamber. She closed the door but did not bolt it. Tascela was beyond the grip of habit, as she was beyond the touch of other human instincts and emotions.

Valeria sat dumbly, watching the woman in whose slim hands, the pirate realized, her destiny now rested.

Tascela grasped her yellow locks and forced back her head, looking impersonally down into her face. But the glitter in her dark eyes was not impersonal.

"I have chosen you for a great honor," she said. "You shall restore the youth of Tascela. Oh, you stare at that! My appearance is that of youth, but through my veins creeps the sluggish chill of approaching age, as I have felt it a thousand times before. I am old, so old I do not remember my childhood. But I was a girl once, and a priest of Stygia loved me, and gave me the secret of immortality and youth everlasting. He died, then— some said by poison. But I dwelt in my palace by the shores of Lake Zuad and the passing years touched me not. So at last a king of Stygia desired me, and my people rebelled and brought me to this land. Olmec called me a princess. I am not of royal blood. I am greater than a princess. I am Tascela, whose youth your own glorious youth shall restore."

Valeria's tongue clove to the roof of her mouth. She sensed here a mystery darker than the degeneracy she had anticipated.

The taller woman unbound the Aquilonian's wrists and pulled her to her feet. It was not fear of the dominant strength that lurked in the princess' limbs that made Valeria a helpless, quivering captive in her hands. It was the burning, hypnotic, terrible eyes of Tascela.

7. He Comes from the Dark

"WELL, I'M A KUSHITE!"

Conan glared down at the man on the iron rack.

"What the devil are *you* doing on that thing?"

Incoherent sounds issued from behind the gag and Conan bent and tore it away, evoking a bellow of fear from the captive; for his action caused the iron ball to lurch down until it nearly touched the broad breast.

"Be careful, for Set's sake!" begged Olmec.

"What for?" demanded Conan. "Do you think I care what happens to you? I only wish I had time to stay here and watch that chunk of iron grind your guts out. But I'm in a hurry. Where's Valeria?"

"Loose me!" urged Olmec. "I will tell you all!"

"Tell me first."

"Never!" The prince's heavy jaws set stubbornly.

"All right." Conan seated himself on a near-by bench. "I'll find her myself, after you've been reduced to a jelly. I believe I can speed up that process by twisting my sword-point around in your ear," he added, extending the weapon experimentally.

"Wait!" Words came in a rush from the captive's ashy lips. "Tascela took her from me. I've never been anything but a puppet in Tascela's hands."

"Tascela?" snorted Conan, and spat. "Why, the filthy—"

"No, no!" panted Olmec. "It's worse than you think. Tascela is old—centuries old. She renews her life and her youth by the sacrifice of beautiful young women. That's one thing that has reduced the clan to its present state. She will draw the essence of Valeria's life into her own body, and bloom with fresh vigor and beauty."

"Are the doors locked?" asked Conan, thumbing his sword edge.

"Aye! But I know a way to get into Tecuhlt!i. Only Tascela and I know, and she thinks me helpless and you slain. Free me and I swear I will help you rescue Valcria. Without my help you cannot win into Techultli; for even if you tortured me into revealing the secret, you couldn't work it. Let me go, and we will steal on Tascela and kill her before she can work magic—before she can fix her eyes on us. A knife thrown from behind will do the work. I should have killed her thus long ago, but I feared that without her to aid us the Xotalancas would overcome us. She needed my help, too; that's the only reason she let me live this long. Now neither needs the other, and one must die. I swear that when we have slain the witch, you and Valeria shall go free without harm. My people will obey me when Tascela is dead."

Conan stooped and cut the ropes that held the prince, and Olmec slid cautiously from under the great ball and rose, shaking his head like a bull and muttering imprecations as he fingered his lacerated scalp. Standing shoulder to shoulder the two men presented a formidable picture of primitive power. Olmec was as tall as Conan, and heavier; but there was something repellent about the Tlazitlan, something abysmal and monstrous that contrasted unfavorably with the clean-cut, compact hardness of the Cimmerian. Conan had discarded the remnants of his tattered, blood-soaked shirt, and stood with his remarkable muscular development impressively revealed. His great shoulders were as broad as those of Olmec, and more cleanly outlined, and his huge breast arched with a more impressive sweep to a hard waist that lacked the paunchy thickness of Olmec's midsection. He might have been an image of primal strength cut out of bronze. Olmec was darker, but not from the burning of the sun. If Conan was a figure out of the dawn of Time, Olmec was a shambling, somber shape from the darkness of Time's pre-dawn.

"Lead on," demanded Conan. "And keep ahead of me. I don't trust you any farther than I can throw a bull by the tail."

Olmec turned and stalked on ahead of him, one hand twitching slightly as it plucked at his matted beard.

Olmec did not lead Conan back to the bronze door, which the prince naturally supposed Tascela had locked, but to a certain chamber on the border of Tecuhltli.

"This secret has been guarded for half a century," he said. "Not even our own clan knew of it, and the Xotalancas never learned. Tecuhltli himself built this secret entrance, afterward slaying the slaves who did the work; for he feared that he might find himself locked out of his own kingdom some day because of the spite of Tascela, whose passion for him soon changed to hate. But she discovered the secret, and barred the hidden door against him one day as he fled back from an unsuccessful raid, and the Xotalancas took him and flayed him. But once, spying upon her, I saw her enter Tecuhltli by this route, and so learned the secret."

He pressed upon a gold ornament in the wall, and a panel swung inward, disclosing an ivory stair leading upward.

"This stair is built within the wall," said Olmec. "It leads up to a tower upon the roof, and thence other stairs wind down to the various chambers. Hasten!"

"After you, comrade!" retorted Conan satirically, swaying his broadsword as he spoke, and Olmec shrugged his shoulders and stepped onto the staircase. Conan instantly followed him, and the door shut behind them. Far above a cluster of fire-jewels made the staircase a well of dusky dragon-light.

They mounted until Conan estimated that they were above the level of the fourth floor, and then came out into a cylindrical tower, in the domed roof of which was set the bunch of fire-jewels that lighted the stair. Through gold-barred windows, set with unbreakable crystal panes, the first windows he had seen in Xuchotl, Conan got a glimpse of high ridges, domes and more towers, looming darkly against the stars. He was looking across the roofs of Xuchotl.

Olmec did not look through the windows. He hurried down one of the several stairs that wound down from the tower, and when they had descended a few feet, this stair changed into a narrow corridor that wound tortuously on for some distance. It ceased at a steep flight of steps leading downward. There Olmec paused.

Up from below, muffled, but unmistakable, welled a woman's scream, edged with fright, fury and shame. And Conan recognized Valeria's voice.

In the swift rage roused by that cry, and the amazement of wondering what peril could wring such a shriek from Valeria's reckless lips, Conan forgot Olmec. He pushed past the prince and started down the stair. Awakening instinct brought him about again, just as Olmec struck with his great mallet-like fist. The blow, fierce and silent, was aimed at the base of Conan's brain. But the Cimmerian wheeled in time to receive the buffet on the side of his neck instead. The impact would have snapped the vertebrae of a lesser man. As it was, Conan swayed backward, but even as he reeled he dropped his sword, useless at such close quarters, and grasped Olmec's extended arm, dragging the prince with him as he fell. Headlong they went down the steps together, in a revolving whirl of limbs and heads and bodies. And as they went Conan's iron fingers found and locked in Olmec's bull-throat.

The barbarian's neck and shoulder felt numb from the sledge-like impact of Olmec's huge fist, which had carried all the strength of the massive forearm, thick triceps and great shoulder. But this did not affect his ferocity to any appreciable extent. Like a bulldog he hung on grimly, shaken and battered and beaten against the steps as they rolled, until at last they struck an ivory panel-door at the bottom with such an impact that they splintered it its full length and crashed through its ruins. But Olmec was already dead, for those iron fingers had crushed out his life and broken his neck as they fell.

Conan rose, shaking the splinters from his great shoulder, blinking blood and dust out of his eyes.

He was in the great throneroom. There were fifteen people in that room besides himself. The first person he saw was Valeria. A curious black altar stood before the throne-dais. Ranged about it, seven black candles in golden candlesticks sent up oozing spirals of thick green smoke, disturbingly scented. These spirals united in a cloud near the ceiling, forming a smoky arch above the altar. On that altar lay Valeria, stark naked, her white flesh gleaming in shocking contrast to the glistening ebon stone. She was not bound. She lay at full length, her arms stretched out above her head to their fullest extent. At the head of the altar knelt a young man, holding her wrists firmly. A young woman knelt at the other end of the altar, grasping her ankles. Between them she could neither rise nor move.

Eleven men and women of Tecuhltli knelt dumbly in

a semicircle, watching the scene with hot, lustful eyes.

On the ivory throne-seat Tascela lolled. Bronze bowls of incense rolled their spirals about her; the wisps of smoke curled about her naked limbs like caressing fingers. She could not sit still; she squirmed and shifted about with sensuous abandon, as if finding pleasure in the contact of the smooth ivory with her sleek flesh.

The crash of the door as it broke beneath the impact of the hurtling bodies caused no change in the scene. The kneeling men and women merely glanced incuriously at the corpse of their prince and at the man who rose from the ruins of the door, then swung their eyes greedily back to the writhing white shape on the black altar. Tascela looked insolently at him, and sprawled back on her seat, laughing mockingly.

"Slut!" Conan saw red. His hands clenched into iron hammers as he started for her. With his first step something clanged loudly and steel bit savagely into his leg. He stumbled and almost fell, checked in his headlong stride. The jaws of an iron trap had closed on his leg, with teeth that sank deep and held. Only the ridged muscles of his calf saved the bone from being splintered. The accursed thing had sprung out of the smoldering floor without warning. He saw the slots now, in the floor where the jaws had lain, perfectly camouflaged.

"Fool!" laughed Tascela. "Did you think I would not guard against your possible return? Every door in this chamber is guarded by such traps. Stand there and watch now, while I fulfill the destiny of your handsome friend! Then I will decide your own."

Conan's hand instinctively sought his belt, only to encounter an empty scabbard. His sword was on the stair behind him. His poniard was lying back in the forest, where the dragon had torn it from his jaw. The steel teeth in his leg were like burning coals, but the pain was not as savage as the fury that seethed in his soul. He was trapped, like a wolf. If he had had his sword he would have hewn off his leg and crawled across the floor to slay Tascela. Valeria's eyes rolled toward him with mute appeal, and his own helplessness sent red waves of madness surging through his brain.

Dropping on the knee of his free leg, he strove to get his fingers between the jaws of the trap, to tear them apart by sheer strength. Blood started from beneath his finger nails, but the jaws fitted close about his leg in a circle whose segments jointed perfectly, contracted until there was no space between his mangled flesh and the fanged iron. The sight of Valeria's naked body added flame to the fire of his rage.

Tascela ignored him. Rising languidly from her seat she swept the ranks of her subjects with a searching glance, and asked: "Where are Xamec, Zlanath and Tachic?"

"They did not return from the catacombs, princess," answered a man. "Like the rest of us, they bore the bodies of the slain into the crypts, but they have not returned. Perhaps the ghost of Tolkemec took them."

"Be silent, fool!" she ordered harshly. "The ghost is a myth."

She came down from her dais, playing with a thin gold-hilted dagger. Her eyes burned like nothing on the hither side of hell. She paused beside the altar and spoke in the tense stillness.

"Your life shall make me young, white woman!" she said. "I shall lean upon your bosom and place my lips over yours, and slowly—ah, slowly!—sink this blade through your heart, so that your life, fleeing your stiffening body, shall enter mine, making me bloom again with youth and with life everlasting!"

Slowly, like a serpent arching toward its victim, she bent down through the writhing smoke, closer and closer over the now motionless woman who stared up into her glowing dark eyes—eyes that grew larger and deeper, blazing like black moons in the swirling smoke.

The kneeling people gripped their hands and held their breath, tense for the bloody climax, and the only sound was Conan's fierce panting as he strove to tear his leg from the trap.

All eyes were glued on the altar and the white figure there; the crash of a thunderbolt could hardly have broken the spell, yet it was only a low cry that shattered the fixity of the scene and brought all whirling about— a low cry, yet one to make the hair stand up stiffly on the scalp. They looked, and they saw.

Framed in the door to the left of the dais stood a nightmare figure. It was a man, with a tangle of white hair and a matted white beard that fell over his breast. Rags only partly covered his gaunt frame, revealing half-naked limbs strangely unnatural in appearance. The skin was not like that of a normal human. There was a suggestion of *scaliness* about it, as if the owner had dwelt long under conditions almost antithetical to those conditions under which human life ordinarily thrives. And there was nothing at all human about the eyes that blazed from the tangle of white hair. They were great gleaming disks that stared unwinkingly, luminous, whitish, and without a hint of normal emotion or sanity. The mouth gaped, but no coherent words issued—only a high-pitched tittering.

"Tolkemec!" whispered Tascela, livid, while the others crouched in speechless horror. "No myth, then, no ghost! Set! You have dwelt for twelve years in darkness! Twelve years among the bones of the dead!

What grisly food did you find? What mad travesty of life did you live, in the stark blackness of that eternal night? I see now why Xamec and Zlanath and Tachic did not return from the catacombs—and never will return. But why have you waited so long to strike? Were you seeking something, in the pits? Some secret weapon you knew was hidden there? And have you found it at last?"

That hideous tittering was Tolkemec's only reply, as he bounded into the room with a long leap that carried him over the secret trap before the door—by chance, or by some faint recollection of the ways of Xuchotl. He was not mad, as a man is mad. He had dwelt apart from humanity so long that he was no longer human. Only an unbroken thread of memory embodied in hate and the urge for vengeance had connected him with the humanity from which he had been cut off, and held him lurking near the people he hated. Only that thin string had kept him from racing and prancing off for ever into the black corridors and realms of the subterranean world he had discovered, long ago.

"You sought something hidden!" whispered Tascela, cringing back. "And you have found it! You remember the feud! After all these years of blackness, you remember!"

For in the lean hand of Tolkemec now waved a curious jade-hued wand, on the end of which glowed a knob of crimson shaped like a pomegranate. She sprang aside as he thrust it out like a spear, and a beam of crimson fire lanced from the pomegranate. It missed Tascela, but the woman holding Valeria's ankles was in the way. It smote between her shoulders. There was a sharp crackling sound and the ray of fire flashed from her bosom and struck the black altar, with a snapping of blue sparks. The woman toppled sidewise, shriveling and withering like a mummy even as she fell.

Valeria rolled from the altar on the other side, and started for the opposite wall on all fours. For hell had burst loose in the throneroom of dead Olmec.

The man who had held Valeria's hands was the next to die. He turned to run, but before he had taken half a dozen steps, Tolkemec, with an agility appalling in such a frame, bounded around to a position that placed the man between him and the altar. Again the red fire-beam flashed and the Tecuhltli rolled lifeless to the floor, as the beam completed its course with a burst of blue sparks against the altar.

Then began slaughter. Screaming insanely the people rushed about the chamber, caroming from one another, stumbling and falling. And among them Tolkemec capered and pranced, dealing death. They could not escape by the doors; for apparently the metal of the portals served like the metal-veined stone altar to complete the circuit for whatever hellish power flashed like thunderbolts from the witch-wand the ancient waved in his hand. When he caught a man or a woman between him and a door or the altar, that one died instantly. He chose no special victim. He took them as they came, with his rags flapping about his wildly gyrating limbs, and the gusty echoes of his tittering sweeping the room above the screams. And bodies fell like falling leaves about the altar and at the doors. One warrior in desperation rushed at him, lifting a dagger, only to fall before he could strike. But the rest were like crazed cattle, with no thought for resistance, and no chance of escape.

The last Tecuhltli except Tascela had fallen when the princess reached the Cimmerian and the girl who had taken refuge beside him. Tascela bent and touched the floor, pressing a design upon it. Instantly the iron jaws released the bleeding limb and sank back into the floor.

"Slay him if you can!" she panted, and pressed a heavy knife into his hand. "I have no magic to withstand him!"

With a grunt he sprang before the women, not heeding his lacerated leg in the heat of the fighting-lust. Tolkemec was coming toward him, his weird eyes ablaze, but he hesitated at the gleam of the knife in Conan's hand. Then began a grim game, as Tolkemec sought to circle about Conan and get the barbarian between him and the altar or a metal door, while Conan sought to avoid this and drive home his knife. The women watched tensely, holding their breath.

There was no sound except the rustle and scrape of quick-shifting feet. Tolkemec pranced and capered no more. He realized that grimmer game confronted him than the people who had died screaming and fleeing. In the elemental blaze of the barbarian's eyes he read an intent deadly as his own. Back and forth they weaved, and when one moved the other moved as if invisible threads bound them together. But all the time Conan was getting closer and closer to his enemy. Already the coiled muscles of his thighs were beginning to flex for a spring, when Valeria cried out. For a fleeting instant a bronze door was in line with Conan's moving body. The red line leaped, searing Conan's flank as he twisted aside, and even as he shifted he hurled the knife. Old Tolkemec went down, truly slain at last, the hilt vibrating on his breast.

Tascela sprang—not toward Conan, but toward the wand where it shimmered like a live thing on the floor. But as she leaped, so did Valeria, with a dagger snatched from a dead man, and the blade, driven with all the power of the pirate's muscles, impaled the princess of Tecuhltli so that the point stood out between her breasts. Tascela screamed once and fell dead, and Valeria spurned the body with her heel as it fell.

"I had to do that much, for my own self-respect!" panted Valeria, facing Conan across the limp corpse.

"Well, this cleans up the feud," he grunted. "It's been a hell of a night! Where did these people keep their food? I'm hungry."

"You need a bandage on that leg." Valeria ripped a length of silk from a hanging and knotted it about her waist, then tore off some smaller strips which she bound efficiently about the barbarian's lacerated limb.

"I can walk on it," he assured her. "Let's begone. It's dawn, outside this infernal city. I've had enough of Xuchotl. It's well the breed exterminated itself. I don't want any of their accursed jewels. They might be haunted."

"There is enough clean loot in the world for you and me," she said, straightening to stand tall and splendid before him.

The old blaze came back in his eyes, and this time she did not resist as he caught her fiercely in his arms.

"It's a long way to the coast," she said presently, withdrawing her lips from his.

"What matter?" he laughed. "There's nothing we can't conquer. We'll have our feet on a ship's deck before the Stygians open their ports for the trading season. And then we'll show the world what plundering means!"

The Hyborian Age

(NOTHING IN THIS article is to be considered as an attempt to advance any theory in opposition to accepted history. It is simply a fictional back-ground for a series of fiction-stories. When I began writing the Conan stories a few years ago, I prepared this "history" of his age and the peoples of that age, in order to lend him and his sagas a greater aspect of realness. And I found that by adhering to the "facts" and spirit of that history, in writing the stories, it was easier to visualize (and therefore to present) him as a real flesh-and-blood character rather than a ready-made product. In writing about him and his adventures in the various kingdoms of his Age, I have never violated the "facts" or spirit of the "history" here set down, but have followed the lines of that history as closely as the writer of actual historical-fiction follows the lines of actual history. I have used this "history" as a guide in all the stories in this series that I have written.)

Of that epoch known by the Nemedian chroniclers as the Pre-Cataclysmic Age, little is known except the latter part, and that is veiled in the mists of legendry. Known history begins with the waning of the Pre-Cataclysmic civilization, dominated by the kingdoms of Kamelia, Valusia, Verulia, Grondar, Thule, and Commoria. These peoples spoke a similar language, arguing a common origin. There were other kingdoms, equally civilized, but inhabited by different, and apparently older races.

The barbarians of that age were the Picts, who lived on islands far out on the western ocean; the Atlanteans, who dwelt on a small continent between the Pictish Islands and the main, or Thurian Continent; and the Lemurians, who inhabited a chain of large islands in the eastern hesisphere.

There were vast regions of unexplored land. The civilized kingdoms, though enormous in extent, occupied a comparatively small portion of the whole planet. Valusia was the western-most kingdom of the Thurian Continent; Grondar the eastern-most. East of Grondar, whose people were less highly cultured than those of their kindred kingdoms, stretched a wild and barren expanse of deserts. Among the less arid stretches of desert, in the jungles, and among the mountains, lived scattered clans and tribes of primitive savages. Far to the south there was a mysterious civilization, unconnected with the Thurian culture, and apparently pre-human in its nature. On the far eastern shores of the Continent there lived another race, human, but mysterious and non-Thurian, with which the Lemurians from time to time came in contact. They apparently came from a shadowy and nameless continent lying somewhere east of the Lemurian Islands.

The Thurian civilization was crumbling; their armies were composed largely of barbarian mercenaries. Picts, Atlanteans, and Lemurians were their generals, their statesmen, often their kings. Of the bickerings of the kingdoms, and the wars between Valusia and Commoria, as well as the conquests by which the Atlanteans founded a kingdom on the mainland, there are more legends than accurate history.

Then the Cataclysm rocked the world. Atlantis and Lemuria sank, and the Pictish Islands were heaved up to form the mountain peaks of a new continent. Sections of the Thurian Continent vanished under the waves, or sinking, formed great inland lakes and seas. Volcanoes broke forth and terrific earthquakes shook down the shining cities of the empires. Whole nations were blotted out.

The barbarians fared a little better than the civilized races. The inhabitants of the Pictish Islands were destroyed, but a great colony of them, settled among the mountains of Valusia's southern frontier, to serve as a buffer against foreign invasion, was untouched. The Continental kingdom of the Atlanteans likewise escaped the common ruin, and to it came thousands of their tribesmen in ships from the sinking land. Many Lemurians escaped to the eastern coast of the Thurian Continent, which was comparatively untouched. There they were enslaved by the ancient race which already dwelt there, and their history, for thousands of years, is a history of brutal servitude.

In the western part of the Continent, changing conditions created strange forms of plant and animal life. Thick jungles covered the plains, great rivers cut their roads to the sea, wild mountains were heaved up, and lakes covered the ruins of old cities in fertile valleys. To the continental kingdom of the Atlanteans, from sunken areas, swarmed myriads of beasts and savages—ape-men and apes. Forced to battle continually for their lives, they yet managed to retain vestiges of their former state of highly-advanced barbarism. Robbed of metals and ores, they became workers in stone like their distant ancestors, and had attained a real artistic level, when their struggling culture came into contact with the powerful Pictish nation. The Picts had also reverted to flint, but had advanced more rapidly in the matter of population and war-science. They had none of the Atlanteans' artistic nature; they were a ruder, more practical, more prolific race. They left no pictures painted or carved on ivory, as did their enemies, but they left remarkably efficient flint weapons in plenty.

These stone age kingdoms clashed, and in a series of bloody wars, the outnumbered Atlanteans were hurled back into a state of savagery, and the evolution of the Picts was halted. Five hundred years after the Cataclysm the barbaric kingdoms have vanished. It is now a nation of savages—the Picts—carrying on continual warfare with tribes of savages—the Atlanteans. The Picts had the advantage of numbers and unity whereas the Atlanteans had fallen into loosely-knit clans. That was the west of that day.

In the distant east, cut off from the rest of the world by the heaving up of gigantic mountains and the forming of a chain of vast lakes, the Lemurians are toiling as slaves of their ancient masters. The far south is still veiled in mystery. Untouched by the Cataclysm its destiny is still pre-human. Of the civilized races of the Thurian Continent, a remnant of one of the non Valusian nations dwells among the low mountains of the southeast—the Zhemri. Here and there about the world are scattered clans of apish savages, entirely ignorant of the rise and fall of the great civilizations. But in the far north another people are slowly coming into existence.

At the time of the Cataclysm, a band of savages whose development was not much above that of the Neanderthal, fled to the north to escape destruction. They found the snow-countries inhabited only by a species of ferocious snow-apes—huge shaggy white animals, apparently native to that climate. These they fought and drove beyond the arctic circle, to perish, as the savages thought. The latter, then, adapted themselves to their hardy new environment and throve.

After the Pictish-Atlantean wars had destroyed the

beginnings of what might have been a new culture, another, lesser cataclysm further altered the appearance of the original continent, left a great inland sea where the chain of lakes had been, to further separate west from east, and the attendant earthquakes, floods and volcanoes completed the ruin of the barbarians which their tribal wars had begun.

A thousand years after the lesser cataclysm, the western world is seen to be a wild country of jungles and lakes and torrential rivers. Among the forest-covered hills of the northwest exist wandering bands of ape-men, without human speech, or the knowledge of fire or the use of implements. They are the descendants of the Atlanteans, sunk back into the squalling chaos of jungle-bestiality from which ages ago their ancestors so laboriously crawled. To the southwest dwell scattered clans of degraded, cave-dwelling savages, whose speech is of the most primitive form, yet who still retain the name of Picts, which has come to mean merely a term designating men—themselves, to distinguish them from the true beasts with which they contend for life and food. It is their only link with their former stage. Neither the squalid Picts nor the apish Atlanteans have any contact with other tribes or peoples.

Far to the east, the Lemurians, levelled almost to a bestial plane themselves by the brutishness of their slavery, have risen and destroyed their masters. They are savages stalking among the ruins of a strange civilization. The survivors of that civilization, who have escaped the fury of their slaves, have come westward. They fall upon that mysterious pre-human kingdom of the south and overthrow it, substituting their own culture, modified by contact with the older one. The newer kingdom is called Stygia, and remnants of the older nation seemed to have survived, and even been worshipped, after the race as a whole had been destroyed.

Here and there in the world small groups of savages are showing signs of an upward trend; these are scattered and unclassified. But in the north, the tribes are growing. These people are called Hyborians, or Hybori; their god was Bori—some great chief, whom legend made even more ancient as the king who led them into the north, in the days of the great Cataclysm, which the tribes remember only in distorted folklore.

They have spread over the north, and are pushing southward in leisurely treks. So far they have not come in contact with any other races; their wars have been with one another. Fifteen hundred years in the north country have made them a tall, tawny-haired, grey-eyed race, vigorous and warlike, and already exhibiting a well-defined artistry and poetism of nature. They still live mostly by the hunt, but the southern tribes have been raising cattle for some centuries. There is one exception in their so far complete isolation from other races: a wanderer into the far north returned with the news that the supposedly deserted ice wastes were inhabited by an extensive tribe of ape-like men, descended, he swore, from the beasts driven out of the more habitable land by the ancestors of the Hyborians. He urged that a large war-party be sent beyond the arctic circle to exterminate these beasts, whom he swore were evolving into true men. He was jeered at; a small band of adventurous young warriors followed him into the north, but none returned.

But tribes of the Hyborians were drifting south, and as the population increased this movement became extensive. The following age was an epoch of wandering and conquest. Across the history of the world tribes and drifts of tribes move and shift in an everchanging panorama.

Look at the world five hundred years later. Tribes of tawny-haired Hyborians have moved southward and westward, conquering and destroying many of the small unclassified clans. Absorbing the blood of conquered races, already the descendants of the older drifts have begun to show modified racial traits, and these mixed races are attacked fiercely by new, purer-blooded drifts, and swept before them, as a broom sweeps debris impartially, to become even more mixed and mingled in the tangled debris of races and tag-ends of races.

As yet the conquerors have not come in contact with the older races. To the southeast the descendants of the Zhemri, given impetus by new blood resulting from admixture with some unclassified tribe, are beginning to seek to revive some faint shadow of their ancient culture. To the west the apish Atlanteans are beginning the long climb upward. They have completed the cycle of existence; they have long forgotten their former existence as men; unaware of any other former state, they are starting the climb unhelped and unhindered by human memories. To the south of them the Picts remain savages, apparently defying the laws of Nature by neither progressing nor retrogressing. Far to the south dreams the ancient mysterious kingdom of Stygia. On its eastern borders wander clans of nomadic savages, already known as the Sons of Shem.

Next to the Picts, in the broad valley of Zingg, protected by great mountains, a nameless band of primitives, tentatively classified as akin to the Shemites, has evolved an advanced agricultural system and existence.

Another factor has added to the impetus of

Hyborian drift. A tribe of that race has discovered the use of stone in building, and the first Hyborian kingdom has come into being—the rude and barbaric kingdom of Hyperborea, which had its beginning in a crude fortress of boulders heaped to repel tribal attack. The people of this tribe soon abandoned their horse-hide tents for stone houses, crudely but mightily built, and thus protected, they grew strong. There are few more dramatic events in history than the rise of the rude, fierce kingdom of Hyperborea, whose people turned abruptly from their nomadic life to rear dwellings of naked stone, surrounded by cyclopean walls—a race scarcely emerged from the polished stone age, who had by a freak of chance, learned the first rude principles of architecture.

The rise of this kingdom drove forth many other tribes, for, defeated in war, or refusing to become tributary to their castle-dwelling kinsmen, many clans set forth on long treks that took them half-way around the world. And already the more northern tribes are beginning to be harried by gigantic blond savages, not much more advanced than ape-men.

The tale of the next thousand years is the tale of the rise of the Hyborians, whose warlike tribes dominate the western world. Rude kingdoms are taking shape. The tawny-haired invaders have encountered the Picts, driving them into the barren lands of the west. To the northwest, the descendants of the Atlanteans, climbing unaided from apedom into primitive savagery, have not yet met the conquerors. Far to the east the Lemurians are evolving a strange semi-civilization of their own. To the south the Hyborians have founded the kingdom of Koth, on the borders of those pastoral countries known as the Lands of Shem, and the savages of those lands, partly through contact with the

Hyborians, partly through contact with the Stygians who have ravaged them for centuries, are emerging from barbarism. The blond savages of the far north have grown in power and numbers so that the northern Hyborian tribes move southward, driving their kindred clans before them. The ancient kingdom of Hyperborea is overthrown by one of these northern tribes, which, however, retains the old name. Southeast of Hyperborea a kingdom of the Zhemri has come into being, under the name of Zamora. To the southwest, a tribe of Picts have invaded the fertile valley of Zingg, conquered the agricultural people there, and settled among them. This mixed race was in turn conquered later by a roving tribe of Hybori, and from these mingled elements came the kingdom of Zingara.

Five hundred years later the kingdoms of the world are clearly defined. The kingdoms of the Hyborians—Aquilonia, Nemedia, Brythunia, Hyperborea, Koth, Ophir, Argos, Corinthia, and one known as the Border Kingdom—dominate the western world. Zamora lies to the east, and Zingara to the southwest of these kingdoms—peoples alike in darkness of complexion and exotic habits, but otherwise unrelated. Far to the south sleeps Stygia, untouched by foreign invasion, but the peoples of Shem have exchanged the Stygian yoke for the less galling one of Koth. The dusky masters have been driven south of the great river Styx, Nilus, or Nile, which, flowing north from the shadowy hinterlands, turns almost at right angles and flows almost due west through the pastoral meadowlands of Shem, to empty into the great sea. North of Aquilonia, the westernmost Hyborian kingdom, are the Cimmerians, ferocious savages, untamed by the invaders, but advancing rapidly because of contact with them; they are the descendants of the Atlanteans, now progressing more steadily than their old enemies the Picts, who dwell in the wilderness west of Aquilonia.

Another five centuries and the Hybori peoples are the possessors of a civilization so virile that contact with it virtually snatched out of the wallow of savagery such tribes as it touched. The most powerful kingdom is Aquilonia, but others vie with it in strength and splendor. The Hyborians have become a considerably mixed race; the nearest to the ancient root-stock are the Gundermen of Gunderland, a northern province of Aquilonia. But this mixing has not weakened the race. They are supreme in the western world, though the barbarians of the wastelands are growing in strength.

In the north, golden-haired, blue-eyed barbarians, descendants of the blond arctic savages, have driven the remaining Hyborian tribes out of the snow countries, except the ancient kingdom of Hyperborea, which resists their onslaught. Their country is called Nordheim, and they are divided into the red-haired Vanir of Vanaheim, and the yellow-haired AEsir of Asgard.

Now the Lemurians enter history again as Hyrkanians. Through the centuries they have pushed steadily westward, and now a tribe skirts the southern end of the great inland sea—Vilayet—and establishes the kingdom of Turan on the southwestern shore. Between the inland sea and the eastern borders of the native kingdoms lie vast expanses of steppes and in the extreme north and extreme south, deserts. The non-Hyrkanian dwellers of these territories are scattered and pastoral, unclassified in the north, Shemitish in the south, aboriginal, with a thin strain of Hyborian blood from wandering conquerors. Toward the latter part of the period other Hyrkanian clans push westward, around the northern extremity of the inland sea, and clash with the eastern outposts of the Hyperboreans.

Glance briefly at the peoples of that age. The dominant Hyborians are no longer uniformly tawny-haired and grey-eyed. They have mixed with other races. There is a strong Shemitish, even a Stygian strain among the peoples of Koth, and to a lesser extent, of Argos, while in the case of the latter, admixture with the Zingarans has been more extensive than with the Shemites. The eastern Brythunians have intermarried with the dark-skinned Zamorians, and the people of southern Aquilonia have mixed with the brown Zingarans until black hair and brown eyes are the dominant type in Poitain, the southern-most province. The ancient kingdom of Hyperborea is more aloof than the others, yet there is alien blood in plenty in its veins, from the capture of foreign women—Hyrkanians, AEsir, and Zamorians. Only in the province of Gunderland, where the people keep no slaves, is the pure Hyborian stock found unblemished. But the barbarians have kept their bloodstream pure; the Cimmerians are tall and powerful, with dark hair and blue or grey eyes. The people of Nordheim are of similar build, but with white skins, blue eyes and golden or red hair. The Picts are of the same type as they always were—short, very dark, with black eyes and hair. The Hyrkanians are dark and generally tall and slender, though a squat slant-eyed type is more and more common among them, resulting from mixture with a curious race of intelligent, though stunted, aborigines, conquered by them among the mountains east of Vilayet, on their westward drift. The Shemites are generally of medium height, though sometimes when mixed with Stygian blood, gigantic, broadly and strongly built, with hook hoses, dark eyes and blue-black hair. The Stygians are tall and well-made, dusky, straight-featured—at least the ruling classes are of that type. The lower classes are a down-trodden, mongrel horde, a mixture of negroid, Stygian, Shemitish, even Hyborian bloods. South of Stygia are the vast black kingdoms of the Amazons, the Kushites, the Atlaians, and the hybrid empire of Zimbabwe.

Between Aquilonia and the Pictish wilderness lie the Bossonian marches, peopled by descendants of an aboriginal race, conquered by a tribe of Hyborians, early in the first ages of the Hyborian drift. This mixed people never attained the civilization of the purer Hyborians, and was pushed by them to the very fringe of the civilized world. The Bossonians are of medium height and complexion, their eyes brown or grey, and they are mesocephalic. They live mainly by agriculture, in large walled villages, and are part of the Aquilonian kingdom. Their marches extend from the Border kingdom in the north to Zingara in the southwest, forming a bulwark for Aquilonia against both the Cimmerians and the Picts. They are stubborn defensive fighters, and centuries of warfare against northern and western barbarians have caused them to evolve a type of defense almost impregnable against direct attack.

Five hundred years later the Hyborian civilization was swept away. Its fall was unique in that it was not brought about by internal decay, but by the growing power of the barbarian nations, and the Hyrkanians. The Hyborian peoples were overthrown while their vigorous culture was in its prime.

Yet it was Aquilonia's greed which brought about that overthrow, though indirectly. Wishing to extend their empire, her kings made war on their neighbors. Zingara, Argos and Ophir were annexed outright, with the western cities of Shem, which had, with their more eastern kindred, recently thrown off the yoke of Koth.

Koth itself, with Corinthia and the eastern Shemitish tribes, was forced to pay Aquilonia tribute and lend aid in wars. An ancient feud had existed between Aquilonia and Hyperborea, and the latter now marched to meet the armies of her western rival. The plains of the Border Kingdom were the scene of a great and savage battle, in which the northern hosts were utterly defeated, and retreated into their snowy fastnesses, whither the victorious Aquilonians did not pursue them. Nemedia, which had successfully resisted the western kingdom for centuries, now drew Brythunia and Zamora, and secretly, Koth, into an alliance which bade fair to crush the rising empire. But before their armies could join battle, a new enemy appeared in the east, as the Hyrkanians made their first real thrust at the western world. Reinforced by adventurers from east of Vilayet, the riders of Turan swept over Zamora, devastated eastern Corinthia, and were met on the plains of Brythunia by the Aquilonians who defeated them and hurled them flying eastward. But the back of the alliance was broken, and Nemedia took the defensive in future wars, aided occasionally by Brythunia, and Hyperborea, and, secretly as usual, by Koth. This defeat of the Hyrkanians showed the nations the real power of the western kingdom, whose splendid armies were augmented by mercenaries, many of them recruited among the alien Zingarans, and the barbaric Picts and Shemites. Zamora was reconquered from the Hyrkanians, but the people discovered that they had merely exchanged an eastern master for a western master. Aquilonian soldiers were quartered there, not only to protect the ravaged country, but also to keep the people in subjection. The Hyrkanians were not convinced; three more invasions burst upon the Zamorian borders, and the Lands of Shem, and were hurled back by the Aquilonians, though the Turanian armies grew larger as hordes of steel-clad riders rode out of the east, skirting the southern extremity of the inland sea.

But it was in the west that a power was growing destined to throw down the kings of Aquilonia from their high places. In the north there was incessant bickering along the Cimmerian borders between the black-haired warriors and the Nordheimr; and the Æsir, between wars with the Vanir, assailed Hyperborea and pushed back the frontier, destroying city after city. The Cimmerians also fought the Picts and Bossonians impartially, and several times raided into Aquilonia itself, but their wars were less invasions than mere plundering forays.

But the Picts were growing amazingly in population and power. By a strange twist of fate, it was largely due to the efforts of one man, and he an alien, that they set their feet upon the ways that led to eventual empire. This man was Arus, a Nemedian priest, a natural-born reformer. What turned his mind toward the Picts is not certain, but this much is history—he determined to go into the western wilderness and modify the rude ways of the heathen by the introduction of the gentle worship of Mitra. He was not daunted by the grisly tales of what had happened to traders and explorers before him, and by some whim of fate he came among the people he sought, alone and unarmed, and was not instantly speared.

The Picts had benefitted by contact with Hyborian civilization, but they had always fiercely resisted that contact. That is to say, they had learned to work crudely in copper and tin, which was found scantily in their country, and for which latter metal they raided into the mountains of Zingara, or traded hides, whale's teeth, walrus tusks and such few things as savages have to trade. They no longer lived in caves and tree-shelters, but built tents of hides, and crude huts, copied from those of the Bossonians. They still lived mainly by the chase, since their wilds swarmed with game of all sorts, and the rivers and sea with fish, but they had learned how to plant grain, which they did sketchily, preferring to steal it from their neighbors the Bossonians and Zingarans. They dwelt in clans which were generally at feud with each other, and their simple customs were blood-thirsty and utterly inexplicable to a civilized man, such as Arus of Nemedia. They had no direct contact with the Hyborians, since the Bossonians acted as a buffer between them. But Arus maintained that they were capable of progress, and events proved the truth of his assertion—though scarcely in the way he meant.

Arus was fortunate in being thrown in with a chief of more than usual intelligence—Gorm by name. Gorm can not be explained, any more than Genghis Khan, Othman, Attila, or any of those individuals, who, born in naked lands among untutored barbarians, yet possess the instinct for conquest and empire-building. In a sort of bastard-Bossonian, the priest made the chief understand his purpose, and though extremely puzzled, Gorm gave him permission to remain among his tribe unbutchered—a case unique in the history of the race. Having learned the language Arus set himself to work to eliminate the more unpleasant phases of Pictish life—such as human sacrifice, blood-feud, and the burning alive of captives. He harangued Gorm at length, whom he found to be an interested, if unresponsive listener. Imagination reconstructs the scene—the black-haired chief, in his tiger-skins and necklace of human teeth, squatting on the dirt floor of the wattle hut, listening intently to the eloquence of the priest, who probably sat on a carven, skin-covered block of mahogany provided in his honor—clad in the silken robes of a Nemedian priest, gesturing with his slender white hands as he expounded the eternal rights and justices which were the truths of Mitra. Doubtless he pointed with repugnance at the rows of skulls which adorned the walls of the hut and urged Gorm to forgive his enemies instead of putting their bleached remnants to such use. Arus was the highest product of an innately artistic race, refined by centuries of civilization; Gorm had behind him a heritage of a hundred thousand years of screaming savagery—the pad of the tiger was in his stealthy step, the grip of the gorilla in his black-nailed hands, the fire that burns in a leopard's eyes burned in his.

Arus was a practical man. He appealed to the savage's sense of material gain; he pointed out the power and splendor of the Hyborian kingdoms, as an example of the power of Mitra, whose teachings and works had lifted them up to their high places. And he spoke of cities, and fertile plains, marble walls and iron chariots, jeweled towers, and horsemen in their glittering armor riding to battle. And Gorm, with the unerring instinct of the barbarian, passed over his words regarding gods and their teachings, and fixed on the material powers thus vividly described. There in that mud-floored wattle hut, with the silk-robed priest on the mahogany block, and the dark-skinned chief crouching in his tiger-hides, was laid the foundations of empire.

As has been said, Arus was a practical man. He dwelt among the Picts and found much that an intelligent man could do to aid humanity, even when that humanity was cloaked in tiger-skins and wore necklaces of human teeth. Like all priests of Mitra, he was instructed in many things. He found that there were vast deposits of iron ore in the Pictish hills, and he taught the natives to mine, smelt and work it into implements—agricultural implements, as he fondly believed. He instituted other reforms, but these were the most important things he did: he instilled in Gorm a desire to see the civilized lands of the world; he taught the Picts how to work in iron; and he established contact between them and the civilized world. At the chief's request he conducted him and some of his warriors through the Bossonian marches, where the honest villagers stared in amazement, into the glittering outer world.

Arus no doubt thought that he was making converts right and left, because the Picts listened to him, and refrained from smiting him with their copper axes. But the Pict was little calculated to seriously regard teachings which bade him forgive his enemy and abandon the warpath for the ways of honest drudgery. It has been said that he lacked artistic sense; his whole nature led to war and slaughter. When the priest talked of the glories of the civilized nations, his dark-skinned listeners were intent, not on the ideals of his religion, but on the loot which he unconsciously described in the narration of rich cities and shining lands. When he told how Mitra aided certain kings to overcome their enemies, they paid scant heed to the miracles of Mitra, but they hung on the description of battle-lines, mounted knights, and maneuvers of archers and spearmen. They harkened with keen dark eyes and inscrutable countenances, and they went their ways without comment, and heeded with flattering intentness his instructions as to the working of iron, and kindred arts.

Before his coming they had filched steel weapons and armor from the Bossonians and Zingarans, or had hammered out their own crude arms from copper and bronze. Now a new world opened to them, and the clang of sledges re-echoed throughout the land. And Gorm, by virtue of this new craft, began to assert his dominance over other clans, partly by war, partly by craft and diplomacy, in which latter art he excelled all other barbarians.

Picts now came and went freely into Aquilonia, under safe-conduct, and they returned with more information as to armor-forging and sword-making. More, they entered Aquilonia's mercenary armies, to the unspeakable disgust of the sturdy Bossonians. Aquilonia's kings toyed with the idea of playing the Picts against the Cimmerians, and possibly thus destroying both menaces, but they were too busy with their policies of aggression in the south and east to pay much heed to the vaguely-known lands of the west, from which more and more stocky warriors swarmed to take service among the mercenaries.

These warriors, their service completed, went back to their wilderness with good ideas of civilized warfare, and that contempt for civilization which arises from familiarity with it. Drums began to beat in the hills, gathering-fires smoked on the heights, and savage sword-makers hammered their steel on a thousand anvils. By intrigues and forays too numerous and devious to enumerate, Gorm became chief of chiefs, the nearest approach to a king the Picts had had in thousands of years. He had waited long; he was past middle age. But now he moved against the frontiers, not in trade, but in war.

Arus saw his mistake too late; he had not touched the soul of the pagan, in which lurked the hard fierceness of all the ages. His persuasive eloquence had not caused a ripple in the Pictish conscience. Gorm wore a corselet of silvered mail now, instead of the tiger-skin, but underneath he was unchanged—the everlasting barbarian, unmoved by theology or philosophy, his instincts fixed unerringly on rapine and plunder.

The Picts burst on the Bossonian frontiers with fire and sword, not clad in tiger-skins and brandishing copper axes as of yore, but in scale-mail, wielding weapons of keen steel. As for Arus, he was brained by a drunken Pict, while making a last effort to undo the work he had unwittingly done. Gorm was not without gratitude; he caused the skull of the slayer to be set on the top of the priest's cairn. And it is one of the grim ironies of the universe that the stones which covered Arus' body should have been adorned with that last touch of barbarity—above a man to whom violence and blood-vengeance were revolting.

But the newer weapons and mail were not enough to break the lines. For years the superior armaments and sturdy courage of the Bossonians held the invaders at bay, aided, when necessary, by imperial Aquilonian troops. During this time the Hyrkanians came and went, and Zamora was added to the empire.

Then treachery from an unexpected source broke the Bossonian lines. Before chronicling this treachery, it might be well to glance briefly at the Aquilonian empire. Always a rich kingdom, untold wealth had been rolled in by conquest, and sumptuous splendor had taken the place of simple and hardy living. But degeneracy had not yet sapped the kings and the people; though clad in silks and cloth-of-gold, they were still a vital, virile race. But arrogance was supplanting their former simplicity. They treated less powerful people with growing contempt, levying more and more tributes on the conquered. Argos, Zingara, Ophir, Zamora and the Shemite countries were treated as subjugated provinces, which was especially galling to the proud Zingarans, who often revolted, despite savage retaliations.

Koth was practically tributary, being under Aquilonia's "protection" against the Hyrkanians. But Nemedia the western empire had never been able to subdue, although the latter's triumphs were of the defensive sort, and were generally attained with the aid of Hyperborean armies. During this period Aquilonia's only defeats were: her failure to annex Nemedia; the rout of an army sent into Cimmeria; and the almost complete destruction of an army by the AEsir. Just as the Hyrkanians found themselves unable to withstand the heavy cavalry charges of the Aquilonians, so the latter, invading the snow-countries, were overwhelmed by the ferocious hand-to-hand fighting of the Nordics. But Aquilonia's conquests were pushed to the Nilus, where a Stygian army was defeated with great slaughter, and the king of Stygia sent tribute—once at least—to divert invasion of his kingdom. Brythunia was reduced in a series of whirlwind wars, and preparations were made to subjugate the ancient rival at last—Nemedia.

With their glittering hosts greatly increased by mercenaries, the Aquilonians moved against their old-time foe, and it seemed as if the thrust were destined to crush the last shadow of Nemedian independence. But contentions arose between the Aquilonians and their Bossonian auxillaries.

As the inevitable result of imperial expansion, the Aquilonians had become haughty and intolerant. They derided the ruder, unsophisticated Bossonians, and hard feeling grew between them—the Aquilonians despising the Bossonians, and the latter resenting the attitude of their masters—who now boldly called themselves such, and treated the Bossonians like conquered subjects, taxing them exorbitantly, and conscripting them for their wars of territorial expansion—wars the profits of which the Bossonians shared little. Scarcely enough men were left in the marches to guard the frontier, and hearing of Pictish outrages in their homelands, whole Bossonian regiments quit the Nemedian campaign and marched to the western frontier, where they defeated the dark-skinned invaders in a great battle.

This desertion, however, was the direct cause of Aquilonia's defeat by the desperate Nemedians, and brought down on the Bossonians the cruel wrath of the imperialists—intolerant and short-sighted as imperialists invariably are. Aquilonian regiments were secretly brought to the borders of the marches, the Bossonian chiefs were invited to attend a great conclave, and, in the guise of an expedition against the Picts, bands of savage Shemitish soldiers were quartered among the unsuspecting villagers. The unarmed chiefs were massacred, the Shemites turned on their stunned hosts with torch and sword, and the armored imperial hosts were hurled ruthlessly on the unsuspecting people. From north to south the marches were ravaged and the Aquilonian armies marched back from the borders, leaving a ruined and devastated land behind them.

And then the Pictish invasion burst in full power along those borders. It was no mere raid, but the concerted rush of a whole nation, led by chiefs who had served in Aquilonian armies, and planned and directed by Gorm—an old man now, but with the fire of his fierce ambition undimmed. This time there were no strong walled villages in their path, manned by sturdy archers, to hold back the rush until the imperial troops could be brought up. The remnants of the Bossonians were swept out of existence, and the blood-mad barbarians swarmed into Aquilonia, looting and burning, before the legions, warring again with the Nemedians, could be marched into the west. Zingara seized this opportunity to throw off the yoke, which example was followed by Corinthia and the Shemites. Whole regiments of mercenaries and vassals mutinied and marched back to their own countries, looting and burning as they went. The Picts surged irresistibly eastward, and host after host was trampled beneath their feet. Without their Bossonian archers the Aquilonians found themselves unable to cope with the terrible arrow-fire of the barbarians. From all parts of the empire legions were recalled to resist the onrush, while from the wilderness horde after horde swarmed forth, in apparently inexhaustible supply. And in the midst of this chaos, the Cimmerians swept down from their hills, completing the ruin. They looted cities, devastated the country, and retired into the hills with their plunder, but the Picts occupied the land they had over-run. And the Aquilonian empire went down in fire and blood.

Then again the Hyrkanians rode from the blue east. The withdrawal of the imperial legions from Zamora was their incitement. Zamora fell easy prey to their thrusts, and the Hyrkanian king established his capital in the largest city of the country. This invasion was from the ancient Hyrkanian kingdom of Turan, on the shores of the inland sea, but another, more savage Hyrkanian thrust came from the north. Hosts of steel-clad riders galloped around the northern extremity of the inland sea, traversed the icy deserts, entered the steppes, driving the aborigines before them, and launched themselves against the western kingdoms. These new-comers were not at first allies with the Turanians, but skirmished with them as with the Hyborians; new drifts of eastern warriors bickered and fought, until all were united under a great chief, who came riding from the very shores of the eastern ocean. With no Aquilonian armies to oppose them, they were invincible. They swept over and subjugated Brythunia, and devastated southern Hyperborea, and Corinthia. They swept into the Cimmerian hills, driving the black-haired barbarians before them, but among the hills, where cavalry was less effectual, the Cimmerians turned on them, and only a disorderly retreat, at the end of a whole day of bloody fighting, saved the Hyrkanian hosts from complete annihilation.

While these events had been transpiring, the kingdoms of Shem had conquered their ancient master, Koth, and had been defeated in an attempted invasion of Stygia. But scarcely had they completed their degradation of Koth, when they were over-run by the Hyrkanians, and found themselves subjugated by sterner masters than the Hyborians had ever been. Meanwhile the Picts had made themselves complete masters of Aquilonia, practically blotting out the inhabitants. They had broken over the borders of Zingara, and thousands of Zingarans, fleeing the slaughter into Argos, threw themselves on the mercy of the westward-sweeping Hyrkanians, who settled them in Zamora as subjects. Behind them as they fled, Argos was enveloped in the flame and slaughter of Pictish conquest, and the slayers swept into Ophir and clashed with the westward-riding Hyrkanians. The latter, after their conquest of Shem, had overthrown a Stygian army at the Nilus and over-run the country as far south as the black kingdom of Amazon, of whose people they brought back thousands as captives, settling them among the Shemites. Possibly they would have completed their conquests in Stygia, adding it to their widening empire, but for the fierce thrusts of the Picts against their western conquests.

Nemedia, unconquerable by Hyborians, reeled between the riders of the east, and the swordsmen of the west, when a tribe of AEsir, wandering down from their snowy lands, came into the kingdom, and were engaged as mercenaries; they proved such able warriors that they not only beat off the Hyrkanians, but halted the eastward advance of the Picts.

The world at that time presents some such picture: a vast Pictish empire, wild, rude and barbaric, stretches from the coasts of Vanaheim in the north to the southern-most shores of Zingara. It stretches east to include all Aquilonia except Gunderland, the northern-most province, which, as a separate kingdom in the hills, survived the fall of the empire, and still maintains its independence. The Pictish empire also includes Argos, Ophir, the western part of Koth, and the western-most lands of Shem. Opposed to this barbaric empire is the empire of the Hyrkanians, of which the northern boundaries are the ravaged lines of Hyperborea, and the southern, the deserts south of the lands of Shem. Zamora, Brythunia, the Border Kingdom, Corinthia, most of Koth, and all the eastern lands of Shem are included in this empire. The borders of Cimmeria are intact; neither Pict nor Hyrkanian has been able to subdue these warlike barbarians. Nemedia, dominated by the AEsir mercenaries, resists all invasions. In the north Nordheim, Cimmeria and Nemedia separate the conquering races, but in the south, Koth has become a battle-ground where Picts and Hyrkanians war incessantly. Sometimes the eastern warriors expel the barbarians from the kingdom entirely; again the plains and cities are in the hands of the western invaders. In the far south Stygia, shaken by the Hyrkanian invasion, is being encroached upon by the great black kingdoms. And in the far north, the Nordic tribes are restless, warring continually with the Cimmerians, and sweeping the Hyperborean frontiers.

Gorm was slain by Hialmar, a chief of the Nemedian AEsir. He was a very old man, nearly a hundred years old. In the seventy-five years which had elapsed since he first heard the tale of empires from the lips of Arus— a long time in the life of a man, but a brief space in the tale of nations—he had welded an empire from straying savage clans, he had overthrown a civilization. He who had been born in a mud-walled, wattle-roofed hut, in his old age sat on golden thrones, and gnawed joints of beef presented to him on golden dishes by naked slave-girls who were the daughters of kings. Conquest and the acquiring of wealth altered not the Pict; out of the ruins of the crushed civilization no new culture arose phoenix-like. The dark hands which shattered the artistic glories of the conquered never tried to copy them. Though he sat among the glittering ruins of shattered palaces and clad his hard body in the silks of vanquished kings, the Pict remained the eternal barbarian, ferocious, elemental, interested only in the naked primal principles of life, unchanging, unerring in his instincts which were all for war and plunder, and in which arts and the cultured progress of humanity had no place. Not so with the AEsir who settled in Nemedia. These soon adopted many of the ways of their civilized allies, modified powerfully, however, by their own intensely virile and alien culture.

For a short age Pict and Hyrkanian snarled at each other over the ruins of the world they had conquered. Then began the glacier ages, and the great Nordic drift. Before the southward moving ice-fields the northern tribes drifted, driving kindred clans before them. The AEsir blotted out the ancient kingdom of Hyperborea, and across its ruins came to grips with the Hyrkanians. Nemedia had already become a Nordic kingdom, ruled by the descendants of the AEsir mercenaries. Driven before the onrushing tides of Nordic invasion, the Cimmerians were on the march, and neither army nor city stood before them. They surged across and completely destroyed the kingdom of Gunderland, and marched across ancient Aquilonia, hewing their irresistible way through the Pictish hosts. They defeated the Nordic-Nemedians and sacked some of their cities, but did not halt. They continued eastward, overthrowing an Hyrkanian army on the borders of Brythunia.

Behind them hordes of AEsir and Vanir swarmed into the lands, and the Pictish empire reeled beneath their strokes. Nemedia was overthrown, and the half-civilized Nordics fled before their wilder kinsmen, leaving the cities of Nemedia ruined and deserted. These fleeing Nordics, who had adopted the name of the older kingdom, and to whom the term Nemedian henceforth refers, came into the ancient land of Koth, expelled both Picts and Hyrkanians, and aided the people of Shem to throw off the Hyrkanian yoke. All over the western world, the Picts and Hyrkanians were staggering before this younger, fiercer people. A band of AEsir drove the eastern riders from Brythunia and settled there themselves, adopting the name for themselves. The Nordics who had conquered Hyperborea assailed their eastern enemies so savagely that the dark-skinned descendants of the Lemurians retreated into the steppes, pushed irresistibly back toward Vilayet.

Meanwhile the Cimmerians, wandering southeast-ward, destroyed the ancient Hyrkanian kingdom of Turan, and settled on the southwestern shores of the inland sea. The power of the eastern conquerors was broken. Before the attacks of the Nordheimr and the Cimmerians, they destroyed all their cities, butchered such captives as were not fit to make the long march, and then, herding thousands of slaves before them, rode back into the mysterious east, skirting the northern edge of the sea, and vanishing from western history, until they rode out of the east again, thousands of years later, as Huns, Mongols, Tatars and Turks. With them in their retreat went thousands of Zamorians and Zingarans, who were settled together far to the east, formed a mixed race, and emerged ages afterward as gypsies.

Meanwhile, also, a tribe of Vanir adventurers had passed along the Pictish coast southward, ravaged ancient Zingara, and come into Stygia, which, oppressed by a cruel aristocratic ruling class, was staggering under the thrusts of the black kingdoms to the south. The red-haired Vanir led the slaves in a general revolt, overthrew the reigning class, and set themselves up as a caste of conquerors. They subjugated the northern-most black kingdoms, and built a vast southern empire, which they called Egypt. From these red-haired conquerors the earlier Pharaohs boasted descent.

The western world was now dominated by Nordic barbarians. The Picts still held Aquilonia and part of Zingara, and the western coast of the continent. But east to Vilayet, and from the arctic circle to the lands of

Shem, the only inhabitants were roving tribes of Nordheimr, excepting the Cimmerians, settled in the old Turanian kingdom. There were no cities anywhere, except in Stygia and the lands of Shem; the invading tides of Picts, Hyrkanians, Cimmerians and Nordics had levelled them in ruins, and the once dominant Hyborians had vanished from the earth, leaving scarcely a trace of their blood in the veins of their conquerors. Only a few names of lands, tribes and cities remained in the languages of the barbarians, to come down through the centuries connected with distorted legend and fable, until the whole history of the Hyborian age was lost sight of in a cloud of myths and fantasies. Thus in the speech of the gypsies lingered the terms Zingara and Zamora; the AEsir who dominated Nemedia were called Nemedians, and later figured in Irish history, and the Nordics who settled in Brythunia were known as Brythunians, Brythons, or Britons.

There was no such thing, at that time, as a consolidated Nordic empire. As always, the tribes had each its own chief or king, and they fought savagely among themselves. What their destiny might have been will not be known, because another terrific convulsion of the earth, carving out the lands as they are known to moderns, hurled all into chaos again. Great strips of the western coast sank; Vanaheim and western Asgard—uninhabited and glacier-haunted wastes for a hundred years—vanished beneath the waves. The ocean flowed around the mountains of western Cimmeria to form the North Sea; these mountains became the islands later known as England, Scotland and Ireland, and the waves rolled over what had been the Pictish wilderness and the Bossonian marches. In the north the Baltic Sea was formed, cutting Asgard into the peninsulas later known as Norway, Sweden and Denmark, and far to the south the Stygian continent was broken away from the rest of the world, on the line of cleavage formed by the river Nilus in its westward trend. Over Argos, western Koth and the western lands of Shem, washed the blue ocean men later called the Mediterranean. But where land sank elsewhere, a vast expanse west of Stygia rose out of the waves, forming the whole western half of the continent of Africa.

The buckling of the land thrust up great mountain ranges in the central part of the northern continent. Whole Nordic tribes were blotted out, and the rest retreated eastward. The territory about the slowly drying inland sea was not affected, and there, on the western shores, the Nordic tribes began a pastoral existence, living in more or less peace with the Cimmerians, and gradually mixing with them. In the west the remnants of the Picts, reduced by the cataclysm once more to the status of stone age savages, began, with the incredible virility of their race, once more to possess the land, until, at a later age, they were overthrown by the westward drift of the Cimmerians and Nordics. This was so long after the breaking-up of the continent that only meaningless legends told of former empires.

This drift comes within the reach of modern history and need not be repeated. It resulted from a growing population which thronged the steppes west of the inland sea—which still later, much reduced in size, was known as the Caspian—to such an extent that migration became an economic necessity. The tribes moved southward, northward and westward, into those lands now known as India, Asia Minor, and central and western Europe.

They came into these countries as Aryans. But there were variations among these primitive Aryans, some of which are still recognized today, others which have long been forgotten. The blond Achaians, Gauls and Britons, for instance, were descendants of pure-blooded AEsir. The Nemedians of Irish legendry were the Nemedian AEsir. The Danes were descendants of pure-blooded Vanir; the Goths—ancestors of the other Scandinavian and Germanic tribes, including the Anglo-Saxons—were descendants of a mixed race whose elements contained Vanir, AEsir and Cimmerian strains. The Gaels, ancestors of the Irish and Highland Scotch, descended from pure-blooded Cimmerian clans. The Cymric tribes of Britain were a mixed Nordic-Cimmerian race which preceded the purely Nordic Britons into the isles, and thus gave rise to a legend of Gaelic priority. The Cimbri who fought Rome were of the same blood, as well as the Gimmerai of the Assyrians and Grecians, and Gomer of the Hebrews. Other clans of the Cimmerians adventured east of the drying inland sea, and a few centuries later, mixed with Hyrkanian blood, returned westward as Scythians. The original ancestors of the Gaels gave their name to modern Crimea.

The ancient Sumerians had no connection with the western race. They were a mixed people, of Hyrkanian and Shemitish bloods, who were not taken with the conquerors in their retreat. Many tribes of Shem escaped that captivity, and from pure-blooded Shemites, or Shemites mixed with Hyborian or Nordic blood, were descended the Arabs, Israelites, and other straighter-featured Semites. The Canaanites, or Alpine Semites, traced their descent from Shemitish ancestors mixed with the Kushites settled among them by their Hyrkanian masters; the Elamites were a typical race of this type. The short, thick-limbed Etruscans, base of the Roman race, were descendants of a people of mixed

278

Stygian, Hyrkanian and Pictish strains, and originally lived in the ancient kingdom of Koth. The Hyrkanians, retreating to the eastern shores of the continent, evolved into the tribes later known as Tatars, Huns, Mongols and Turks.

The origins of other races of the modern world may be similarly traced; in almost every case, older far than they realize, their history stretches back into the mists of the forgotten Hyborian age.. : . . . .

"It blotted out furniture, walls, and the smiling countenance of Baal-pteor."

Original *Weird Tales* illustration by Vincent Napoli

Afterword

"BEYOND THE BLACK RIVER" was the second of Conan's four serial-length appearances in *Weird Tales*, this a two-part short novel that ran in the May and June 1935 issues. For a change, Conan did not make the cover. Wright seems to have been experimenting: the issue featured "a weird Craig Kennedy murder-mystery" by Arthur B. Reeve, set off by a non-erotic Margaret Brundage cover that was possibly her worst ever. Also unusual for a Howard serial, "Beyond the Black River" was without fanfare, relegated to the midsection of the issue. It did claim two excellent Hugh Rankin interior drawings—the last time Rankin would illustrate Conan.

Perhaps Wright was feeling guilty over the more than $800 *Weird Tales* now owed Howard for published stories. Possibly more readers were seconding Robert Bloch's move to impeach Conan. More likely, Howard had disdained to provide a semi-clad lovely whose distress would have rated the cover. Breaking convention, "Beyond the Black River" contained no romantic interest for whom Conan could perform deeds of daring. Howard was aware of the risk he ran in denying his readers the traditional imperiled beauty in brass bra and silk knickers: "My latest sales have been . . . a two-part Conan serial to Weird Tales; no sex in the latter. I wanted to see if I could write an interesting Conan yarn without sex interest."

Howard appears to have grown bored with the Arabian Nights approach to epic fantasy, and was consciously experimenting: "My latest sales to Weird

Tales have been a two-part Conan serial, 'Beyond the Black River'—a frontier story, and a novelet dealing with Mississippi negroes, etc., 'The Moon of Zambebwei,' which I understand will be changed to 'The Grisly Horror.' In the Conan story I've attempted a new style and setting entirely—abandoned the exotic settings of lost cities, decaying civilizations, golden domes, marble palaces, silk-clad dancing girls, etc., and thrown my story against a background of forests and rivers, log cabins, frontier outposts, buckskin-clad settlers, and painted tribesmen. Some day I'm going to try my hand at a longer yarn of the same style, a serial of four or five parts."

This last reference apparently is to "The Black Stranger," an unsold Conan short novel of 33,000 words, that mixes Conan and pirates and Picts and a doomed stockade. It was rejected, and Howard unsuccessfully attempted salvage by rewriting it into a tale of Black Vulmea and pirates and Indians and a doomed stockade. The Black Vulmea revision, "Swords of the Red Brotherhood," finally was published by Donald Grant in 1976 as part of the collection, *Black Vulmea's Vengeance*. A heavily "edited" version of "The Black Stranger" came out in *Fantasy Magazine* for March 1953 (March on the spine, February on the contents page—if you're keeping score). Unfortunately "The Black Stranger" has never been published except in an "edited" version that attempts to connect the tale to Conan's usurpation of the Aquilonian throne. We have Howard's original manuscripts for this and the other three Conan tales that were discovered after his death, and it is hoped that we will be able to present the stories *as Howard wrote them* once present contractual matters are resolved.

For Howard's experiment is a successful one. Prior to this we have seen Conan in Hyborian Age versions of Nordic sagas, pirate yarns, Eastern adventures, classical/medieval intrigues and battles. "Beyond the Black River" proposes a Hyborian Age variant of the American frontier. For the first time Howard has turned from the stock mélange of classical and medieval Europe, with trappings of *The Thief of Bagdad* and Sir Richard Francis Burton—a distillation of books and movies—in favor of a framework which he knew from immediate contact—that of the American frontier. It has been proposed that "Beyond the Black River" was influenced by Robert W. Chambers' novels of Indian warfare in colonial New York. The notion is comparable to suggesting that Sir Richard Francis Burton based his writings on Rudyard Kipling. To begin with, Howard ranked Zane Grey and Jack London among his favorite authors. But more to the point, Howard was Texas-born and Texas-bred. His ancestors were pioneer stock; he was steeped in the traditions of the American frontier; his letters recount grim and bloody tales of settlers, Indians, and outlaws that were told to him by sources closer to reality than a Chambers' novel. When he chose to write of Conan as a scout on a savage frontier, Howard for the first time was writing about characters and situations that he *knew* about—not reflections of page or screen.

It is a distinction that gives "Beyond the Black River" a sense of conviction and mounting power that few of the other Conan stories can match. Often Conan seems a dream of the Arabian Nights—entertaining, but no more real than any other dream. In "Beyond the Black River" Conan and his world seem real.

"Beyond the Black River" is a story that Conan fans probably react to with more mixed feeling than any other in the series. The charges have been made that the story is nothing more than a western yarn with swords taking the place of rifles, and a dash of sorcery stirred in; that here the Picts are not Howard's usual portrayal of a mystic, dawn-age savage race, but are American Indians with axes instead of tomahawks and dark (though still white) skins instead of red; that Conan has become so much of a superman that Howard has to resort to a secondary character, Balthus, in order to have a sympathetic viewpoint character. All true, but ... It comes down to whether this experiment succeeds or fails in the imagination of each reader; whether he is attracted by the reality of this presentation, or more at home in the conventional milieu *à la The Thief of Bagdad*.

Fritz Leiber, the dean of present writers of epic fantasy, has called "Beyond the Black River" "the truest and most satisfying of the Conan stories." George H. Scithers, editor of the long-running Conan fanzine, *Arma*, ranks it as "one of the best stories of the Conan series." Robert Weinberg, noted pulp fan and student of the fantasy genre, considers this tale "one of those stories that elevates Howard's sword-and-sorcery fiction well above any other that has ever been written."

I'll drink to that. "Beyond the Black River" was the first Conan story I ever read; first loves are slow to fade, but I think there is justification in singling out this story from the rest of the series. Howard might have set the tale at Fort Ghori on the Sea of Vilayet, pitted the *kozaki* against King Yezdigerd's Turanian advance, changed Balthus into an endangered wench in harem costume, and retitled it "Beyond the Zaporoska River." He might have copped the cover, but the story would have been standard fare. "Beyond the Black

River" succeeds because the story has a conviction and power that carry it beyond its routine plot.

Scithers suggests that Balthus is Howard's persona—the author deliberately writing himself into the story as one of the characters. His argument is a strong one, and Scithers further proposes that the dog, Slasher, is a literary incarnation of Howard's dog, Patch—a companion of twelve years whose death was a severe loss to Howard. Perhaps so. It is interesting to think of Howard stepping into his own story to meet Conan face-to-face. It might explain the intense feeling of personal involvement "Beyond the Black River" imparts.

In his lifetime Howard was virtually ignored by the regional press. A rare acknowledgment of his existence and burgeoning career appeared in a chatty column, *Burkett News*, in the *Coleman Democrat-Voice* for April 25, 1935. The columnist nostalgically chirps: "Robert, a little tow-headed boy, with his dog, Patches, roamed these hills and probably dreamed of the time when he could carve his name even higher than he could carve it. . . ." I think it more likely that his dreams were of facing down a horde of savage Picts, his valiant dog fighting at his side.

Robert and Patch would finally enter the world of Conan as Balthus and Slasher. It is a world that demands a hero of Conan's might to survive.

Vows Conan: "He was a man. I drink to his shade, and to the shade of the dog, who knew no fear. The heads of ten Picts shall pay for his, and seven heads for the dog, who was a better warrior than many a man."

And the forester observes: "Barbarism is the natural state of mankind. Civilization is unnatural. It is a whim of circumstance. And barbarism must always ultimately triumph."

Howard was absent entirely from the next four issues of *Weird Tales*, but a Conan tale was featured on the cover of the November 1935 issue—one of Margaret Brundage's best pastels: a nude Nafertari cowering amidst four cobras. "Shadows in Zamboula" was again the lead story, with interior art by Vincent Napoli, one of *Weird Tales'* best artists, although Howard considered Napoli's Conan to have too much of a Latin cast. This time the readers voted the Conan story second-best in the issue, edged for top spot by "The Way Home" by Paul Frederick Stern (a pseudonym of pulpster Paul Ernst, whose Doctor Satan series was running in *Weird Tales* at the time).

Howard's own title for the story was "The Man-Eaters of Zamboula"—but as often happened, the editor had a better idea. "Shadows in Zamboula" is a good Conan adventure—fast-paced and enjoyable. While it lacks the power of the best of the series, most Conan fans list it among their favorites. The plot twists make it more than a simple rescue-the-girl exercise, and Conan is shown to be no fool when it comes to civilized court intrigue. It is really a story with two separate menaces—the cannibals who hunt their prey amidst the darkened city, and the ambitious priest, Totrasmek. For that matter, there is a sinister side to both Nafertari and Jungir Khan, and Conan is wise to skip town. It is significant that, to Conan, the cannibals are less evil than the treacherous innkeeper, Aram Baksh; Conan's vengeance is no less gruesome and fitting than the fate he reserved for Constantius at the end of "A Witch Shall Be Born."

Howard seems to have been having some fun of his own in writing "Shadows in Zamboula." Baal-pteor, who spares no details as to the training of a strangler of Yota-pong, is a bit more mysterious with his name: "I am Baal-pteor.... Once, long ago and in another land, I had another name. But this is a good name, and why Totrasmek gave it to me, any temple wench can tell you." *Baal*, sure, *ba'al*, means *lord*, you knew that. Earlier, in "Jewels of Gwahlur," Howard described "the monstrous and obscene Pteor, the god of the Pelishtim, wrought in brass, with his exaggerated attributes reflecting the grossness of his cult." Farnsworth Wright must not have been keeping score.

The following issue contained the first installment of a five-part Conan serial, *The Hour of the Dragon*. At 75,000 words, it is twice as long as any other Conan tale. Howard's only completed novel, it is also the final episode in Conan's career. *The Hour of the Dragon* has been published as a separate volume in this present edition of the Conan series, to which the reader is referred.

The Hour of the Dragon concluded with the April 1936 issue of *Weird Tales*. Conan returned in the July 1936 issue with a new three-part serial, "Red Nails." As usual, Howard claimed the cover spot—once more Margaret Brundage portraying a rather languid sacrifice of Valeria. Harold DeLay rendered the three interior drawings this time—Conan was appropriately swashbuckling and granite-jawed, Valeria was the only girl in the crowd who didn't wear a bra.

"Red Nails" had been completed in July of 1935. It was the last Conan story Howard wrote—for that matter, it was the last fantasy story Howard ever completed, although he would not take his life for another year.

The problem was not that Howard had grown bored with Conan. Although looking toward better-paying markets, he was still quite enthusiastic over the Cimmerian. His letter to fellow fantasy writer Clark

Ashton Smith, dated July 23, 1935, sheds light on his plans and on Conan:

"I've been concentrating on adventure stuff recently, trying to break into that field permanently. I've made a start, with yarns published in Action, Thrilling Adventures, and Top-Notch; got a couple of cover designs in a row with Top-Notch and am toiling manfully to become a regular contributor. Sent a three-part serial to Wright yesterday: "Red Nails," which I devoutly hope he'll like. A Conan yarn, and the grimmest, bloodiest and most merciless story of the series so far. Too much raw meat, maybe, but I merely portrayed what I honestly believe would be the reactions of certain types of people in the situations on which the plot of the story hung. It may sound fantastic to link the term 'realism' with Conan, but as a matter of fact—his supernatural adventures aside—he is the most realistic character I ever evolved. He is simply a combination of a number of men I have known, and I think that's why he seemed to step full-grown into my consciousness when I wrote the first yarn of the series. Some mechanism in my sub-consciousness took the dominant characteristics of various prize-fighters, gunmen, bootleggers, oil field bullies, gamblers, and honest workmen I had come in contact with, and combining them all, produced the amalgamation I call Conan the Cimmerian."

The problem was one of finances. *Weird Tales* was one of the poorest-paying markets in the pulp field—average payment being 1¢ a word, on publication. The Depression killed several of Howard's better markets during 1932 and 1933, forcing him to hire an agent and to seek out new markets. In trouble itself (*Oriental Stories* and its retitled continuation, *The Magic Carpet Magazine*, were costly failures), *Weird Tales* became increasingly slow with payments. By 1935 Howard had broken into new markets. With his mother's hospital bills mounting, and *Weird Tales* owing him more and more money, he was forced to devote his time to these paying markets.

Howard's letter to Farnsworth Wright, dated May 6, 1935, conveys the desperation he felt, as well as his reluctance to leave the magazine that had launched his career:

"For some time now I have been receiving a check regularly each month from Weird Tales—half checks, it is true, but by practicing the most rigid economy I have managed to keep my head above the water; that I was able to do so was largely because of, not the size but the regularity of the checks. I came to depend upon them and to expect them, as I felt justified in so doing. But this month, at a very time when I need money so desperately bad, I did not receive a check. Somehow, some way, my family and I have struggled along this far, but if you cut off my monthly checks now, I don't know what in God's name we'll do. . . .

"I do not feel that my request is unreasonable. As you know, it has been six months since 'The People of the Black Circle' (the story the check for which is now due me) appeared in Weird Tales. Weird Tales owes me over eight hundred dollars for stories already published and supposed to be paid for on publication— enough to pay all my debts and get me back on my feet again if I could receive it all at once. Perhaps this is impossible. I have no wish to be unreasonable; I know times are hard for everybody. But I don't believe I am being unreasonable in asking you to pay me a check each month until the accounts are squared. Honestly, at the rate we're going now, I'll be an old man before I get paid up! And my need for money now is urgent.

"Of course, I sell to other magazines from time to time, but these sales are uncertain; to make markets regularly requires much time and effort, and for years most of my time and effort has been devoted to the stories I have written for Weird Tales. I may not—may never be a great writer, but no writer ever worked with more earnest sincerity than I have worked on the tales that have appeared in Weird Tales. I have grown up in the magazine, so to speak, and it is as much a part of my life as are my hands and arms. But to a poor man the money he makes is his life's blood, and of late when I write of Conan's adventures I have to struggle against the disheartening reflection that if the story is accepted, it may be years before I get paid for it.

"This is a statement of my case, spoken in the only way I know how to speak, that is to say frankly. I trust that my bluntness has given no offense. Necessity drives me. A monthly check from Weird Tales may well mean for me the difference between a life that is at least endurable—and God alone knows what."

At the time of Howard's suicide, thirteen months later, *Weird Tales* owed him some $1350 for published stories.

Howard's disillusionment is understandable, expressed in a letter dated December 5, 1935: "The last yarn I sold to Weird Tales—and it may well be the last fantasy I'll ever write—was a three-part Conan serial which was the bloodiest and most sexy weird story I ever wrote. I have been dissatisfied with my handling of decaying races in stories, for the reason that degeneracy is so prevalent in such races that even in fiction it can not be ignored as a motive and as a fact if the fiction is to have any claim to realism. I have ignored it in all other stories, as one of the taboos, but I did not ignore it in this story. When, or if, you ever read it, I'd like to know how you like my handling of the subject of lesbianism."

For all that, "Red Nails" is not appreciably more heavily laden with gore and sex than some of the others of the Conan series. The short novel calls to mind Howard's earlier tale, "The Slithering Shadow," which also places Conan in an enclosed city, Xuthal (once again, lost and labyrinthine and lurking with horrors), ruled by a Stygian princess, Thalis (beautiful and sinister and fond of flogging naked girls). The bloodshed is no more than usual, no more graphic than most—nor is this the only tale in which only Conan and the girl are left standing. Valeria is deadly with a blade, but so was Bêlit of "Queen of the Black Coast." Nor is the sex any more explicit than in some of the earlier tales. Nude and semi-nude girls are stock characters in the series; flagellation, graphic or implied, is commonplace in Howard's stories, frequently with lesbian overtones—e.g., "The Slithering Shadow," "A Witch Shall Be Born," "The Black Stranger," "The Vale of Lost Women."

It was a matter of realism in part—if the story calls for decadence, let there be decadence; if a battle is joined, let's see some blood. And it was also a case of Howard knowing his markets—both how far he could go, and how to slip in that *one* scene that would demand both a cover and his readers' enrapt attention:

"One problem in writing bloody literature is to present it in such a manner as to avoid a suggestion of cheap blood-and-thunder melodrama—which is what some people will always call action, regardless of how realistic and true it is. So many people never have any action in their own placid lives, and therefore can't believe it exists anywhere or in any age. Another problem is how far you can go without shocking the readers into distaste for your stuff—and therefore cutting down sales. I've always held myself down in writing action stories; I never let my stories be as bloody and brutal as the ages and the incidents I was trying to depict actually were. I think sometimes I'll let myself go—possibly in a yarn of the Middle Ages—and see if I can sell the thing. I don't know how much slaughter and butchery the readers will endure. Their capacity for grisly details seems unlimited, when the cruelty is the torturing of some naked girl, such as Seabury Quinn's stories abound in—no reflection intended on Quinn; he knows what they want and gives it to them. The torture of a naked writhing wretch, utterly helpless—and especially when of the feminine sex amid voluptuous surroundings—seems to excite keen pleasure in some people who have a distaste for wholesale butchery in the heat and fury of a battlefield. Well, to me the former seems much more abominable than the cutting down of armed men—even the slaughter of prisoners in the madness of fighting lust."

Seabury Quinn was the author of the Jules de Grandin series, the only character whose popularity outshone Conan's in *Weird Tales'* long history. De Grandin was an occult investigator who was constantly battling fiends whose foul designs were frequently cribbed from Krafft-Ebing. Quinn knew about covers and readers too.

Withal, "Red Nails" remains something of a disappointment. Too much of the story is familiar Conan fare. Although "Red Nails" can be said to present Howard's recurrent concept of a vast, entirely enclosed, lost city far more effectively than the previous versions, we have read it before. The two warring factions are appropriately maniacal—but Fritz Leiber comments that their feud "suggests the war games of two bands of boys in a huge haunted house." Still, Xuchotl *is* a splendid variant of the haunted palace theme, and Howard visualizes it very well. The crypts are as demon-haunted as any in the series. Tascela is an alluringly evil witch-queen of the Theda Bara school. Valeria—another of Howard's numerous sword-wielding female adventurers—is one of Conan's better girl-friends, and she requires rescuing only part of the time.

"Red Nails" is a good Conan story, but somehow it just doesn't seem as good as it should be. Robert Weinberg has pointed out that Valeria may be the reason. While she is an intriguing character and an excellent match for Conan—whose girl-friends usually do little more than lose their clothes and require constant rescuing—she is still *the girl*. On his own, Conan is sombre and violent; cast with *the girl*, he is prone to dashing deeds of derring-do. Such adventures usually have upbeat endings: Conan riding off with the gold and the girl into the sunset. A sense of light-hearted adventure destroys the mood of epic fantasy. Like the cartoons you chuckled over as a kid, they are experienced and forgotten. You remember those experiences that moved you through terror or grief. The best Conan tales are those in which Howard's own mood of pessimism and fatalism is conveyed to the reader. Imagine "Beyond the Black River" if the cavalry got there in time; "Queen of the Black Coast" with Conan and Bêlit sailing off with the treasure.

For myself, I think the disappointment lies in knowing that "Red Nails" is the last Conan story Howard wrote. As such, it's an anticlimax, emotionally. Conan deserved a better farewell. A hero of his stature should have earned a *Götterdämmerung*, not just a kiss.

"The Hyborian Age," as Howard explains in his introductory paragraph, is a "history" of Conan's world which he prepared when he began writing of Conan. The essay explains Howard's amazing consistency with regard to the Hyborian kingdoms and races throughout the twenty-one Conan tales. "The Hyborian Age" was run as a serial in Donald Wollheim's amateur journal, *The Phantagraph*, where it ran in the February, August, and October-November 1936 issues. The fanzine published only the first half of the essay, halting just before the paragraph beginning "Five hundred years later the Hyborian civilization was swept away." In *The Phantagraph*, a line was inserted (to conclude the third installment): "This was the world of Conan's time." This sentence does not appear in the corresponding section of the complete essay, published as a mimeographed booklet, *The Hyborian Age*, in 1938 by LANY Cooperative Publications. The text presented in this edition is that of the 1938 booklet.

H.P. Lovecraft called "The Hyborian Age" "a detailed quasi-historical sketch of infinite cleverness and imaginative fertility."

E. Hoffman Price has another assessment: "Bob's history and map of the Hyborian Age was a nightmarish and irritating thing, and his nomenclature was the supreme affront."

Well, "The Hyborian Age" *is* a pseudo-history of an imaginary age and world. While Howard did propose the Hyborian Age as an epoch "which men have forgotten, but which remains in classical names, and distorted myths," he clearly states that his concept is simply a fictional background. A reader's reaction to the quasi-history depends on whether he views it as just that—a fictional device—or whether his own knowledge of ancient civilizations is outraged by the liberties Howard has taken.

"The Hyborian Age" is a fantasy, the same as the Conan tales are fantasy—the essay even includes the bones of an epic, in the history of Gorm's conquests. It is interesting to compare this pseudo-history of lost ages with Howard's much earlier version of mankind's unhistoried past, as narrated by Gonar in the Bran Mak Morn tale, "Men of the Shadows." The two concepts present interesting contrasts and similarities, particularly since the Picts feature prominently in both. A brilliant imaginative creation, or muddled mysticism and sham ethnology—"The Hyborian Age" gave Conan's age a real-world unity, and the concept has served as the inspiration for most of the imaginary universes that later writers of epic fantasy created for their own characters.

"Red Nails" ran in the July, August-September, and October 1936 issues of *Weird Tales*. Howard's suicide was on June 11 of that same year, and the August-September issue carried the notice of his death. "The Eyrie" reflected the readers' admiration for Howard and their stunned sense of loss at his death—even as the final Conan tale thundered on to its gory conclusion.

"Red Nails" ended halfway down the page. The remaining space of *Weird Tales*, page 353, bore a sonnet: "R.E.H.," by the gifted R.H. Barlow:

"And as of mythic kings our words must speak
Of Conan now, who roves where dreamers seek."
Karl Edward Wagner
Chapel Hill, North Carolina
February, 1977

FRANK HERBERT
...is science fiction

THE JESUS INCIDENT Frank Herbert with Bill Ransom	04504-8—$2.50
CHILDREN OF DUNE	04075-5—$2.25
DESTINATION: VOID (revised ed.)	03922-6—$1.95
THE DOSADI EXPERIMENT	03834-3—$2.25
DUNE	04376-2—$2.50
DUNE MESSIAH	04346-0—$2.25
EYES OF HEISENBERG	04237-5—$1.75
THE GODMAKERS	03919-6—$1.95
THE SANTAROGA BARRIER	03824-6—$1.75
SOUL CATCHER	04250-2—$1.95
WHIPPING STAR	04116-6—$1.95
THE WORLDS OF FRANK HERBERT	03502-6—$1.75

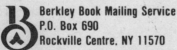

Berkley Book Mailing Service
P.O. Box 690
Rockville Centre. NY 11570

Please send me the above titles. I am enclosing $_____
(Please add 50¢ per copy to cover postage and handling). Send check or
money order—no cash or C.O.D.'s. Allow three weeks for delivery

NAME_____

ADDRESS_____

CITY_____ STATE/ZIP_____

49 A